LIMESTONE AND CLAY

LIMESTONE AND CLAY

Lesley Glaister

Chivers Press • Thorndike Press
Bath, Avon, England   Thorndike, Maine USA

This Large Print edition is published by Chivers Press, England, and by Thorndike Press, USA.

Published in 1994 in the U.K. by arrangement with Reed Consumer Books Limited.

Published in 1994 in the U.S. by arrangement with Atheneum Publishers, a division of Macmillan Publishing Company, Inc.

U.K. Hardcover ISBN 0–7451–2383–X (Chivers Large Print)
U.K. Softcover ISBN 0–7451–2602–2 (Camden Large Print)
U.S. Softcover ISBN 0–7862–0247–5 (General Series Edition)

The author and publishers are grateful to Faber & Faber Ltd for permission to quote from 'You're' by Sylvia Plath, from *Collected Poems* ed. Ted Hughes; and to Screen Gems EMI for permission to quote from 'I feel the Earth Move' by Carole King, from *Tapestry*

The text of this Large Print edition is unabridged.
Other aspects of the book may vary from the original edition.

Set in 16pt. New Times Roman.

Printed in the U.K. on acid-free paper.

British Library Cataloguing in Publication Data available

Library of Congress Cataloging-in-Publication Data

Glaister, Lesley, 1956–
   Limestone and clay / Lesley Glaister.
     p.   cm.
   ISBN 0–7862–0247–5 (alk. paper : lg. print)
   1. Large type books. 2. Marriage—Fiction.   I. Title.
[PR6057.L27L56   1994]   94–20366
823'.914—dc20

For Leo *with love*

LIMESTONE AND CLAY

SALT

From the bedroom, Nadia can hear Simon clattering in the kitchen, as he prepares Sunday lunch. Poised on her shoulders, black nylon-clad legs straightened above her head, she inhales the meaty smell. This moment reminds her of moments in her parents' house. Sunday morning was a long plain space, a light tunnel until lunchtime. It was a roasty flesh-scented boredom, quiet but for the sluggish ticking of the pendulum clock and the light tapping of her mother's whisk against the side of the batter bowl.

Nadia exhales and lowers her legs over her head so that her toes touch the floor. The stretch in her thighs is exquisite and the blood pulses in her ears. The Plough.

The lamb is for Simon's friends, Miles and Celia and Celia's husband Dan. There will be roast potatoes too, and Nadia knows that Simon is at the sink peeling them, his brow furrowed with concentration as he attempts to peel a potato in one long unbroken spiral. It is a silly ambition. But harmless. Unlike some.

Nadia turns onto her stomach. She bends her knees up and reaches back to grasp her feet. She inhales and draws herself up into a taut rocking arch. Her hipbones are two sharp points against the floor. The Bow.

1

'Shit,' Simon says and she lets her legs go and flops, smiling, knowing he's broken the peel. She turns over and lies supine, drawing air deep into her lungs, flattening her diaphragm, holding the air tight and trapped and then letting it out in one long smooth stream. She hears the pop of the cork from a winebottle.

Nadia draws in another breath and smells rosemary. She sits up and draws each foot in turn up to bounce on the opposite thigh. And then she stands before the full-length mirror. She is short and well-built—'stocky' is her mother's unflattering description. Her breasts are large and her hips curved above strong thighs. Her belly is a sad hollow. No, no, not sad: it is a scoop of space, of freedom, look at it that way. She turns her back on the mirror and shakes out her hair. It is long, wiry hair, and it stands out around her head in a brown bush. She puts on her red dress and catches her hair back with a black ribbon. She notices the calendar, a photograph of stalagmites; among them, dwarfed by their glittering immensity, a small caver. She keeps her eyes on the picture rather than the date.

Simon is beating something now in a bowl. The tap, tap, tap of the whisk reminds her again of her mother in the steamy Sunday-morning kitchen, the radio on very softly, hardly audible above the cooking sounds, the bubbling and simmering and the spitting of the roast. *Family Favourites* it would be, with the

2

names of unknown people in places with unknown names that made her both restless and glad to be at home. Her mother would sometimes join in with the radio, singing softly, beating time with her whisk or tapping with a spoon. When lunch was almost ready, the pressure cooker would give a fierce, startling hiss and fill the kitchen with the sudden wet aroma of cauliflower or Brussels sprouts.

Nadia stares at her face in the mirror. Her hazel eyes are insignificant without make-up. Her nose is small and sharp. She draws black lines around her eyes, and fills her pale lips in with scarlet, like sheeny poppy petals. Better, she thinks, and pokes shiny red hoops through the holes in her earlobes.

Simon is sipping wine, standing by the kitchen table flicking through the colour supplement. He looks up. 'Nice,' he says.

I didn't put it on for you, she'd like to say. The sharp half of her would like to say. But that can't be true for she knows it is his favourite dress, a dress he bought her, insisting that it was just her colour. 'It makes you glow,' he'd said. He indicates the winebottle and she shakes her head.

'Not yet. Anything I can do?'

'All under control.'

It is April. The window of the flat is on a level with the tops of flowering cherry trees in the park across the road. They make her think of snow. It is April. On Friday, Simon and Miles and Celia are going caving. They are seeking a way between Curlew Cavern and Boss Hole. They will drop down beneath the buzzing sunlit moorland, far down to places never seen, dead places gurgling with sinister streams, places where water rises without warning, where slabs of rock fall and crush and block the way without a sign on the surface. Where people disappear. They are planning to penetrate the secret places of the earth, to find a way between one cave and another a mile beyond. This is their ambition. She thinks of grubs wriggling; she thinks of worms.

Simon opens the oven door to check the progress of the lunch. The kitchen fills with the hot fragrance of lamb and rosemary. Nadia's stomach growls. 'Look at this,' Simon says, holding out the colour supplement. Nadia doesn't look at the glossy page. She looks instead at him. He is stubbornly good-looking. Even with her eyes narrowed with resentment, she can't see anything that displeases her. He is tall and golden, hair curls over the collar of his old denim shirt, his cheeks are sharp with a half-grown indecisive beard. His lack of effort annoys her and yet she is impressed.

'Anything up?' he asks. His eyes are pale grey and capable of probing.

'No,' she sighs, 'there's nothing up.'

'You don't mind them coming?'

'Of course I don't. You haven't set the table.' She turns away to find a tablecloth.

4

*　　*　　*

Celia is as much Simon's type of woman as Nadia is not. Celia is tall and smooth and fair with a dry ironic voice. Whenever Simon and Celia stand together, Nadia thinks spitefully of the Master Race. They could be models for a eugenics campaign. Indeed, they were lovers once, long ago; and although it didn't work— they were too alike, fought like tigers—Nadia resents the warmth that passes between them, the meeting of their eyes, the way Simon will always spring to Celia's defence.

'Why is she always so brittle? Such a smart-arse?' Nadia has often complained.

'It's just her way, a sort of shell, you'd see if you got to know her ...' And Nadia has scowled, twisting her fingers in her rough brown hair.

*　　*　　*

Simon carves the lamb into thick pink slices. Celia leans forward, breathes in the smell and groans appreciatively.

'Why don't you come?' Miles says to Nadia. 'Not on Friday, but we could organise a trip, just get you down there to see. You ought to know ...'

'Who says?' Nadia asks.

'Oh Nadia, Nadia ...' Miles stretches out his hand.

5

'Catch me underground!' Nadia shudders.

'And Yorkshire pudding,' sighs Celia. 'What a little gem he is.'

'Open another bottle of red, my darling,' Simon says. Nadia reaches for the corkscrew, flicking him an irritated glance. He only ever calls her 'my darling' when Celia is there, and always with a dry inflection mimicked from her.

'You're looking great, Nadia,' Miles says. 'How's life?'

'Fine.' Nadia thrusts the corkscrew viciously into the cork.

'Dan sends profuse apologies,' Celia says. 'Sorry, but speleological talk is not his forte over Sunday lunch. Causes acute dyspepsia. The whole business, actually. You two ought to get together.' She smiles once more at Nadia, who avoids her eyes, pouring out the wine. 'Yes, on at me to pack it in, actually.'

'No ...' says Miles.

'Yes. Oh don't worry. After this jaunt we're going in for a sprog, if that's the appropriate terminology nowadays. Had to solemnly promise Dan to stay on terra firma, *supra* terra firma, actually. Quaintly superstitious as always, he fears me giving birth to a troglodyte.'

'More a trog than a sprog in that case!' Miles winces at his own weak joke.

Nadia presses her lips together, feeling them turn papery thin in an imitation smile.

6

'Well, congratulations.' Miles raises his glass.

Nadia waits for Simon's response, but 'Gravy?' is all he says, offering Celia the jug.

'Hold your horses, Miles, mission not accomplished yet,' Celia says, looking at Simon through her fair lashes.

Nadia splashes wine on the tablecloth. 'Bloody hell,' she says.

'Salt,' cries Celia. She stretches over for the salt mill and grinds a little heap onto the red pool.

'All right?' Miles covers Nadia's hand with his own.

'All right,' she says. She watches the redness creep through the loose grains. There is enough wine in her to stave off the worst of her feelings. Miles has the sensitivity Celia lacks. She looks at him gratefully. *He* remembers, that is clear. She narrows her eyes at Celia, who is clinking her glass against Simon's and laughing. Celia catches the look.

'Oh hell,' she says, putting down her glass. 'I didn't think. Oh shit.'

Nadia shrugs. 'Let's eat.' The meat is tender in her mouth and the talk is carefully general. Miles asks her about her work, Celia admires the clay masks that hang upon the walls. They are primitive faces, glazed pewter-blue and green. All their eyes are sad shadows, only holes, and Nadia knows she will never make another. As the meal progresses the talk slides

7

inevitably down through pottery and clay into rock and caves, and Nadia closes her mind to it.

*   *   *

The earth turns and the sun shifts across the diners at the table and leaves the room. Clouds gather. Nadia flicks on the light as she makes coffee. Her lunch hangs in her stomach like a greasy ball. There are shreds of lamb caught between her teeth, a rotting, intimate taste. She grinds coffee, her hand on the lid of the grinder, the hard vibration travelling up her arm and making her teeth rattle as the pungent fragrance is released. There is something she won't tell Simon, there is something she will not even let herself think. She smothers the moth-wings of hope under a blanketing sadness.

It has happened before, too many times to count.

She tips the grounds into the coffee pot and pours in boiling water. She arranges four cups and saucers, of her own making, green and white marbled glaze. She pours thin cream into a jug and knows she cannot drink coffee herself. She puts a peppermint teabag into one of the cups.

'Doing much teaching?' Miles asks.

'No,' Nadia sighs. 'I want more ... there isn't the money for "non-vocational skills"

8

nowadays. I might get a few hours in September.'

'Shame.'

'It is. I'd like to be teaching now. I'm not doing much else.'

'If you can, do, if you can't, teach,' says Celia, inevitably.

'Watch it,' says Simon, who is a geography teacher.

'But Nadia *can*,' Miles objects, and Simon grunts his agreement.

'I *know*,' Celia says.

'The inside of this flat is bloody proof of that. Masks, vases,' Miles casts around, 'cups ...'

Nadia squashes the teabag against the side of her cup with a spoon and watches the greenness spread through the water. 'I *could*,' she corrects.

'Potter's block?' asks Celia.

'I don't know ... maybe.'

Miles leans towards her, his brown eyes searching. Nadia wishes, not for the first time, that she could fancy him. He would be so *safe*. He would do all the worrying for her, all the bolstering and massaging of her ego. But he has a long shiny nose, dented on either side where he constantly jams his glasses back, and all she can possibly feel is fond.

'Teaching *is* easier,' Simon concedes. Celia, who tried it once, splutters.

'Not *easier* exactly, but clearer-cut,' Nadia

9

ponders. 'You go, you teach, you come home, the job is done. And pottery's a good thing to teach. It's a skill that anyone can learn. There's evidence of progress. People are *pleased*. It's satisfying to please people. And it's tactile ... there's something about that, using the hands, playing with mud ...'

'Sounds horribly like some sort of icky primal therapy,' Celia remarks.

Nadia shrugs, suppressing her irritation. 'Whereas I don't know where I'm going with my pots. I've lost the ... oh, I can't explain ... I've lost the *point* somehow.'

'Points failure!' says Celia, 'also the bane of British Rail ...'

'Oh do shut up, Celia,' says Simon, and Nadia would have been grateful if his exasperation didn't sound so affectionate.

'It'll come back,' Miles comforts. 'Don't force it.'

'S'pose so,' Nadia says. She stands up. 'I'll leave you three to it. I'm going out for some fresh air ... said I might call in on Sue.'

'Thanks for lunch,' Celia says.

'Thank Simon. Bye, Miles. See you.' Nadia pushes her feet into her boots and buttons up her coat on the way downstairs. The amount of irritation she feels is quite out of proportion, she tells herself, but still there is adrenaline in her arms and legs that screams to be spent and she strides fiercely along, swinging her arms, punching holes in the air with clenched fists. It is Celia who rubs her up the wrong way—one of her mother's favourite expressions, and it is very apt. She feels like a cat that has been foolishly ruffled.

It is not just Celia. It is the pathetic flutter of hope that a tiny spurt of nausea, an extra day on the calendar can provoke. If Celia hadn't said ... but it is that sort of subject, always lurking, always a snare. Just forget it, just manage not to register the date, and someone will be there, pregnant, or breast-feeding, or talking about babies. And Celia, no doubt, will have no trouble. There she'll be this time next year, a baby in her arms, and Simon will want to hold it too, will be bound to. 'Uncle Simon', Celia will call him with a self-mocking laugh, and he'll look with his grey eyes, pupils flared, at the baby at Celia's white breast, and he will think, will be bound to think, of what might have been. Oh yes, Nadia can see it all.

There has been hope after hope after hope. Late periods, false alarms—only they weren't alarms but quite the opposite—and then, worse, real confirmed pregnancies that lasted a few weeks until her body mutinied and rejected them. And there was the one that was longer, the last one, the five-month pregnancy that really had her fooled. She hesitates outside the park gates, and enters. Usually she avoids the park on Sundays for that is the time when people parade their fertility. The duck-pond is glassy under the cold sky. It will rain, there is just a rustle of wind, a goose-pimpling of the water, a stirring in the trees which sprinkles blossom like confetti. Nadia's mother hates ornamental cherry trees for their messiness, their brief spring triumph and then its aftermath: the soggy, brownish, slippery mess of petals. A waste of time, she says, give me a good old laurel any day. Dependable. Nadia finds a smile on her face at this memory of her mother who detests the muckiness of nature, can't abide autumn, the scruffiest of all the seasons, the most wasteful.

By the water a row of small muffled children throw bread to the quacking ducks. Seagulls wheel greedily overhead, briefly mirrored in the water. A sparrow hops, cocking its head, eager for crumbs. 'Mu-um,' a child complains, 'Sacha's not giving hers to the ducks, she's *eating* it.'

April, May, June, July, August, September, October, November, December, January. If Celia gets pregnant straight away, as she is bound to, it will be a new-year baby. Blossom floats past Nadia and sticks to the surface of the water. She walks on, leaving her hope, a little woolly shape, invisible at the water's edge.

*   *   *

'Be seeing you,' calls Miles as he clatters down the stairs.

Simon hugs Celia and kisses her cheek. She

12

turns her lips towards his, but he pats her awkwardly and steps back.

'Got right up Nadia's nose, didn't I?' she says, grinning in her sheepish way.

'Well you can be a prize pain in the neck,' he says. 'You can't blame her. I'd have expected more diplomacy from a personnel manager...'

'Maybe it's a reaction. I can't seem to help it.' Celia buttons up her coat and lifts her hair clear of the collar. 'I don't mean anything. I *do* like her. And, Si,' she touches his arm, 'I am sorry about the baby thing. That was clumsy.'

'Yes,' says Simon, 'well.' He looks away. 'Say hello to Dan for me. And see you on Friday.' At this thought he smiles. 'And we'll do it. I feel it in my bones this time, we'll find the way through.'

'We'll have a bloody good try,' Celia says, 'and if we don't we'll try again.' She leans forward and succeeds in kissing him lightly on the lips. She looks at him in her level, amused way, as if aware of her power, using it judiciously.

Simon listens to her running down the stairs and banging the door. He is irritated. She is wrong to think she still has that power. And she should know that now. Recent events should have shown her that. It is true that the scent of her skin and her clean soft hair can stir desire in him, but not more so than any lovely woman who stands so close. He remembers her long body, pale and almost featureless, small

13

breasts with white nipples, just the faintest pink at the tips, the shallow indentation of her navel, the merest scrap of colourless pubic hair. Her body has a childish smell and it was touching to find the truth of her inside the brittle smart-arsed shell. But he found her unwomanly in an almost perverted way, an elongated child. And eventually, with familiarity, he found her, at least undressed and available, hopelessly unerotic. He never said that, of course, she never knew, and their parting was for other reasons, *her* reasons, more convenient for him to let her think that, except for this look she gives him that says, We have secrets, there is still something between us. And there is a secret. But nothing else. He fervently hopes there is nothing. Wishes nothing.

He wanders into the bathroom. Nadia's things are everywhere: her brush, its bristles clogged with wiry hairs; her mascara, powder and eye-pencils; tweezers; a packet of sanitary towels; an ear-ring; some tortoiseshell combs, breath freshener, the red varnish with which she paints her toenails. He has never known a woman to have so much feminine clutter. His other women, Celia included, have been natural, soap-and-water types. Friends who happen to have female bodies.

In the kitchen he looks at the piles of greasy crockery and cutlery, the crusty roasting-tin, and sighs. Strictly speaking it's Nadia's job.

Cook doesn't wash. But she's not there and they were his friends. He picks potato peelings and coffee grounds from the blocked plughole and runs the taps.

Nadia wears a strong musky perfume in the crooks of her elbows and between her breasts. She is darkly, strongly female in a way that used to scare him. Not his type. The first time they made love had been completely unexpected. He had gatecrashed a party at her house, along with some friends. They'd never even met before, and exchanged no more than a cursory word all evening, but somehow he'd been left behind at the end of the party among the bottles and overflowing ashtrays. She'd started to clear up around him, assuming he was asleep, but he was watching. And there was something about her, something about the way her breasts pressed against the stretchy velvet stuff of her dress, or about the way the damp tendrils of her hair made ringlets against her neck, or just about the unselfconscious way she moved that moved *him*, and he had reached out, half hopefully. She had hesitated and then let him pull her down beside him and hold her. He had been surprised by her softness and her womanly smell, amazed by the way his body responded, a Pavlovian response which seemed to bypass his brain altogether. He had followed her into her bedroom and found the experience of her almost too intense, the dark shadows, the soft depths, the scented puff of

15

hair that crinkled against his belly making him want to yelp at the sensation. It had been like the first time all over again for him. It *was* the first time he had been so engulfed in sensation, lost himself completely.

In the morning he had woken and seen that her sleeping face was smudged with mascara and lipstick, which he ought to have disapproved of, but which moved him instead to tenderness. She lay on her side, facing him, so that her breasts were squashed together, a dark crease between them. Her nipples were pinkish-brown, large as pansies, and around them were little wisps of hair. He touched one of her nipples experimentally with his fingertip and watched, amazed at the way it crinkled, stirring like a growing thing. He looked at her face then and saw that her eyes were open and that she was grinning. As he kissed her smudgy face he experienced a slithering sensation, both exhilarating and exasperating, that he only recognised later as the beginning of falling in love.

Five years. He squirts detergent in the water and whips up a foam with his fingertips. And something needs to happen now. A child might do, might prove the catalyst they need to propel them forward. He washes the wineglasses first in the clean water and rinses the bubbles off under the tap. He looks up and catches the empty eyes of one of Nadia's masks, a mask with a lopsided smirk. He

16

echoes the expression and loads the sink with plates.

* * *

Nadia walks and walks. She is hot inside her coat though her fingers and her ears are cold. She walks down a road of semi-detached houses and hesitates outside Sue's. The lights are on and she can see the bright cartoon blinking of the television set. The children will be sitting round it—even Robin, the baby, watches. Nadia's baby, the five-month one, would be due about now. She should be bulky now, walking with difficulty, her coat buttoned tight around the bulge. May 1 was the date. Has Simon thought of that? She could not talk about it without tears—and there have been enough of those already. If, by some miracle, this time ... She walks on. She cannot bear to go in. Not that she resents Sue's family, or begrudges her her children. But just now Robin would tear at Nadia's heart with his round brown eyes and his way of snuggling on her lap. Sunday is not a day for calling on families, anyway. Sunday is a day for family patterns, fathers and mothers and knives and forks, strolls and bathtimes and stories. Nobody visited on Sundays, she remembers— except proper visitors, uncles and aunts who stayed overnight. Nobody dropped in casually. That was more a Saturday thing. Her father

17

would have hated it. He liked to sleep late on Sunday mornings and then wake up and wallow in the bath. He'd walk to the pub before lunch, for a snifter, he said, and come home smelling lovely, of whisky and cigar smoke, benign and ready for lunch. After lunch he'd wash up, with Nadia and Michael drying and putting away, and then they would all drive out into the country to pick strawberries or kick a football about or sledge. Or if the weather was really terrible they'd watch old films on the television and eat slices of home-made cake. It would have been awful if anyone had dropped in. An intrusion.

It is still light, but there is the feeling that it should, by rights, be dark. Lights are on and leaves flutter darkly, and there is the irritable twitter of invisible birds. Nadia walks until she feels the first spots of rain, and then she turns towards home, hoping that Miles and Celia have gone. She thinks about a cup of tea, a bath, something soothing on the television, an early night.

*   *   *

'You weren't serious about your pots?' Simon says. He is pouring tea. 'Anything to eat?'

'No. I'm still stuffed. Half serious. I *am* stuck. And as I said, I can't see the point any more.' Simon frowns and hands her her tea. 'I mean, I think of a new shape, a new idea, something to hang on the wall, or some functional thing. I invent it. I make it. And there it is, tra-la, another *thing*. Do we need more things?'

Simon considers. 'More beautiful things, I think, yes.'

Nadia frowns. 'Yes, well. Thanks for washing up. I would have done it.' She takes her tea and sits in the sitting room in front of the gas fire. She feels her shins warm up and remembers the mottled blue of her grandmother's shins, plain to see even through thick mouse-coloured stockings. 'She's cooked her legs,' her mother had said when asked, 'sitting so close to the fire. Legs *in* the fire near as damn it. It's a wonder she hasn't gone up in smoke.' And Nadia had imagined meat, dead cooked meat on her grandmother's shinbones, and been sickened as well as fascinated. She picks a last shred of lamb from between her teeth and sits in the Lotus position instead, smoothing her dress in a warm tent over her knees.

Simon sits down on the sofa behind her. 'You might just as well say what's the point of exploring, of what I do, of what I'm going to do. Of finding a way through.'

'I do say that.'

'And discovery. What's the point of that? Finding a new species, say, bats or something.'

'Well?' Nadia unfolds her legs and turns to face him.

19

'Well it's obvious. It increases human knowledge and, in a way, power.'

'Power!'

'Yes. Don't scoff. Over nature.'

'Ah, so that's it.' Nadia points her toes and reaches over to grasp them, her face flattened against her knees.

'No. Or not just that.'

Nadia sits up straight, raising her arms above her head. She exhales loudly, letting her hands flop to her lap. 'I suppose you'd say then, by the same token, that by moulding something out of clay I'm exercising power over nature.'

'Depends how you want to look at it.' Simon looks at her irritably. 'By creating something beautiful you're increasing the world's stock of beauty.'

'Maybe,' Nadia says. She lies on her back and pushes herself up on her hands and feet. The Crab. She cannot be bothered to argue. 'Ouch,' she says, and lowers herself to the floor. 'Belly still too full.' She gets up and sits on the sofa beside him. 'I suppose you're all ready for Friday? The Three Musketeers.'

'Shut up.'

'Sorry.' Nadia puts her hand on his knee. 'I really can't stick Celia,' she says, without really meaning to. '*She* makes me go like this. That's why I went out.'

'I know.'

'It's the way she goes on I can't bear.'

20

'Yes,' Simon agrees, and Nadia looks at him with sharp surprise. They sit quietly for a moment listening to the vague murmuring of the television in the flat downstairs.

'Did I tell you about the goose?' Simon asks.

'Goose?'

'It fell down Boss Hole—in the eighteenth century I think it was—and three days later it emerged from Curlew Cavern with its feathers all singed—by the fires of hell, they said. That was the first inkling that there was a way through.'

'But if it's never been found in all this time!'

'Doesn't mean it isn't there.'

'Doesn't mean it is, either, Simon.'

'It *is* there. It just hasn't been traversed, that's all.'

'I don't want to argue about this again, but,' but she can feel the anger rising, the wheel of the argument creaking round again as it has creaked round periodically throughout their time together, 'but is it worth risking your life for ... for a hole? Would Roland say it had been worth it, do you suppose?'

'I know what I'm doing. And anyway, I'm not sure that he wouldn't think it was worth it.' Simon draws into himself, with a stubborn set look that Nadia recognises and which drives her irresistibly to goad him, to wipe the look off his face, to make him think.

'It's perverted,' she says.

'Perverted! That's a new one. How do you

work that out?'

'To put yourself in danger for the fun of it ...'

'Fun!'

'What then? Oh yes, sorry, the physical challenge, the physical *and* mental challenge. It *is* perverted, well decadent at least, to do that when other people have no choice but to put themselves in danger. What about miners? What a cushy life you must lead if you have to set up these challenges, flirt with death ...'

'Oh give it a rest.' Simon reaches for the remote control and switches on the television. He flicks through the channels: hymns, wildlife, shrieking comedy, hymns. He settles for the wildlife programme and they stare together at a translucent magnified shrimp building a home from huge crystalline grains of sand. Inside, as it works, the tiny engine of its innards vibrates and pumps, and its long whiskers wave.

'This minute creature,' explains the narrator, 'works ceaselessly to create ideal conditions for the survival of its young.'

'Christ!' exclaims Nadia. 'I'm having a bath.'

Simon watches a starving salmon beat itself to death in an effort to reach the right place to lay its eggs. It loses its fat sleekness and grows an ugly hook of a jaw so that it cannot eat, only fight for survival in the battle for the next generation.

He flicks through the channels once more. There is a roar of synthetic laughter; a well-heeled congregation, their mouths agape at the climax of a hymn; a fat man singing on a hillside. He switches the television off and unfolds a large hand-executed underground map. A diagram of two cave systems with a maddening gap between them. It is for him to join the ends; not join them, of course, but discover the link. That is what he must do, and then there will be time to think. For it *is* dangerous, what he proposes to do, and no, it is not worth dying for. But he has to do it. He is set on it. All the things that Nadia says may be true. Some of them, but not what she says about decadence. For how can adventure, discovery, be decadent?

He wanders into the bathroom. He likes to see her in the bath, compact and wet. The scented bath-foam she uses glistens on her body, catches in her pubic hair in a thousand points of light. She wears a silly bath hat, and lies back with her eyes closed, ignoring him. He dabbles his finger in the water and she slaps it away as if it is a fly.

'Was Scott of the Antarctic decadent?' he asks. 'Or Ranulph Fiennes?'

'Yes,' Nadia says.

She is impossible. He gives an exasperated snort and returns to his map.

Nadia is the first, the only, lover Simon has had who wasn't a friend first. Most of them

23

have been cavers. And he has shared with them the dangerous risk of trust. You have to let go, let yourself go into it, trust your fellows, know your safety is uppermost in their minds, just as theirs is in your own. Comradeship is nearer the truth than friendship, though Simon balks at the sentimental ring of the word—a clean exchange—unlike romantic love with its sticky emotional residue. And there is never more sense of achievement than in the exhausted jubilation at the end of a successful expedition. And more so, the nearer danger has approached; for then there is the feeling of having got away with something. He shakes that thought away. Most of his other lovers have been a part of this, and their love-making has never been so much an end in itself as it is with Nadia. More an affirmation of survival. Not for a long time has he been unfaithful to Nadia, not since he accepted that she had him. He has not been what he considers unfaithful, at least.

He studies the map. It is a sort of puzzle. And he thinks he has the answer. It has only to be proved. There must be a link between the two systems: he is convinced there is a link. It is a way which has been tried. Five years ago a caver died—as Nadia never fails to remind him. His body was never recovered. He was simply lost. There is a place at the end of the mapped section of Curlew Cavern where it is necessary to duck under the surface of an underground stream for a few metres. Beyond that, the roof opens out and there is a dark hole, a crawl that slopes up, away from the water. Simon believes that this crawl must lead to the long shaft that is the end of the Boss Hole System, but the aperture is not visible there. Poring over maps, pacing the springing surface of the moor, Simon is more than ever convinced.

He had been down there with Roland Charles, the caver who died. Together they had mapped the caves, experienced the excitement of almost, only-to-be-proved discovery. But Roland's last attempt had been solo. Stupid. And he had paid the price. A solo death among the limestone, bones whitening in the rock. Since then, out of respect for Roland's memory, as well as fear, no one has been back. It has taken Simon years to regain his determination, and months to persuade Celia and Miles that it is not foolhardiness to try again. Celia is the most cautious. It is she who is most often the voice of reason, the most fastidious checker of equipment, maddening often but slow and safe. A reassurance. And she is the slimmest, too, the lithest, the one most likely to be able to squeeze herself through the tiny gaps between the plates of rock.

It will be done this time. The stubborn earth will not hold out again. Underneath the tussocky moor there is a way and it will be traversed. And Simon will be there.

He avoids the word 'obsession'. In the context of caving, it's a word that suggests hazard and irrational action. But still, in Simon's dreams, night after night, the limestone yields to him. He penetrates the whiteness. It gives way to the probing of his torch beam. The water parts for him, the air is pocketed sweetly against the cave roof, and the squeeze is no squeeze but an easy crawl which opens into triumph. This is the happy dream he has, a bright dream: after the easy crawl there is a rimstone pool, the water is so clear it is invisible, still as no surface water can ever be. Under the water is a round blue bowl, and in the bowl is a heap of golden coins. Treasure glints in the crystal water and an eyeless fish of palest pink swims round and round the bowl. All around are white stalactite straws, pencils of frost reaching from ceiling to floor. He shivers with the cold beauty and then he awakes. If dreams are omens, he does not believe this, but if they *are* to be considered omens, then surely this is a good one?

*　　　*　　　*

In the dark, in the rain and the wind that scour the moorland, a lost sheep stumbles. Its woolly legs bend under it and the heather gives way, a pad of fibrous earth splits over a gap between rocks and with a startled bleat the sheep

26

plummets down a deep vertical shaft. Its back is broken by the fall. It lies on loose shale in the utter darkness. Its feeble mind makes no sense, sees no shape, and because of the merciful snapping of its cervical vertebrae it feels no pain. In the black cold numbness it closes its eyes and knows no more.

SAND

Nadia wakes with a sour taste in her mouth. It is early. She watches the cold light extend through the gloom, illuminating the open wardrobe, the hanging clothes, sharpening the narrow black shadows and folds.

Between her legs there is a stickiness. If it is blood then it is over. Once again. She lies still. All that is visible of Simon is one shoulder, grey in this light, and the ruffled back of his head. After five years she can still be moved by his beauty, the soft wing of shadow cast by his shoulderblade onto the smoothness of his back. The strong curve of Simon's shoulder is like marble in the early light, a virtuoso sculpture, solidity and life captured in dawn and grey. She imagines this shape in clay, massive, hollowed, glazed grey with a tinge of pink to indicate dawn, or life.

There is a definite dampness. She gets up carefully, imagining the brownish map she will leave behind on the pale green sheet, but in the

27

gloom there are no colours and she cannot see. In the bathroom she finds no blood, only a white moisture. As she sits on the toilet she feels sick, an awful, definite nausea. Recognisable, undeniable. The silly hope is there again, flapping its wings against her diaphragm. But she is tired of it, the rhythm of hope, despair and resignation that prints its pattern over her months and years. She should have learnt not to hope by now. Think about something else.

Her feet are cold on the kitchen floor. It is not yet seven o'clock. She lets up the blind and finds the sky flushing with just the pink she'd like to use for a glaze if she was to sculpt the shoulder, an impossibly subtle rosiness which glints on wet slate roofs and makes them glow, which plays with the cherry blossom, spreading a faint shadowy blush on its whiteness like the warmth of skin.

Nadia makes a pot of tea and returns to the bathroom while it brews. She runs hot water in the basin, splashes her face, and, feeling sluttish, scrubs inside her nightshirt at her armpits. She rubs cream into her face and brushes her hair. She frowns at her reflection. There is a dark hair growing on her upper lip. She tweezes it out and the sharp sensation brings tears jumping to her eyes.

She pours the tea and takes it in to Simon. 'Time,' she says. He groans. He has moved, hunched himself under the quilt so that his

28

shoulder is hidden. Nadia sits crosslegged on the bed. She runs her hand over her legs, shaved smooth last night. Her toenails are coral pink. The tea tastes dirty. This is familiar, but she drinks it resolutely. Simon is sensitised to every clue. She will not let the stupid hope out of herself, she will not infect him. She thinks of a drawstring bag, the neck tightly drawn up to trap its wriggling contents. She purses her lips to match.

'OK?' Simon asks, eventually pulling himself into a half-sitting position and reaching for his tea.

'Fine,' Nadia replies. Her fingers smell strongly of soap, a comforting smell.

'Period started?'

'Uh huh.'

'All right?' Simon asks carefully. He is wary. Her reactions vary at this time, sometimes she cries, sometimes she is fiercely bright, but she has turned away so he cannot see her face. She pulls on a pair of black tights.

'Fine.'

Simon has been looking at houses. This is a secret. Family houses with gardens and extra bedrooms. It is not only Nadia who suffers a loss of hope each time she bleeds. He had thought she looked pale, noticed she avoided coffee, thought perhaps ... but she is like bloody clockwork. It is only recently that it has become real, the possibility of fatherhood and thus the disappointment.

He remembers a woman called Grace, a girl really. He and Grace and several others—all student teachers—had shared a tall damp house in Tooting Bec. He closes his eyes against Nadia leaning forward and shaking her breasts into a scarlet bra. He sees Grace, Grace who never wore, was far from needing to wear, a bra. Her hair was short and blond, neat as a swimming cap, and she had a wide pale mouth. In his memory Grace sits at the table eating toast and golden syrup. She wears a long woolly jersey—his—and hockey socks, but her thighs are naked. Grace had a gangly, sexy style. Cool thighs. They had become lovers just because they were both there, and house-sharing somehow became living together without him noticing. Simon remembers a 'coming to' in a supermarket, holding the wire basket while Grace chose cheese and fruit. He realised that they must seem to be, to other shoppers, a couple. That indeed they were a couple. He looked at the way the short hairs lay on the back of her neck, the way she frowned and fingered an avocado for ripeness and handed it to him for his opinion, and panicked. This was not it, not what he meant, or wanted. He had dropped the avocado and turned to bolt, but Grace had grabbed him by the arm. 'What's up with you? Aren't you well?' And he had had to say, 'I'm fine,' and follow her round the shop, his heart thudding dully.

He had planned to tell her that evening that

he wanted to go, but she had cooked steak and opened a bottle of wine and he couldn't spoil the evening for her. And she had turned on the gas fire and worn a silky petticoat she'd bought at a jumble sale and her nipples stood out against the silk like beads and he hadn't been able to say anything at all. And he has always been convinced that that was the night he impregnated her.

That was a terrible time. He opens his eyes and there is Nadia fluffing her hair with her fingers. She feels his eyes upon her and turns round. 'I thought you were going in early,' she says.

'Just getting up.' He closes his eyes again to see Grace's white face. 'Pregnant,' she is saying. And he feels his real self peel away and his false self staying calm, talking about the sensible thing, casting around for sources of cash while his real self panics, its face the face of Munch's scream. She had resisted, but he was resolute. Escape was purchased. He could never touch her again. A sliver of him, a sliver which he doesn't countenance, despised her for her obedience. He had stayed with her for the six weeks in which they weren't allowed to make love and then they parted, cleanly, for it turned out that she despised him too for causing her to snuff out, with no apparent regret, their future.

It had never been a baby in his mind. It had been the threat of chains. There had been the flicker of pleasure in the proof that he was fertile—though it had never seriously crossed his mind that he might not be. Apart from that the whole episode had been a narrow squeak, a door flung open at the last minute, a reprieve. Now that he wants a baby, experiences a foolish almost-broodiness when he sees little boys with their kites in the park, little girls on swings, he thinks for the first time of that problem as a child who could have been. Who would be thirteen now. He doesn't regret what happened, it is simply that his imagination has only just caught up with it. He has only just grasped what it meant.

Simon gets swiftly up, sickened by this sleepy emotional soup. He stands under the hot needles of the shower thinking of clean uncomplicated things: rocks and water and sky. There is a week of work to get through—five days of geography: meanders and oxbow lakes, contour lines and gross national products—and then the trip.

*   *   *

When Simon has gone, Nadia goes back into the bathroom. She cleans her teeth, watching herself in the mirror, wiping off the toothpaste spatters. In the early days, when she first moved in with Simon, Nadia would stand like this, brushing her teeth, her face reflected near the bottom of the mirror, imagining Celia's face, slightly higher up, overlapping. For Celia had lived briefly with Simon in this flat too. And then Nadia would see, like tissue-paper masks, the faces of all the lovers that had ever been here, brushing their teeth in front of this mirror. And she had bought a new mirror and smashed the old one before she threw it away.

Nadia opens the window to breathe in the fresh air and sees the woman from the bottom flat outside, sweeping the steps to the front door. There is just the round grey circle that is the top of her head and beneath it the shoulders and arms, solid in a blue nylon housecoat, moving in and out with the rhythm of her sweeping. The broom makes a shushing sound on the step. Nadia closes the window quietly, feeling guilty. She never sweeps the step or cleans the communal staircase. But it is Simon's flat, after all, and neither does he. She has never spoken to the woman downstairs, only nodded in passing.

'She talks,' Simon had warned. 'And talks and talks and talks. Steer clear.' And so Nadia had contrived to avoid her, listened on the landing for a moment before going down, retreating if there was a sound until the door banged shut.

Nadia makes herself a cup of peppermint tea and, sighing, carries it to her studio. She cannot put it off any longer. She must work, point or no point. She makes her living selling pots at craft fairs. The masks sell well, and the

33

mugs and the candlesticks. There are rows of them, leather-hard clay, waiting to be fired. Spring is a slow time. In the autumn and up to Christmas she can sell hundreds of pots, as many as she can make. At first this was a thrill. It was all that she had ever wanted—to make money from her craft. Now ... she watches the light on the rows of dull things. Tired shapes, easy, repetitive. She should make another batch before she fires them. Bored, she thinks. Is that what I am? It is just a job. Simon is bored with his job too—trying to cram adolescent heads with maps and charts. But then he has his caving. That is his challenge. And this is not supposed to be just a job, it is supposed to be her life, all she ever wanted. She remembers the excitement when the kiln arrived, how she hardly left her studio for weeks, how Simon had to come and find her at bedtime, how they made love, her hands on his flesh, her head full of clay so that the glistening slickness between them became confused in her mind with the act of her creation. When did that leak away?

She opens the lid of the plastic-lined dustbin where she keeps her clay, looks at the cold, inert mass. She has not the heart for it today. Instead she cleans the basin, which is pocked and smeared with clay splashes. She begins to clean the window, which is almost obscured to half-way up by splashes from the wheel, and as she stretches and rubs she feels a familiar sensation. She stops. No. It cannot be. Let it not be. She feels the pulling ache in her belly that heralds the onset of her period.

*   *   *

Nadia curls in bed, her breasts pressed against her knees. One hand is clamped between her thighs against the pad, pressing as if forcing back the flow. There was blood, not bright, but old. Not much, but the sight of the brownness made her weak. There's nothing you can do. That's what the doctor would say if she was to ring. Go to bed and wait, he'd say, and it is true. No power on earth can alter what is happening. She has been here so many times before, in this bed, in this position, experiencing the seeping-away of her hope. The other times are there in bed beside her. They curl like the petals of a rose behind her, each folded into each, all the memories, all her babies. The taste of tears is in her mouth, a salt-sea taste. She closes her eyes, each in turn, and the colour of the curtains changes, the colour of the light itself. With the left eye it is bluish and sharp, with the right, pink and soft. Which is correct? She closes them both.

The sea-taste of unspent tears brings her the memory of a beach, somewhere in Wales. It was a summer holiday, her mother and father were sitting on towels beside a blue-and-orange-striped windbreak. There was a

35

thermos flask and sandwiches crunchy with sand. The beach stretched long and wide, the sea was miles away, a flat distant glint. The sand was licked and carved into shallow hollows and ridges like a giant map, sprawling, textured with ripples, shards of shells and the curly casts of sand-worms. When the tide turned, the sea just rolled in, unimaginably, just rolled in, no indeterminate lapping forward and back. No warning. It rolled in, wafers of water, deceptively shallow and inviting, a thin shiny skin, warm from the warmth of the sunny sand. It didn't come in evenly but followed the ways it had carved, stealthily filling the hollows, making long tentacles of water that could creep round an unwary paddling child, wrap around and join and tighten and deepen until the child found itself stranded. And then the sand could give way, simply fall away beneath the feet of the child, dissolve, sand that had seemed so solid a moment before. Most years a child was drowned, Nadia's mother warned. And Nadia wondered why they had come here in that case, and watched, anxiously, her brother with his fishing net, a tiny distant figure, smaller than her little finger if she held it up to measure.

The telephone rings. Nadia is shaken from her memory by its rude double blurt. She almost doesn't answer, but it does not give up and she hauls herself up to answer it.

'Hello stranger,' Sue says accusingly. 'I

36

thought I'd see you at the weekend.'

Nadia is pleased to hear her voice. She is pulled out of herself. 'Sorry,' she says.

'Have you done another firing yet? Someone from the council rang and asked if we wanted to do a stall at some function. Could you manage some egg-cups?'

Nadia laughs. 'Yes, I expect so. Oh, it's nice to hear your voice. How about lunch, Sue?'

'Oh I'd love to, Nad, but ... is everything all right?'

'Oh, fine.'

'It's just that you sound a bit ... Simon all right?'

'Fine. Tomorrow?'

'Oh Nad, we're off to Devon tomorrow to stay with Matthew's shitty uncle.'

'I forgot.'

'*Sure* you're all right? I could nip out for an hour tonight, get someone to sit.'

'No.'

'Sure?' Sue sounds relieved. 'I'll send you a postcard.'

'Love to the kids. Have a good holiday.' Nadia puts down the phone and looks at it resentfully. Talking to a friend would lift the lid off her box now, but then she has talked and talked. Sue has heard this story so often, listened to her cry. What else could she say? She must be tired of Nadia's misery. She's got enough of her own to deal with, with the doings of her soddish husband and three rumbustious

37

kids. This time it is not up to her friends, it is up to Nadia.

*   *   *

On the hills mist thickens and clings. Cumulonimbus, the rain-bearing cloud, drags its heavy belly through the heather. Sheep the colour of rocks, the colour of cloud, huddle close in the wetness. Drips hang from the wizened fingertips of stunted trees. In burrows newborn rabbits curl blindly in the dim, grey-furred warmth. And through the spongy earth there is the probing of furled fronds, obedient to the season, pushing up out of the darkness into the heavy grey light.

NOODLES

It is dark. There is red flock wallpaper but it is flaking into velvet feathers. There is a churning, a grumbling, a low threat. Reptiles fighting, scaly skull pressed against scaly skull, flat teeth grinding. Nadia wakes. The dream lurks in her pillow and she pulls her head out of it—a terrible, squashing, dissolving dream. And now there is fresh blood. And it is over, if ever there was anything more than imagination.

    She washes and puts the kettle on for tea. There is a dark murmurous pain in the small of her back. She swallows paracetamol with water. Simon has gone to work, left a note: *Didn't want to wake you, see you, love Si.* Nadia pulls up the blind. Cherry petals blown by the wind are splattered on the windowpane. Rain pelts, the petals slide. There is the sound of her dream, which has become the faint blustery moan of the wind. The shiny branches of the trees lash and struggle. If there was sunshine, perhaps, she could cope. The kettle switches itself off and falls quiet. She makes tea with a bag in a cup. Something about the ordinary process of fishing the wet brown teabag out of the cup, the useless wodge leaking thick brown onto the silver surface of the draining-board, causes her to moan. She listens as if outside herself to the animal sound, sadness that any creature would recognise. She lets her head hang back and howls, thinking of the soft tube of a howling dog's muzzle, the full-throated, heart-rending sound. Is this madness? the detached part of her wonders. But she need not do it, would not do it if Simon, if anyone, was here. She wonders if she is audible in the flat below, and stops. She drinks her tea, still standing, watching the dismal spring weather. She feels blood flowing and soaking her pad. Inside, the wings of hope shrivel as if they have flapped against a flame. All the silly bubbles burst and she lets her legs go, she actually sinks to the floor, feeling ridiculous and melodramatic. She lies for a short time on the cork tiles. It is a reasonably clean kitchen but under the refrigerator and the cupboards she can see dark bits and pieces, movements even, dust-clogged webs. In such small spaces whole worlds are living, feeding on crumbs and fat splashes, living and breeding. Whole worlds of life underneath the refrigerator, and yet no life in Nadia's womb.

It is cold lying on the floor. It needs sweeping and washing. Nadia thinks of a bright housewife in an advertisement with her mop and detergent, cutting hygienic swathes through the grease, a shiny smile upon her face. It would be children's footprints she'd be mopping up, and the muddy skids of a puppy-dog's paws. There is a wine cork under the fridge and some once-frozen peas. She gets up, shivering, and goes back to bed.

Nadia lies curled and dozing, thinking of yesterday, when she lay like this and there was still some hope. She would ring Sue if she were not off to Devon. If she could have seen her yesterday and talked, she might have gained some perspective. Sue is good at putting things in perspective, and Nadia likes listening to Sue's stories of muddly family life with unreliable Matthew. Instead she'd stayed at home and thrown some silly egg-cups on the wheel. She had moulded little chicken's beaks onto some of them, and ducks' on the others, and given them quirky expressions on their faces, and outsize feet. And now they must wait

40

for the firing.

She could ring someone else. There are other friends—even Miles—who would be glad to help. But why should anyone want to know? Why spread the misery? She can manage it, swaddle it and stow it away. It only needs time. She cannot bear the thought of pity; there is enough of that in herself.

She gets up and changes her pad, averting her eyes from the dark clotted wetness. She opens the bathroom window. The rain has paused and the wind dropped. A rag of blue shows in the sky, a handkerchief waving. Below the window are greenish daffodils almost open; one blast of sunshine and they'll ripen and split, yell out their colour.

The doorbell rings. Nadia hesitates. She fluffs up her hair with her fingers and presses her lips together to give them colour. She goes to the door and looks through the peephole. She sees the distorted fishy face of the woman from downstairs swimming through the glass. Curious, she opens the door.

The woman looks surprised and clears her throat. 'Good-morning,' she says, 'I'm your local Intrigue representative. I wonder if I could interest you ...' She thrusts forth a rain-spattered cosmetics catalogue.

'Oh, no thanks,' says Nadia and begins to close the door.

'Bugger it,' the woman says. 'Pardon me. I knew I wouldn't be any good at this.'

41

Nadia smiles and pauses, her interest caught. 'Just started?'

'Yes, thought it might be a good side-line, but I haven't mastered my "sales technique".' The woman regards her closely. 'Didn't think you'd be in, duck. Been all down the street. Haven't sold a sodding thing. Are you all right?' She has odd-coloured eyes, one brown, one blue, and a cheerful doughy face.

'Fine . . .' Nadia falters under her scrutiny.

'Only you don't look it. Have I got you out of bed?'

'Oh no . . .'

'Why don't you let me in duck, and have a look at my samples? There might be something to bring a bit of colour to your cheeks. There's all sorts in here . . .' She flicks through the pages of lipsticks and creams. 'Some of them aren't too bad. Go on . . . be a devil.'

'Oh all right then,' says Nadia. After all she has nothing else to do but mope and mourn.

'Have you a dog?' the woman asks, looking past her into the hall.

'No . . . it's no pets allowed, isn't it?'

'Strictly speaking, but I have Darling . . . no harm done, more part of the family than a pet.'

'Darling?'

'My crow.'

'Crow . . . what, *inside*, flying about?'

'No! In a cage . . .' Nadia leads the way into the kitchen. 'Drives Derek barmy with his racket.'

42

'Derek?'

'My old man. Claims he does. Really, you know, he's quite partial to him. Derek that is. Can't speak for Darling. I'm Iris, by the way.'

'Nadia. Coffee? Tea?'

'Please.'

Nadia switches the kettle on again. 'Is it legal? Keeping a crow in a cage? Isn't there some law about wild birds?'

'Don't ask me. Can't have him flying about loose, can I? Imagine the mess! And he was a present. Can't turn your nose up at a gift horse, can you?' Iris has taken off her raincoat. She is a stout woman with a hard, corseted body under her lacy pink cardigan. 'Mind if I take my shoes off?' she asks, easing her feet free of her tight high-heels. There is a dent in the fat on the top of each. She wiggles and stretches her toes.

Nadia spoons instant coffee into two mugs. She is dazed by Iris. 'Sugar? Milk?' she asks.

'Please.' There is a faint odour of nylon and leather. 'Been on my feet since first thing. If I don't crack it today, I said to Derek, I'm packing it in. And what have I done? Sod-all.' She smiles ruefully.

A pale sunbeam escapes from behind the clouds and shines through the window onto her grey hair.

'Cheering up,' Iris observes. 'Said it would.'

Nadia sips her coffee. Her belly is aching, and her back. She is filled with a sensation of

43

falling and loss. She could easily cry. She wishes Iris would go. She closes her eyes and sees a star falling, a silvery trail.

'Poorly,' says Iris. 'Knew you were. What is it? Flu? There's a lot of it about.'

'I'm all right,' Nadia says.

'Look ...' Iris opens her case and brings out a fistful of lipsticks. 'Apricot, Amber, Bee-Sting, Coraline and Plum ... frosted or gloss ... Pumpkin Pie, Rhubarb, Sunset ... and ...' she squints at the tiny label on the bottom of a tube, 'Fandango ... that one's not bad actually. Want to try?' She winds up the stubby orange stick.

Nadia shakes her head. 'Sorry, not in the mood.'

'Fair enough. Just have a whiff of this.' She squirts Nadia's neck with an aerosal spray. '"Addiction", they call it. I ask you! Who dreams up these names!'

Nadia winces at the sickly artificial smell.

'Does smell like bog cleaner, doesn't it?' Iris says cheerfully, and Nadia finds herself laughing. She is weak and light-headed. 'Oh I know it's all a load of crap—do excuse me—but it is a job. A side-line, at least. And people do buy it apparently.' She looks mystified.

'Side-line to what?' Nadia asks.

'Fortune-telling.' Iris grins. 'That's my main job. I'm on Enterprise Allowance. It doesn't make *me* a fortune, unfortunately, but *c'est la vie*. Hence the side-line.' She flicks her hand

44

disdainfully over the lipsticks.

'Do you advertise?' Nadia asks. 'I mean how do you find your customers?'

'Clients, I like to call them. Word of mouth, duck. And ads in shop windows.'

'I'd never have guessed,' Nadia says. 'I mean you don't ...'

'Don't look the part? No. Maybe I should. What do you think? I'm thinking of changing my image. I could dye my hair black. What about some scarves? I could paint my face with all this muck,' she indicates her samples, 'and Darling could ride on my shoulder ...' Nadia laughs again. She wishes Simon was here. He'd love this. 'Or perhaps not,' Iris adds. 'He's a bit sporadic in the toilet department.'

'How's business?'

'Not booming.'

'How long have you been at it?'

'Always. But I've only just become a business.'

'What do you do?'

'All the usual things. Cards, palmistry, tea-leaves, the crystal ball—though I've never got the hang of that. More of a gimmick. Don't know why I'm telling you this. Too honest, that's my trouble.'

'What's best ... I mean which do you prefer?'

'Hmmm,' Iris frowns.

'Maybe I'm being nosy,' Nadia says.

'No, no ... palms and the leaves, I think. I'll

tell you a secret—Nadia, is it?—it doesn't have to be tea-leaves. I can read anything like that. Soup bowls, toothpaste spits in the sink ...'

'You can't!'

'You'd be surprised,' Iris says, and her blue eye and her brown eye twinkle so that Nadia cannot tell whether or not she's joking. 'You might laugh, but I foretold disaster in my nephew's bowl of Frosties.'

'Disaster?'

'Well, misfortune.'

'What happened? Sorry, I *am* being nosy.'

'Nothing that couldn't be solved. And he's a roofer now. So, shall I do yours?'

'Oh no ... another time perhaps ... I'm really not in the mood.' Nadia suddenly feels terribly tired. Less unhappy, but exhausted. When Iris goes she will make some toast and take it to bed, have a glass of brandy perhaps, that will knock her out, and while she's waiting for sleep she'll read some Sylvia Plath. Simon finds it irritating when she retreats under the quilt to do this. Silly, self-indulgent, neurotic cow, he calls the poet, offended by the fact that a woman could kill herself and leave her babies. And Nadia partly agrees. But still, she loves the voice she hears, and death has crystallised it bright and steady as a star. Nadia has yearned pregnancy and children through her words: she has longed to be cow-heavy and floral in a Victorian gown; she has longed for the clean cat's mouth, the little one, the clear

46

vowels rising like balloons. It is a strange comfort with the draining-away of hope to read the words. It has become part of her ritual.

The sky has darkened again and a flurry of raindrops and petals hit the window as if flung by a fist. Nadia gets up and switches on the light.

'Wish it would make up its mind,' remarks Iris.

'Well, that's spring for you,' Nadia says.

'I'll be off.' Iris forces her feet back into her shoes. 'You look done in. Thanks for the coffee.' She stands up. 'Sure I can't interest you in anything? I didn't show you the eye-compacts did I? On special. Just look ...' She brings from her case two flat eyeshadow compacts. 'Amazon—browns—or Fjord—blues—what do you think? Amazon's more your colour, I'd say.'

'All right,' Nadia says, to hurry her. 'I'll take the Amazon.'

'Really?' Iris looks startled. 'Maybe my luck's on the turn.'

At the door, she turns and looks at Nadia, leans forwards almost as if she is about to kiss her.

'It'll be all right,' she says.

'What?'

'I'll do your palm another time, shall I? Just knock, duck. Any time.'

Nadia listens to her weary feet clumping

47

down the stairs. Then she makes toast and takes it with a glass of brandy to her rumpled bed and before she sleeps she reads a poem. The last lines—*Right, like a well-done sum. A clean slate with your own face on*—make her smile and then cry, and she falls asleep with the prickly sensation of tears drying on her cheeks.

*   *   *

It is late. Simon has a Chinese dinner for two on the passenger seat and a tissue-wrapped bottle of wine on the floor. He gets out of the car, holds the warm greasy package against his chest as he locks it and looks up at the windows of the flat. It is all dark. Out? he wonders, annoyed. The meal and the wine were bought on impulse. The date, April 10, had wagged at him from the staff-room calendar, a vaguely significant date, something or other that he shouldn't forget. He'd remembered Nadia's back turned to him in the morning, disappointment, perhaps. And after his staff meeting and his game of squash he'd stopped at The Golden Dragon and ordered the chef's special dinner for two or three. Only after he'd ordered the meal and was waiting, sipping a glass of lager, had he taken the trouble to think clearly. April 10 was Celia's birthday. A date he'd had branded on his brain once when he'd forgotten. It had nothing to do with Nadia. He'd grinned foolishly into his drink, like a

48

man in a sitcom, feeling tempted to share the joke with the Chinese waiter who brought him his meal. He'd resisted, but stopped at the off-licence on the way home and bought a bottle of sparkling wine to complete the joke.

But it seems she isn't in. The flat is in darkness and the curtains undrawn. He puts the food on the table and switches on the light, irritated to find the table still covered with the remains of Nadia's breakfast. He turns the oven on low and puts the brown-paper package inside.

He goes into the bathroom to pee and sees blood in the toilet, a dried spot on the seat, a bright red pool under the water, startling against the white porcelain, and experiences terror and pity. Menstruation frightens him. In theory it's all right, but the actuality of the blood, the terrible intimacy of sharing a bathroom with a menstruating woman, the peculiar blood tang in the air, he cannot bear, or can only bear by hardly thinking, hardly breathing in. It is more now than that too, it is a scarlet punctuation, a regular full-stop.

He flushes the toilet and washes his hands. He goes into the bedroom and flicks on the light. He is surprised to see Nadia crumpled in the bed. She opens her eyes blearily.

'Hello! I thought you were out.'

Nadia grunts something unintelligible. She looks dazed, a waker from a deep dream. Simon sits down beside her on the bed. Her hair is a wild bush and her cheeks flushed. He is pleased that she is there. 'Belly ache?' he asks sympathetically. 'Had a good snooze?' Nadia nods. 'Tea? Wine? I've bought us a take-away. Chinese.'

'Good,' Nadia says and her voice is soft and scratchy with sleep. 'Tea first.'

Simon makes tea for her and watches her as she sips it, her hands wrapped round the mug. She looks happy in a tremulous way, like a child after tears.

'Been in bed all day?' Simon asks.

'No ... what time is it?'

'Nineish.'

'Really? Oh, I forgot it was your squash night. Oh ... good ...'

'Why good?'

'The day is nearly over, that's all ...' Nadia gets up. She is wearing the long T-shirt she uses as a nightie, and leggings too, all baggy at the knees. As she passes him, Simon gets a whiff of some terrible perfume. While she's in the bathroom, he straightens the bed, finds Sylvia Plath's *Collected Poems* and frowns in Nadia's direction. When there has been a loss before, she has taken to her bed like this and read Plath. But she wasn't pregnant. She wasn't even late. Or perhaps she was. She never said.

The kitchen is full of the smell of scorching brown paper. Nadia rescues the meal from the oven and, burning her fingers on the sharp edges, opens the silver-foil trays and arranges

50

them on the table: beef and black beans; chicken and cashew nuts; sweet-and-sour pork; Cantonese noodles; prawn crackers; spring rolls. The hot smells quarrel in the air.

'How did you know?' Nadia asks Simon.

'What?'

'That I hadn't cooked?'

'Intuition,' Simon says, grinning as he eases his thumbs under the wired wine-cork.

'But what if I had?'

'But you haven't ...'

Nadia accepts this, quells her irritation. After all, this is a treat. 'Are we celebrating?' she asks, and the cork pops out and hits the window. It's a softening-up, she thinks, because of Friday, because I disapprove so much of what he is going to do. Not disapprove; because I am terrified. The wine fizzes into the glasses. Simon's chin and cheeks are flecked with golden stubble. The light catches the ends of his long lashes. She cannot bear to think of him below the earth, crushed in the dead rock, or drowned in secret water. But that is more important to him than her. I *am* jealous, she admits to herself, smiling wryly, feeling absurd. Jealous of the earth.

'Here,' says Simon, handing her a glass. 'Cheers.'

The wine is cold, the bubbles sharp as grit. Nadia shivers. 'Cheers.' They clink their glasses together. It is strange to be hauled so abruptly from the fuzzy vagueness of her

51

dreams. All afternoon she has been rising and falling like a seal, her head above the surface for a moment, registering the passage of time, the moan and splatter of the weather, and slipping easily back, sleep closing like a watery skin above her. It is strange to be hauled from that to a mysterious celebration in the harsh electric kitchen light, the sharp bubbles in the icy wine, the raindrops glittering street-lit orange on the black window-glass. Simon follows her eyes, gets up and pulls down the blind. It makes a sharp smacking sound and her mother says, quite distinctly, in her head, 'Pull yourself together,' and she is aware all at once of the mess she is, her unmade-up face, the huge unbrushed blurr of her fuzzy hair. She tries to smooth it around her head.

'Let's eat then,' she says. She spoons noodles and crispy balls and translucent orange sauce onto her plate. 'Good day?' she asks.

Simon fills his own plate, licks black-bean sauce off his fingers. 'The usual. Get anything done?'

Nadia shakes her head. She tells him about Iris and the cosmetics. 'Did you know she was a fortune teller?' she asks.

Simon pulls a face and shakes his head. 'Good God, no. More of a school dinner lady, or a shop assistant.'

'Snob!' Nadia says and flicks him with a noodle.

'Did she tell yours then?' Simon asks.

'No ... but I might have it done. For a laugh. She's really nice, funny. You should meet her. She's got a pet crow.'

'Hmmm.' Simon looks dubious. 'I wouldn't encourage her ... A crow, you say? Isn't that illegal? Don't know if I like the idea of a crow in the building.'

'Oh don't be such a fogey. Simon, I've been thinking, why don't we book a holiday?' Nadia looks at him hopefully. The thing to do is look ahead. Not worry about Simon's safety, forget about babies. Book a holiday somewhere hot and lazy where the wine is cheap. She wouldn't want to be pregnant then, she fools herself, not allowed to drink, exhausted, nauseous.

'Eat some more,' Simon says, wiping his mouth.

'I wonder if she can tell fortunes,' Nadia muses. 'I mean I wonder if anyone can, really.'

'Crete again?' Simon says. 'Or somewhere new?'

'I'll get some brochures,' Nadia promises. She nibbles a prawn cracker that dries the roof of her mouth and sticks to it.

'Finished?' Simon asks. 'Scrabble?'

'I'd rather slump.'

'Oh go on ...'

Nadia sighs. 'All right,' she says, 'but in the other room by the fire.'

Simon is winning and Nadia doesn't care. He has good letters, that much is clear from the way his lips are pressed together in suppressed

53

excitement. He is as transparent, sometimes, as a child. Nadia smiles. Perhaps he is, will have to be, enough. Man enough and child enough too, if there is no other. But she has thought this before. Easy to be philosophical at the beginning of a new cycle.

'Go on then,' Simon prompts.

'It's your turn!'

'No, I put ISTHMUS—double letter, triple word, thirty-two. Didn't you put it down?'

Nadia looks at the scrap of paper she's been writing on. 'Oh yes, sorry.'

'More wine?'

She shakes her head. 'I haven't finished this. I can't go ... oh hang on. What about this—' she puts down her letters, proudly. 'USURY. Sixteen. Not too bad, eh?'

'That's the last of the Us; I bet I get stuck with the sodding Q,' Simon says, frowning now at his letters.

Nadia closes her eyes. The gas fire creaks and pings; Simon's Scrabble pieces click together; she can hear him muttering, testing a word. Outside someone shouts, a car starts up and drives away. Nadia opens her eyes and through a gap in the curtains she glimpses the icy half-eaten moon, revealed for a moment between crumpled black clouds. The telephone rings. Nadia reaches for it. Celia is there, sounding strained, wanting Simon.

'For you,' Nadia says, handing it over.

She goes to the tape player and puts on an

54

old tape, Carole King, and sings along as the rich voice fills the room.

'I feel the earth, move, under my feet,
I feel the sky tumbling down,
I feel earth start to tremble,
Whenever you're arou ... ound.'

She begins to dance, but Simon glares and flaps his hand at her. She turns the music down, still humming, and sits before her letters. She tries not to eavesdrop.

'Oh ...' Simon is saying. His voice is very flat. He catches Nadia's eyes and then looks away, turns away slightly. Giving me the cold shoulder, she thinks. She rearranges her letters. Is GYPS a word?

'Well, that's good I suppose—it's what you wanted—no—no, sorry I can't. No.'

What's the plural of ISTHMUS? Nadia wonders.

'Oooh, darling, when you're near me,
And you tenderly call my name,
I know that, my emotions,
Are something I just can't tame,' she mouths.

'Bye then. Oh, happy birthday. Yes I did. Bye.' Simon puts down the phone and remains where he is for a moment too long, his back slightly turned.

55

'Your go,' Nadia says.

'I feel the sky tumbling down,
a tumbling down,
a tumbling down,
tumbling down,
a tumbling dow—ow—own.'

'Do we have to have that?' he asks.

'I like it,' Nadia says, but she switches it off. She is unsettled by the bleakness in his eyes. 'What's up, Simon? Everything all right?'

He puts his hands over his eyes and holds them there for a moment. When he takes them away she sees that he has mastered his expression. There is even the trace of a smile. 'Not really,' he says.

'What's up?'

'Celia's pulled out.'

Nadia feels a little surge of relief. 'Because of the weather? So it's off?'

Simon shakes his head. He fiddles idly with his letters. 'No and no,' he says. 'Actually it's because she's pregnant.' There is a pause. Nadia finds she is holding her breath. FAT, Simon puts. 'Six.'

'Is that all you can do?' Nadia sits back on the sofa. Energy drains from her, she can feel it, running down through her limbs, leaving her chilled. If it was anyone else . . . She can feel the leak of blood between her legs. 'Pregnant?' she repeats, and her voice has gone flat. 'That was

56

quick.'

'Oh God,' Simon says. He gets up and walks around the room. He goes to the window, pulls the curtain back and stares out at the night.

'She only said they were going to start trying on Sunday,' Nadia says weakly.

'She thought she might be then, apparently. Didn't want to say in case she wasn't. Test result this morning. Promised Dan she'd pull out if it was positive. So that's that.'

'Well, she could have warned you.' Nadia manufactures indignation on Simon's behalf.

'Mmmm,' Simon says. Nadia's belly groans, a sad sound. Simon snorts in half-amused acknowledgement.

'Still playing?' Nadia asks. Simon shakes his head. Nadia begins picking up the letters and dropping them into the bag. 'Lucky old Celia and Dan,' she says, unable to bear Simon's silence, unable to keep an edge of bitterness from her voice. She folds the Scrabble board and puts it in the box. 'You won,' she says. Simon breathes in very deeply as if he has been winded. 'What's up?' she asks. He shakes his head. 'I mean I don't see why you're *so* upset. You and Miles can still go, can't you, if you think it's wise in this weather?'

'Oh yes.' Simon turns towards her. 'I'm not upset.' Nadia swallows the last of her—now flat—wine. Simon sits down beside her and puts his arms around her. She pulls back and looks at him, seeing again the bleakness in his eyes. 'Sorry,' he says.

'Sorry for what?'

'Just sorry.' He holds her tight, burying his face in her neck.

There is something she must ask, though she fears the answer. She looks over his shoulder as she speaks, 'Simon, is it that you still . . .'

'No!' Simon exclaims, quite violently.

'Well then? What's the matter?'

'I don't know, I . . . I'm just sorry it isn't you.'

'Ah.' Nadia closes her eyes again. She lets him hold her, but her own arms are limp. Sorry! she thinks, how trivial a word. But sorrow is apt. It *is* sorrow she feels, but she rebels against pity. She feels, also, rage. But undirected. It is nobody's fault, is it, that Celia's reproductive system is so bloody efficient while her own has proved, so far, duff? What can she do with her rage? Where can she send it?

She does not want him touching her. She moves away, makes herself stiff, her face is like cardboard. He looks at her, puzzled.

'I'm going to bed,' she says.

'Don't be miserable, Nadia.' She doesn't answer, chews viciously on the corner of her thumbnail. 'I see you've been reading Plath again.'

'So?' She has ripped a shred of skin with her teeth, and it hurts. Tears come to her eyes. She gets up quickly to stop him seeing.

'Did you think *you* were?' he asks, but Nadia

will not answer. He follows her into the bathroom.

'Get out, will you. Can't I have some privacy?'

'You should have said,' Simon says. 'Isn't it to do with me? Nadia, are you angry with me?'

'Brilliant!' Nadia shuts the door in his face. She brushes her teeth, spits violent froth in the basin. She feels sick from the dinner and the wine and the news, Celia's wonderful news. She puts on her nightdress, gets into bed and pretends to read, ignoring Simon when he gets in.

'Funny how people who don't like poetry like Sylvia Plath,' he says.

'*And* people who do,' she retorts, turning the page. 'Does it threaten you?'

'Sorry.' Simon snuggles against her but she lies stiff. 'Of course it doesn't. I do love you,' he says miserably.

'I'm trying to read,' says Nadia.

Simon sleeps and Nadia listens resentfully to his breathing. I should not be angry with him, she thinks. My rage is not for him. Not really. But how can he sleep while I am so angry? How can he just slip away? It is evasion. It is a dirty trick. She moves roughly, elbows his ribs, but he does not wake, only sighs in his sleep and turns over. They should have talked. Air your differences, her mother would have said. Bring them out into the open. Did she really say that? And what differences? Celia is pregnant. She

59

can hardly blame Simon for that. Nadia is not pregnant. And that's not his fault either. Is it the caving that is making her so angry? But she always knew he was a caver, how can she be angry with him for being what he is? What he has always been.

We should have talked, she thinks, then I would be able to sleep. But I am not tired, I've been sleeping all day. How can Simon sleep while I'm so awake? He sleeps like a baby— only babies *don't* sleep at night, people complain. Lucky fertile people complain about their broken nights. How she would love to stumble from her bed to soothe a crying child. Simon groans as if he's having a dream. 'Bastard,' she whispers. Lines come into her head:

I was angry with my friend;
I told my wrath, my wrath did end.
I was angry with my foe,
I told it not, my wrath did grow.

I *do* like poetry, she thinks, suddenly sitting up, dragging the quilt off Simon. How dare he imply that I don't!

She gets up and stands glaring at Simon, who lies uncovered on the bed, dimly illuminated by the light from a street lamp outside their window. He sleeps naked, and his precious penis is squashed against his leg, clinging like a leech. She throws the quilt on

60

top of him and goes into the kitchen to heat milk. She drinks it sitting cross-legged in front of the gas fire, wrapped in her dressing gown. There must be a leak in the chimney, for every now and then there is a hiss and shudder from the fire as if a raindrop is finding its way in. There is a low sporadic sound that she cannot identify and then she realises that it is snoring; not Simon, but a rumble from downstairs. Iris's husband, perhaps.

Maybe it's Simon's sperm that's at fault. Simon, lying there so smugly oblivious in his sleep with his soft little leech. She imagines his sperm, inactive or maimed, swimming round in circles, their tails flapping feebly. She wonders if he's thought of that. That it might be his fault. But no. For she *has* conceived. And he told her once about a girl he'd made pregnant, who'd had an abortion. So it can't be him.

She goes into her studio, and looks into the cold cupboard at the drying pots. She could fire them tonight, since she's not asleep. It would take hours for the kiln to heat to temperature. It has to be switched on and off regularly for it mustn't heat too fast. It is a nuisance. Laborious. But it would be a use of the night that hangs so emptily ahead of her.

She picks up and taps the bottom of her pots, listening for the musical clink that tells her that they're quite dry. She hates them, the silly, smug shapes. What do they say? I am a mug. I am mask. I am hand-crafted. Buy me. That is

61

what they are designed to say. I won't make any more, she thinks. The egg-cups are not ready for firing. She should wait for them. But they are such trivial things. She breaks one against her bench. It splits easily.

She loads the kiln, and takes the bungs out to let the first moisture and gases escape as the pots begin to heat. Inside the peep-hole she puts some thermodynamic temperature cones. When the tip of the first one bends the temperature will be right for the bungs to go back in. She switches the kiln on. It hums faintly. She throws the bits of the broken egg-cup into a bin of dried fragments. The good thing about clay is that until it is fired it is green. It can be broken down, robbed of its edges: it can return to formlessness and be remade.

TEA

Nadia wedges some clay, turning it round and round, leaning all her weight on it, pressing into it with the balls of both her hands and then flopping it over, the stiff mass, waking it with her energy into a warmer plasticity. It is slick, grey clay, good, fat, stretchy, strong stuff. She slices through it with a wire, looks with satisfaction at the smoothness of the sliced surfaces, no grit, no pockets of air. It is even and dense. The wedging has tired her arms and shoulders; the muscles complain. She stretches back, one arm over her shoulder, one stretching up between her shoulderblades to catch the other's fingers, a yoga exercise to limber the back and shoulders, but her fingers slip from each other, ungraspable with their flaking film of clay.

And there it sits, a lump waiting to be assigned a form. There is no point, perhaps, but there is no point in leaving it either. No more point in a formless mass in her plastic-lined dustbin than in what it might become. The kiln hums in the corner, there is a little warmth leaking from it despite the insulation, and a hot baked-earth smell. She sat up most of the night waiting for the kiln to heat and now, in the morning, with sharp crumbs of sleep in the corners of her eyes, and undreamt dreams lurking in her head, she works.

And what will she make? She smooths her fingers over the surface of the clay. She thinks of Simon's shoulder, its beauty in the pearly dawn light. And then his sleeping body stripped naked by her anger, anger which for a moment she can't recall. The same body has the power to move her in some moods, anger her in others. And sometimes there is indifference. It is me, she thinks. The capacity of Simon's body to move me depends on my attitude, not on itself. She feels profound for a moment until her mother chips in: 'Beauty is in the eye of the beholder,' the oldest and tritest of her clichés. Said in response to Nadia's complaint about her own lack of beauty. Said, leaning over Nadia's shoulder, gazing into the mirror with her, with an inflection that meant that while she didn't behold beauty *herself*, you never knew what others might see. And Simon thinks she's beautiful; sometimes he says that, and sometimes she is.

She fingers the cold pliant clay. Work, she tells herself, you must work. You must make something. She digs her fingers in and fashions a crude face, hollow eyes, a pinched ridged nose, a gaping mouth. It is an ignorant, frightened face. She screws her fist into it to eradicate the features. Despite the slight warmth from the kiln she is cold. She wraps her hands around the lump, pulls it away from the bench, smooths it into a pleasing shape. It is a curled shape, something entire. A foetus perhaps, snug as a bud and at home like a sprat in a pickle jug—bloody Sylvia bloody Plath. She balls the clay and wanders into the kitchen to put on the kettle.

From the window, she watches Iris on her way out. It is raining slightly. She watches her hesitate before deciding to put up her umbrella, a clear plastic one inside which her head and shoulders are a blur. Is she off to sell fortunes or Intrigue? It will be Intrigue, because she has her sample case in her free hand. She walks quickly, there is optimism in her stride. Today, perhaps, she'll make some

64

sales.

In her studio, Nadia models a hand. She works fast. It is a palm, lying open, all the lines etched clear enough to read. She pauses and relaxes her own left hand on the bench, seeing the way the fingers curl up slightly, the hollowed palm with its net of lines exaggerated by the drying clay. She is curious about the lines, so intricate and so precise, stamped on her palms like brands. With a fine tool she teases the finger-ends into nails like her own, two bitten, one broken, one long. She uses her own long nail as a tool as she works, cleaning out the little wedges of clay from underneath it with her other thumbnail until there is a tiny pile like mouse-droppings scattered around the hand. The wrist is an ugly soft stump. She frowns, slices it off cleanly with a cheese-wire. Is that better? She stands back and considers it. She finds that her coffee is cold and is pleased, for that is a sign of absorption. This hand is the first thing she's been absorbed in for weeks. It may be pointless, but it is there, a fine, cold gesture, reaching out—or beckoning.

She looks through the peep-hole in the kiln. The pots are glowing cherry red. The last cone has bowed its head. She turns off the kiln. It makes a shuddery sigh, as if relieved. Now it will slowly cool, creaking and groaning. It will be a day before she can open it and take out the biscuit-fired pots, ready for their glaze. Once the pots are fired they are like stone again, they cannot be broken down except into useless shards. It is mysterious, the process, circular. First there is rock, which decomposes into clay, and then, after the digging, purifying and working, there is the firing, which transforms it into another kind of stone. But fragile.

She washes the grey clay off her hands, watches them grow pink in the hot water, the basin become filthy with the splashes. She is light-hearted. There is such satisfaction in making use of the morning, having something to show for it. Perhaps this is what she should do. Sculpture, sculpt from the human body. Perhaps she should employ a model, sculpt whole figures, sculpt all the different parts. To capture the language of the body, she thinks, that is it. The hesitations, the confidence, depression, friendliness, tension, exhilaration. Is it possible? As her toasted cheese bubbles under the grill she imagines an exhibition. Body Language? Voice of Clay? The Body Eloquent? There will be rows of faces—not the blank masks—eloquent faces and frozen limbs, held like question marks, exclamation marks, held in the poses that in living bodies are fleeting, are read subliminally. The Sublimation of the Subliminal? No! She grins into her toasted cheese. She eats standing up, gazing out of the window. In the Manner of the Word, perhaps? Iris returns, her umbrella furled under her arm, for it has stopped raining. By the dip of her head and the heavy

way she places her feet, Nadia can see that she
has had no success, that she is tired and fed up.
There is no need to see her face to be able to tell
that. This is what she must capture. Perhaps
she will not use faces, perhaps facial
expressions are too obvious, too easy. Faceless
Voices? Who would be her model? Who would
be grateful for a bit of cash? She hears Iris
banging shut the front door. Iris might. Later
she'll visit and ask her—and perhaps have her
palm read too.

*   *   *

'Hello.' Iris stands back from the door. 'Come
in, duck.'

Nadia can smell cooking. 'Are you eating?
It's nothing important. I can come back later.'

'You look better,' Iris observes. 'No, do
come in, it doesn't matter. Would you like
some?'

'I've eaten.'

'Sure?'

Iris leads her into the kitchen. 'Your
eyeshadow hasn't come yet,' she says.

'Oh no, I didn't expect ...'

'Derek, it's Nadia from upstairs,' she calls
through the wall. 'Just hold on while I dish up,'
she says.

She opens the oven and there is a rush of
brown meaty fragrance. She brings out a Fray
Bentos steak-and-kidney pie risen proud and

crusty from its tin. 'There's plenty for three,' she says, but Nadia shakes her head.

'Perhaps I'll go. You don't want me hovering while you're eating. I'm sure Derek won't.'

'Oh he's oblivious,' Iris says cheerfully. She tips a mound of steaming potatoes into a colander, shakes them and pours three-quarters of them onto one plate, the rest onto the other. She divides the pie into a large and a smaller piece. 'Sure?' she asks, with the knife poised. Nadia nods. 'No greens,' Iris apologises. 'I know they're good for you but we can't stick them. Come through.'

She picks up the heavily laden plate and, pushing sideways through a dangling door-screen of gaudy plastic strips, leads Nadia into the sitting room. It is a dark room, the light muffled by heavy net curtains, the spaces cluttered with spindly bits of dark furniture, every surface crammed with blown-glass animals, seals and parrots and gaudy dogs. The television is switched on and in front of it there is an enormous red moquette armchair, of which Nadia can only see the back, and above it the top of a dark head.

'Derek, this is Nadia; Nadia, Derek.' Iris leads Nadia round. Derek fills the armchair as if he has been modelled to fit it. His hair is long and his beard, luxuriant as any prophet's and liberally clotted with food, cascades over his belly. He nods at Nadia, and returns his eyes to

68

the screen, where an animated fireman is climbing a ladder.

Iris puts a tray with a picture of Buckingham Palace on it onto his lap and then the plate of food. 'We tend, usually, to watch TV while we eat,' he says, and his voice is a delicate well-bred surprise, as if the voice of a wood-pigeon had issued from the mouth of a frog.

'I'll come back later,' Nadia says again, wishing to escape from the overwhelming smell of steak-and-kidney and another, stranger, smell she can't identify. 'Daft of me to come at lunchtime. I get all out of sync., working alone.' Derek nods politely, but keeps his eyes on the screen. He begins shovelling potatoes into his mouth.

Iris beckons her out. 'I'll eat in the kitchen, duck. Then we can talk without that racket. Cup of tea?'

'Well if you're sure.'

Iris fills the kettle.

'No. You sit down. I'll make tea while you eat your lunch,' Nadia says. 'Much luck this morning?'

Iris sighs. 'One stinking deodorant. What shall I do with the profit? World cruise, do you think?'

Nadia smiles. 'I wondered if you'd do something for me. A bit of modelling. I'd pay.'

Iris snorts and a fragment of puff pastry flies across the table. 'Modelling? Me? What for, a shipwreck?'

'Some work I'm doing—some sculpture.'

'I don't know ... I mean I'm hardly Miss sodding World, am I?'

'That doesn't matter.'

'Would I have to strip off?'

'I don't think so. I'm interested in your hands and feet ...'

Iris looks at her rough stubby fingers, splays them in front of her. 'Modelling! Wait till I tell Derek!'

'So you will?'

'Don't see why not.'

'Wonderful. What about tomorrow, could you spare an hour in the morning?'

'I'll have to consult my diary,' Iris says, and grins.

'About ten? The other thing is, I wondered if you'd have time to do my fortune this afternoon—read my palm.'

'Bless you. Course I will.'

'How much?'

'To you, five pounds. I have a sliding scale,' she explains, and licks gravy from her lips. 'That's at the bottom of it. Don't mind Derek,' she says, lowering her voice, 'he's sedentary by habit.' With her fork she mashes a potato into the gravy from her pie. She eats it with a faraway look in her eyes. 'I fret about his heart. He eats like a frigging horse, but he doesn't work like one, that's what I say to him. All he does is sit, sit and eat and sleep. Loves his TV and his papers and a flutter on the horses. Does get into a lather over the horses.'

'Does he get out? I've never seen him before.'

'Tea's in the caddy,' Iris says. Nadia spoons it into the pot and puts on an orange woolly tea-cosy with a pom-pom on the top. 'Out?' Iris laughs briefly and then her face falls and in that change of expression Nadia sees the elusiveness she'd love to capture. But can it be captured, made solid, fired even, into stone? And without the use of the face, is there a corresponding body-signal, the beginning of a gesture ...?

'He gets as far as the bog, and into bed. Like sleeping next to a wart-hog,' she says. 'Snore?' She smiles grimly and lays down her knife and fork. Nadia recalls the rumbling last night, the sound she'd guessed was snoring, which vibrated through the floorboards.

'Can you sleep through it?' she asks.

'I sleep in the gaps,' Iris says. 'I sleep for a second and then wake, all night, sleep/wake, sleep/wake, like one of those lights that flick on and off.'

'A strobe? Can you really do that?'

'I've learnt. Now let's pour the tea and then we'll go through. You can meet Darling. He's in the back today, in my room. Getting on Derek's wick this morning, wouldn't shut up. I'll just take Derek his coffee—he won't drink leaf tea,' she explains, spooning Nescafe into a cup. 'Afraid I'll read something. He likes a biscuit though.' She takes a packet of

Garibaldis from the cupboard. Nadia glimpses, before the cupboard door closes, a stack of tinned pies, and another of biscuits. The kitchen is full of old-fashioned things: a wooden-handled washing-up brush, a handknitted dishcloth, a big slab of green soap, a coronation tea-caddy, things that remind Nadia of her grandmother, although Iris isn't old, can't be more than fifty-five.

'All right, that's him settled. Come through.' They carry their rattling cups and saucers into the back room. It's the room that corresponds to Nadia's studio upstairs, narrow and coldly lit. Nadia blenches at the stifling bird-stench, recognised now. She breathes through her mouth as she looks round. The room looks entirely different from her own, despite having the same shape and light. It is dominated by the crow in its majestic domed cage which is suspended from an elegant lamppost of a stand. But it is a homely room otherwise, with its flowery carpet and fat furniture—or would be if it were not for the liberal splattering of bird droppings and feathers.

'Meet Darling.' Iris taps the bars of the cage.

'Hello Darling,' Nadia says, but the bird looks morosely at the floor of its cage. It has a bald spot on top of its head and looks like a sour, disenchanted vicar.

'He's always shy with strangers,' Iris says. She makes some loving, chuckling noises in her throat. 'Moulting, aren't you? Normally you're a lovely glossy boy, aren't you?'

'Never mind.' Nadia smiles and looks around the room for signs of fortune-telling. Under a blue cloth by the window is what looks like the crystal ball.

The bird shuffles along his perch, sticks his tail through the bars and ejects a long brown dropping onto the carpet.

Iris tuts. 'Naughty boy,' she says. 'I'll put the fire on. Always bloody cold in here.'

'North-facing,' Nadia says.

'Sit down, do.' Iris indicates one of the armchairs by the fire. She switches the fire on and there is an electric flickering under the logs. 'Quite effective, don't you think?' she says, and Nadia doesn't know how to respond. There is an elusive teasing in Iris's voice. Is she serious?

She brushes the feathers off the chair and sits down opposite Iris.

'Drink your tea and I'll do your leaves. Free gift. Sales incentive, they call it,' Iris says.

Nadia sips her tea, avoiding the large leaves floating on the surface. It is weak, grey, strange tea.

'You look better,' Iris remarks, leaning forward and observing her.

'Sort of,' agrees Nadia. She wonders if she is allergic to crows. Her eyes have started to itch.

'China tea,' Iris says. 'Only they usually drink it without milk.'

'Oh?'

'Fortune teller's tea. Better leaves, though as

73

I say, anything will do. Finished? Leave a drop.' Nadia finishes her tea, bracing herself against the cooling slops, the leaves floating up against her lips. She picks a leaf from her mouth and replaces it in the cup.

'Finished.'

Iris looks into the cup. 'That's it. Now, turn the cup three times anti-clockwise. Concentrate. Shut your eyes.' Nadia does so, pinching her lips together against a smile. She's glad Simon can't see her sitting so foolishly between the fake fire and the sulking crow playing make-believe. Through the wall she can hear the drone of a racing commentator rising in excitement and a dull thud which must be Derek in a lather, thumping the arm of his chair or stamping. The crow belches.

'He begs your pardon,' Iris says, taking the cup.

She turns it upside-down. 'It has to drain,' she explains, 'and then ...' She turns the cup over and frowns into it, squinting and muttering. She looks up at Nadia as if puzzled, the electric firelight flickering oddly in her odd-coloured eyes.

'I see a lover ...' She pauses.

'That's Simon, yes.'

'I see a lover in danger. I see darkness. A bad omen ...'

'Oh God,' Nadia goes cold. 'That's the cave. He's a caver.'

Iris looks into the cup again. 'Could be ...

74

sometimes it's not *literal*, if you know what I mean.'

'Metaphorical?'

'I don't know about that. But it might not be a danger like caving, it could be a problem, a secret, a deceit ... that kind of danger.'

'But he is going caving, a dangerous expedition, he's supposed to be going this weekend! It *must* be that.'

'Well, maybe. But keep an open mind. And I see a mother ... your mother?'

'Haven't seen my mother for years.'

'Ah, that's it then,' Iris sits back. 'I see a mother alone. You should get in touch. Could you get in touch?'

'I could,' says Nadia, 'but I doubt I will.'

'Fallen out?'

'Sort of.' Nadia is reluctant to think about it.

'And that's it.'

'All you can see?'

'This *is* a free introductory offer,' Iris reminds her huffily. 'If you're ready to pay, I'll read your palm. I need the money first. I'm not being funny—that's how it's done.'

Nadia brings a five-pound note out of her purse. She is disgruntled by Iris's reading already. Doesn't want to hear more. But she feels committed now. She hands the money over.

'No,' Iris says. 'You hold it in your hand for a moment. Now, shut your eyes again. Relax.' Nadia tries, hoping this won't take long. She is

75

feeling chilly and faintly sick; there is almost a taste of crow in her mouth. She opens her eyes. 'All right?'

Iris nods and takes the money. She holds it in her hand for a moment, rubbing it between her fingers as if she could absorb information through her skin. Then she takes both of Nadia's hands in her own. She does not look at them but gazes unseeingly straight through Nadia, who is unnerved by the intensity of her expression. It is absurd. She wants to laugh. It is either absurd or frightening. It is unnerving the way the eyes are so different; the pale eye, reflecting light, seems candid and friendly, while the dark one soaks up light and secrets. Nadia tries to pull her hands away, but Iris squeezes them hard for a moment, screwing her eyes closed. Her hands are very hot and the pressure almost hurts.

Then she loosens her grip and smiles and her face is ordinary again, plain, doughy, good-natured. 'Now. You're right-handed?' She studies the two palms. 'The left is inheritance, the right what you make of it. Strong hands. Creative. You work with your hands?'

'Iris! I just told you that. I'm a scu—well, potter.'

'But dissatisfied, duck.' Iris rubs her thumbs into Nadia's palms, she seems to be reading them like Braille, hardly glancing at them, looking all the time at Nadia's face for her response. 'Time for a change of direction ...

there is inspiration ... but frustration. You should go for it, whatever it is, duck. Don't be afraid. I see success.'

'Yes?'

'And money ... not much ... no, you'll never be rich, but you'll be comfortable.'

How many people does that apply to? Nadia wonders.

'You're not easily taken in,' Iris says, narrowing her eyes. 'Nobody's fool. But you do have a tendency to trust some people, you should watch that.' She looks away, glances down at the hands. 'A good long life,' she traces her thumb down to Nadia's wrist, 'but there are breaks. Some illness in the abdomen, some weakness ... perhaps some nervous trouble? You take things to heart.' She pauses as if waiting for encouragement, but Nadia keeps her mouth shut. She will not help. 'You're passionate,' Iris continues. 'He's a lucky man—Simon, isn't it? And he's yours for keeps—barring accidents.'

'Is he?'

'You must watch your health.'

'I do yoga, and I don't smoke.'

'Good. I see a move soon. I see water, a move across the water.'

'Can't imagine that.'

Iris shrugs. 'Only telling you what I see. Someone close to you, a woman, will be ill. A problem with a lump ... a relative. Sister? Someone whose name begins with J?'

Nadia shakes her head. 'I've no sisters. No one I can think of.'

'Now, have you a question?'

Nadia hesitates. She clears her throat, tries to keep her voice light, succeeds in sounding utterly unlike herself, like some thin impersonation of Celia. 'What about sprogs?'

'Kiddies? Ah, so that's it.' Iris runs her thumbs up the outsides of Nadia's hands, glances down.

'Just a question.'

'Not important?' Iris gives a knowing smile and Nadia bristles, pulls her hand away. Iris looks searchingly at her. Really she looks almost half-witted with her light and her dark eye, and her unkempt scribbled face.

'I don't see any ... but you can't tell, something like that ...' Tears jump to Nadia's eyes. 'So that's what's up,' Iris says. 'I thought, yesterday, I could see it in your eyes.'

'Must go,' says Nadia standing up.

'Don't rush off, there's more ...'

'No, that's enough.' The crow smell is choking her, making her eyes run.

'I've upset you. Should keep my bleeding mouth shut, shouldn't I? Open it and put my foot right in.'

'No, it's all right, I asked you,' Nadia says in a stifled voice. 'Must go, that's all.'

Iris follows her through into the hall. 'Would you like to talk ...? I do know ...'

'No thanks.'

'Stay for another cup of tea, not leafy muck, proper tea with a teabag.'

'No ...'

'Oh sods,' Iris wails.

'Another time,' Nadia says, desperate to get out. 'Bye, Derek,' she calls. There is an answering yell of fury as a horse loses a race.

'See you in the morning—about ten, shall I?' Iris asks.

'Oh, yes ... Bye.' Nadia flinches away from Iris's extended hand.

'It's all a load of cobblers, Nadia,' Iris calls after her. 'Don't believe a word.'

Nadia almost runs along the road, gulping fresh air deep into her lungs, brushing her hair with her fingers to rid herself of the sensation of dirty feathers. There is something soft on the sole of her shoe, something she picked up from Iris's carpet; she pauses to scrape it off on the kerbstone. It looks like a sliver of meat, or a worm. She shudders, wondering what crows eat.

The sky is heaped with grubby clouds but between them are stretches of tight blue silk. Sunlight glints from puddles in gutters and the soaked grass in the park. She decides to go through the park and breaks into an awkward run. Her feet splash in the puddles, a gardener looks at her curiously. There are no children this morning, a showery schoolday. She stops by the duck-pond, quite breathless. The surface of the water is enamel green and the ducks are suspended motionless within it, their beaks closed, their slick feathers folded around them as tightly as if they were carved. There is soggy bread floating on the surface of the water. The ducks in this city park are spoilt rotten. They ignore her, but sparrows dance about her feet begging for crumbs.

Nadia fumes. How *dare* Iris presume to know her problem when she's more or less a complete stranger? And then, after all that, to call it a load of cobblers. As if it could be anything else! What a fraud the woman is with her odd, mad eyes and her stinking bird. And what did she really say? So obvious, all of it, so generally applicable. That there will be no children is the answer. That's what she really said. And what about the tea-leaves? What about the danger to Simon? Is cobblers all it really is?

She stalks along, hands in her pockets, wishing she hadn't asked Iris to model. She'll always be round now, prying, sticking her nose in. And what does she mean, anyway, she *does* know? Nadia kicks an empty can and it clatters satisfyingly, sending a rabble of pigeons whirring into the trees.

And what is the point of copying lumps of a lumpish woman in clay? She brushes the wetness off a bench with the sleeve of her coat and sits down. There is something wrong with the hand she made, it comes to her as she watches the clouds gathering and dispersing,

80

they make almost-pictures—a castle with a streaming moat becomes a grazing cow becomes a dragon breathing fire becomes a mouse with a fractured tail. The hand is too literal, that is the trouble. It is literally a hand, actually her own hand. It has no flow. There should be a flow, like the flow of clouds. The shapes will be solid, of course, but ideas must be able to flow around them, form and re-form like the pictures in the clouds.

*   *   *

Simon looks at the tops of the heads of his industrious class. A good class to have last thing in the afternoon. Some classes are impossible to control at the end of the day, all ears cocked for the finishing bell. Here, almost everyone is working. There's Laura gazing out of the window, and Joe's head is bobbing. He looks closer, sees the earphones in his ears. Takes a step towards him, and then stops. Let him be. He's not doing any harm. Let him think he's got away with something. Only fifteen minutes to go. Simon is the one all ears for the finishing bell. The class are tracing isobars onto their maps. They have been studying weather.

Simon brushes chalk-dust off his hand onto his trousers. He must ring Miles. There is no reason not to go ahead with the expedition. It has rained, true, and he wouldn't advise

81

inexperienced cavers to take any risks. But he and Miles know what they're doing. Just as well, perhaps, that Celia has pulled out. She is so cautious; the Voice of Reason, they call her. Many times she's called a halt, retreated, insisted that they abandon an expedition. Bloody women, he and Miles have muttered mutinously behind her back. Sometimes— only sometimes—they have had to admit that she was right. But this time nothing will stop them. He looks at his watch, taps it impatiently as if to speed it up.

He follows Laura's eyes. She is gazing out at the daffodils on the school lawn. Most of them are broken off, trampled by trespassers across the green in front of the school. It is a logical short-cut. Whoever designed the entrance? Did they really expect the kids to walk round by the path to the door, twice as far? The sun is shining smugly now, as if it had never stopped. It shines on the daffodils and the window, illuminating the vertical smears the window cleaners have left. It shines on the hair of the children nearest the window. Laura has lovely hair, he notices, toffee-coloured, and long dreamy eyes, beautiful, actually. In a few years' time ... Her cheeks are as soft and full as summer fruits, an apricot bloom.

'Sir?' It is clever Zachary at the front, blinking earnestly through his spectacles.

Simon sighs. 'Yes, Zach?'

'Sir, I've been wondering how maps are

82

made. In the first place, I mean.'

'Good question, we'll come to it later in the course.'

'I mean, how can the world be drawn as if it is flat? Won't it be distorted? And who decides what goes in the centre?'

Simon sighs. Surely it's time for the bell? 'Big questions, Zach. There are different projections—there'll always be some distortion of course ... on a rectangular projection you get distortion of high-latitude areas ... Tell you what, I'll bring some in next time. They come in all shapes, all attempts to reduce distortion. As to who decides the centre ...'

He tails off, but Zach looks satisfied, goes back to his isobars.

The school cat stalks across the green and settles itself down in the sunshine. A woman pushes a push-chair up the school path, pink padded arms and legs wave feebly from it. He thinks of the baby—not baby yet, the blob— inside Celia. He sees Celia by the fire— ridiculously, for it is the last thing she would ever do—knitting a shawl.

There is the premature rumble of chairs being shuffled that always precedes the final bell.

'OK you lot,' Simon says. 'Pack up now.' And then there is the rude but welcome jarring of the bell.

Thank Christ for that, thinks Simon.

*   *   *

Sunshine discovers a soft hollow by the road, and there is a stirring. Green sepals split, spilling thick yellow primrose cream. Furled fern fists lift and splay their fingers. Green life nuzzles out of the earth into the warmth. Small creatures scuttle, brittle wings glint. And the stirring becomes a more vigorous movement. Under the surface, a tangle of snakes is awakening. The sun warms the blood in their sluggish veins and the serpentine struggle back to life after a dormant winter is transmitted from body to sinuous body. There is an orgy of slithery wriggling and then, at once, the creatures separate, glide away through the bracken, pressing their muscular sides against stones and plant stems, winding away, until the writhing place is still, and only the squashed bracken stirs as it rights itself.

CLAY

Nadia brushes her hair vigorously, tearing through the snarls, until it fills with static and flies up to meet the brush. Simon has gone to work. She has a memory of a kiss, and then the bang of the door. She had slept again, woken, wept for the might-have-been child and then got up. Sunlight patches scatter from the window, there is the fruity song of a bird. She is suddenly energetic, enthused with ideas for her new project. She looks at her own body under the shower, solid curves and planes, smoothness and dimples, the roughness of knees and elbows, the sharpness of nails.

Naked, she performs the Sun Salutation, bending and stretching and flexing her whole body, feeling the stiff morning muscles relent, the blood flow. She relaxes on the floor and an oblong of sun stretches across her; there is even a faint warmth through the glass, as if someone has laid a warm towel on her belly. She wriggles, feeling unexpectedly sexy. It is the sun and the exciting sizzle of spring in the air. Simon, Simon, Simon, she thinks. Or somebody.

Tonight he will be off on his adventure. Last night she had to endure his preparations. The sitting-room floor was strewn with his gear, and he was abstracted, not with her at all. She didn't tell him what Iris had seen in the tea-leaves, he'd only have scoffed, looked at her in that disbelieving way that says, Are you really so credulous? And anyway, even Iris said it was cobblers. And it will be all right. She strokes her belly, lit gold in the sun. She sits up and stretches forward, her face against her knees, and she licks her own skin, tastes the clean soapiness. She sees the first hairs beginning to poke through the skin, unevenly. It's ugly the way they grow, stiff with their sliced-off ends like miniature logs. Later she'll shave them.

She shivers. It is time to dress and then to work. She plans to work all day. Iris needn't stay long. She'll work until she's exhausted. Say nothing scathing to Simon, if he goes—will he really go? She must trust his judgement. She will be bright and ordinary, kiss him when he leaves as if he's off to work, or to play squash. She must not mock. The day will go in a flash, and there is no need for any fear.

It's a relief to enjoy work again, to experience enthusiasm in her fingers for the feel of the clay and for what she can make it be. And once Iris has gone, once she has some ideas, a few sketches, she can work speechlessly. All the energy will be in her fingers, the thought and the decision she will trust to their sense.

She sees the lump of clay in the bin as a lump of possibility today. She only has to get Iris over with. Why use Iris? Why not her own self? But she has asked now, and Iris was eager, flattered to be asked.

When the kiln had cooled she'd opened the door to find only a couple of casualties: a mug and a mask both cracked, but the other items are lined up ready for the glaze. And there is no rush.

At ten o'clock Iris arrives. She wears a black-fringed red silky shawl over her brown skirt and cardigan. 'What do you think?' she says, turning round as she enters to give Nadia the full effect.

'Nice.'

'Might as well look the part as not.' Iris throws it over her shoulder. 'This afternoon,' she adds, 'I'm seeing about my hair.'

'Do you want coffee?' Nadia asks, 'or shall we get straight on?'

'Depends if you're paying by the hour,' Iris says. Her voice is smiling, trying to ingratiate. Nadia looks away.

'I'll give you a fiver this morning,' she says. 'It probably won't even be an hour. Is that OK?'

She leads her into the studio. 'If you sit there,' she indicates the chair she's placed by the window, 'and take off your shoes and ... are you wearing tights?'

'Stockings,' Iris says.

'I thought everyone wore tights these days.'

'Give me claustrophobia in my you-know,' Iris replies, hauling up her skirt and fiddling with a pink suspender button. 'Wouldn't have put them on if I'd known ...' she grumbles under her breath. She peels off the stocking and hangs it over the arm of the chair. The stretched foot dangles coyly, toes turned in. 'Cold in here,' she remarks. 'You ought to get yourself a bit of carpet.'

'Can you imagine cleaning the clay off it?'

'That's a point.'

'The heater'll come on in a minute.'

'Wouldn't say no to a coffee, since you ask,' Iris says, sitting heavily down.

'OK.' Nadia goes into the kitchen to make her one.

'I went to university, you know,' Iris says when she returns.

'Really?' Nadia hands her her coffee.

'That's surprised you. Had me down as thick, didn't you?'

'No, not at all,' Nadia says, but she is surprised. 'You're one up on me, then,' she says. 'I went to art school. What did you read?'

'English. At Leeds. But I didn't stick it. Only stayed till the first Christmas, not my cup of tea. Fish out of water, me. I like books, reading, all that ... but they are only books, aren't they, duck? Got it all out of proportion there they had. There was a kerfuffle when I left—after all the effort it took to get there— Dad none too pleased. And then I met Leonard.'

Nadia has picked up her pencil and is roughly sketching the position of Iris's foot, which rests tensely on the low stool as she talks.

'Leonard?'

'My first husband. Lovely man, gentle, generous ... Had this feeling about him, broken head line, bad sign however you read it. Sign of early death. But couldn't help myself. Couldn't wait either—and I was bloody right as it turned out.'

'What happened?'

'Third anniversary, crushed by a ton of cod at Grimsby Harbour.'

88

'Oh dear ...' Nadia feels an alarmed smile jump to her face.

'It's all right, it does sound comical. He'd had *his* chips ...'

'Iris!' Nadia looks at her. Is she joking? Again there is an enigmatic glitter in her eyes.

'Well, you have to laugh,' she says. 'Never regretted it—leaving university I mean, marrying Leonard. Better to have loved and lost than ...'

'And now there's Derek.'

'Yes, well ...' Iris sighs. She leans forward. 'Sorry about yest—' she begins.

'Can you keep still?' Nadia asks.

'Only I *do* know ...'

'I need to concentrate.' Nadia keeps her eyes on Iris's foot.

There is silence for a moment and then the fan heater switches on.

'Clever,' Iris remarks.

'On a thermostat.'

Nadia sneaks a look at Iris's face. She has pressed her lips together, looking sad and perplexed, as if trying to come to some decision.

'I'd rather not talk just for a moment, if you don't mind,' Nadia says. 'Would you like the radio on?'

'I'm all right, duck,' Iris replies. 'You just carry on.'

* * *

Once Iris has gone, Nadia really works. She prepares the clay and then stops, regards it, a grey lump, a cold dead mass. And then she begins. She takes it between her hands and begins to work life into it. Energy and warmth flow through her fingers, press into the structure of the clay until it responds, until it almost begins to take responsibility for its own form, to communicate with her hands. She forgets the sketches she began with and becomes absorbed in the work, in the touch and the smell of the clay, often she closes her eyes as she squeezes and pinches and moulds, for her eyes are too intellectual, too literal. Her eyes bring words into her mind and it is not words she is after, it is a feeling, something there are no words for, a spontaneous rhythm.

She works for hours and it is hunger that brings her to. The form she has made is something like a foot. It is not literally a foot, but it has the tension of a foot about to run, a lifting, so that it seems reluctantly rooted to the bench. Or it could be a plant, a strange yearning shoot, but muscled. It is unlike anything she has ever done or seen. She is exhilarated by it, delighted and alarmed. She shivers. It is cold in the room, the heater has switched itself off again. There is a distant sunlit sheen outside in the world she has temporarily forgotten. Cars are travelling on the road, birds are sending out shrill slivers of sound, gradually the world edges back. Her neck aches, and her wrists. She shakes her hands and feels and hears the tiny clicking of her strained joints.

And here is this—thing—that she has made. The surface of the clay dulls as she watches, the first minute particles drying in the air. And if it works—if for anyone else it works—if it is art, then there need be no end to it. She could do it again. Could she do it again? The transformation of the ordinary—Iris's ordinary lumpish foot—into, what? Art? What's that? The ineffable? She snorts at her own pomposity.

The thing is puzzling to look at, but intriguing. Is it? Or is it simply nonsense? Nadia longs for fresh eyes. It has been part of her all day, there has been no distance. Perhaps it has always been part of her. So how can she tell? She rubs the drying clay between her fingers and thumbs. The doorbell rings. Impatiently and abstractedly, she goes to answer it. It is Celia.

*   *   *

'Oh.' Nadia is caught off guard. 'Simon's out,' she says. She runs her clayey fingers through her rough hair. She is wearing no make-up and she is filthy.

'I know, I've come to see you, not Si,' Celia says.

'I've been working ...'

91

'Have I interrupted?'

'No. Just finished. Come in then,' Nadia says ungraciously, standing back to let Celia past. 'Go into the kitchen. I'll just wash my hands.'

She throws a damp cloth over the thing, for is it finished, or not? And then she washes her hands, letting the water run scalding hot, glimpsing her unmade-up face and her messy hair in the clay-spattered square of mirror above the sink. She is not ready for company, not anybody, most certainly not Celia. She is annoyed to be interrupted, not from the work, which is finished for now, but from the underground river of thought, the almost-contact with her subconscious that a working day, that speechless hours, afford. It is particularly irritating that it is Celia who has barged in. Broken the mood. I should have sent her away, she thinks, shouldn't have answered the door. Should have looked through the spy-hole, and left her outside. But through her dislike is threaded a string of fascination. For Celia was Simon's lover. It is fascinating to try to see what Simon saw.

'I've put the kettle on,' Celia says.

'Fine. I'm having a sandwich. Want anything?' Celia shakes her head. Nadia slices bread and cheese and a tomato. 'Sure? I'm starving.'

'Working hard?'

'All day.'

92

'Found the point?'

'What? Oh yes.' Nadia is surprised Celia remembers Sunday's trivial conversation. 'Don't know about that. Maybe I've invented a new one. For myself I mean. I'm sculpting some ... oh never mind.' Why should she explain what she's doing to Celia? And how can she explain? It would sound so bloody arty and pretentious and trite.

'Sculpting? I thought you were a potter.' Nadia looks at her with sharp dislike. She notices how pale Celia looks, how there are shadows under her eyes. 'Or is that the new point? Art instead of craft?'

'Not exactly.' The kettle hisses and Nadia switches it off, spoons instant coffee into mugs. 'Anyway, what do you want?'

'Have you any sugar?' Celia asks, smiling wryly. 'I've got a sudden craving for the stuff. White death.'

'It'll have to be brown death,' Nadia says, bringing out an ancient, solid bag of muscovado. 'Oh yes. Congratulations. Simon told me. You'll have to chip a bit of that off,' she adds, for Celia's teaspoon has met with resistance.

'Thanks.' Celia sugars her coffee and Nadia sees the teaspoon trembling between her fingers.

She sits down opposite Celia and eats a mouthful of her sandwich. 'God, I'm starving,' she says. Celia watches her. 'So?' Nadia asks.

'What do you want?' She corrects the brusqueness in her voice. There is no need to be quite so rude. 'I mean you've never been to see me before. Only Simon.'

'Well, yes, no. Is he still going tonight?'

'I think so—Miles is a bit dubious. They'll decide at the last minute.'

'Oh.' Celia looks wistful.

'You *could* go,' Nadia says.

'Oh no ... even if I wasn't up the spout I wouldn't, what with the weather. Bloody headbangers. Men.'

Nadia frowns at her. This is not like Celia. Why does she seem so vulnerable? She doesn't even look particularly pretty today, sort of worn down and anxious.

'I hope they don't go,' Celia says.

'Is that what you've come to tell me?'

Celia sips her coffee and wipes her mouth with the back of her hand. 'You said Simon told you? That I'm in the club?'

'Yes.'

Celia takes a deep breath. 'Is that all he told you?'

'Yes. Why?' Celia's face is transfused with a tremulous resolve. Nadia's mouth goes suddenly dry. She puts down her sandwich. 'Why?'

'There's something I want to tell you,' Celia says. 'I mean, not that it will make any difference to any of us. I just feel I have to tell you.'

'What?' Nadia slides her hands under her thighs to stop them shaking. Outside a bicycle bell rings. She notices that her spider plant needs watering. 'What?'

Celia's voice is defensive. 'I don't see *why* it should make any difference.'

'*What?*'

'That Simon is the ... the donor.'

'Donor? What?' Nadia fends off the truth. She squeezes her eyes and sees sparkling darkness.

'Well, the father; only biologically, of course ...' Celia hesitates, looking frightened now. 'You had no idea ... no, I can see ... I thought maybe ...'

Nadia stares hard at the table, at the surface which is so ringed and pocked. Simon is always saying he will sand it. She pulls her hands out from under her thighs and examines the fingertips, which have paled to ivory. The patterns of her fingerprint, the intricate whorls and the hair-like lines, are grey with the faintest tracing of clay. They look like complex pebbles—agate perhaps. Something semi-precious. She slides her eyes down to see Celia's feet under the table, her black shoes, the hems of her jeans. 'Donor?' she says. 'Father?'

She remembers Simon's attitude the evening Celia had rung. How he had missed a beat, kept his back turned a moment too long.

'I really thought you'd know,' Celia pleads. 'Oh Christ, I've done it now. I thought you'd have guessed, or he'd have told you.'

Nadia looks at Celia as if hypnotised, watching the way her face moves, the muscles in her cheeks bunching and flattening as she speaks, her eyes widening and narrowing, the stretching of her lips ... the moist tongue inside, the slight unevenness of her teeth. 'It wasn't romantic,' she is saying, as if offering an excuse. 'You should know that. I mean I admit I tried to make it, you know, nice, natural. I invited him to dinner, but he said no.'

'With Dan too?' Nadia asks.

'No! Si said no to dinner. Said that would make him feel unfaithful. Scrupulous Simon!' She gives a hard little laugh. 'He came round on the day. The day I was ovulating ... Did all that revolting knicker-gazing and temperature-taking for a few weeks to be sure. Rang him. Dan went out. Si came round. Had a drink. Hardly spoke. I mean we'd spoken earlier when I persuaded—well, asked: he hardly needed *persuading*.' She meets Nadia's eyes almost as if this is a collusion but Nadia snatches hers away. She realises she hasn't been breathing and forces breath all the way down inside her to fill her poor shocked flattened lungs.

'We did it very quickly. Almost impersonally—no, *clinically*. We didn't even kiss. I didn't enjoy it, you should know that. It was something he did to me, like artificial respiration or something.'

'Except it wasn't artificial.' Nadia's voice is husky.

'Well, no. And as soon as we'd finished, well, *he'd* finished, he left. He didn't kiss me, not once. I lay in bed for ages, knees up, visualising the little buggers swimming up, egging them on ...' She stops, waiting for Nadia to speak.

'So Dan knows?'

'Of course. Actually it was his idea. Not Si ... but the general idea.' Celia sips her coffee. She has regained her self-possession now that she has spoken.

'Dan's idea,' Nadia repeats. Her mind has gone sluggish. She looks at the bread on her plate, the protruding lip of cheese, a viscous tomato pip which has fallen onto the table.

'Yes. He had the snip years ago—first marriage, one kid. Ten years ago, more. Never dreamt he'd want to do it again, reproduce that is. But then we decided. So it was reversal—expensive, dodgy—or AID, or this.'

'This. Simon.'

'Seemed the best option. No need for doctors, nothing offputting and medical. And I talked him round to considering Si. We both like him. He's good-looking, healthy, intelligent—and there is some similarity between them. I mean, I know Dan's dark and Si's fair, but otherwise ...'

'Interchangeable,' Nadia mutters.

'Well no, but ...' She finishes her coffee. 'And anyway, when Dan came home we made love.'

'Straight after? Didn't you even wash?' Nadia shudders.

'We made love very—well, thoroughly. And that night I conceived. So it does feel a bit like Dan's.'

'Is that what you're planning to pretend? I mean you and Simon when you plotted this...' Nadia's shock is warming into anger. How can Celia be sitting calmly in her kitchen saying these things! 'Are you planning to pretend it's Dan's?'

Celia has not noticed Nadia's anger. She pulls a sad clown's face. 'Don't know. That *was* the idea. Dan's pretty adamant.'

'*Was* the idea? What's changed?'

'Well, I've told you, haven't I? You haven't got a biscuit, have you?'

'No,' Nadia lies. 'Why did you tell me?'

'I don't know ... I suppose when it came to it, I couldn't stand the deception.' Bully for you, thinks Nadia. 'I told Si to tell you, I thought he should. But he said you wouldn't understand ...'

'Too bloody right!' Nadia gets up. She throws her sandwich in the bin. 'So, does Dan know you're telling me? Or Simon?'

'Well, no, not yet. But Nadia, I thought you should know. It is to do with you ... but it really needn't make any difference.'

'Thanks very much,' Nadia snaps. 'And I'm expected to keep mum—ha!—now am I?'

'I would have thought it was in your interests,' says Celia stiffly. 'I didn't think you'd take it like this.'

'Like bloody what? What did you expect!' She pauses, tries to calm herself. 'You do know Simon and I have been trying?'

'Yes.' Celia looks sheepish.

'You do know about the miscarriage?' Celia nods. 'So you can hardly expect me to be overjoyed.'

'Oh Christ, Nadia, I am sorry. I didn't think it through, all that side of it. Only afterwards, that's why I came round.'

'I wouldn't expect *you* to have thought, but I would have expected Simon ...' She feels the back of her throat hollowing with impending tears and grits her teeth against them.

'I've made a mistake,' Celia says dully. 'I shouldn't have told you. Oh shit.'

'You'd better go,' Nadia says. 'I need to work.' She blinks, angry to find that her eyelashes are wet.

'I suppose you'll tell Si that I've been round. What will you say?'

'None of your business,' Nadia says. 'Go.'

Celia goes out of the door. She turns. 'Honestly, I didn't mean to hurt you.'

Nadia slams the door.

MOONMILK

Nadia's anger is like the bright hot embers of a fire. It glimmers under the greyness of ash, but it takes only the slightest stir, the merest breath, to fuel it into brilliant lashing flame. The anger is a painful thing. It burns her stomach. It leaves no room for food. It heats her ribs until they flutter like hot fans against the stone of her heart.

She wanders around the flat. Everything is very still and clear. There are hard edges around every separate object like the black outlines in a child's colouring book. Shadows are precise like neat, scissor-cut cardboard shapes. The eyes in her masks are very dark and neat—and the slice-shaped mouth-holes.

She stands in the kitchen watching water drip from the tap. Each drop gathers round the outside rim of the tap, then forms itself for the splinter of a second into a perfect crystal pear, reflecting in its minuscule life the blur that is Nadia. And then it drops into the half-full bowl. The circles it creates are swollen ridges riding to the margins of the bowl as the drop becomes one with the greasy water, to be replaced by the next fattening drop.

Celia is fattening with the developing child. Of course, it is imperceptible yet. Of course, it has started to rain. Only an April shower—but

100

the sky has blackened. Nadia looks out of the window, disoriented. The light is strange. The sun still shining somewhere finds its way through the cloud like a torch shining yellow under a grey blanket. The lining of Celia's womb will be rich and velvety red with the quilted, unshed blood. It will be a luxurious place for Simon's child.

The trip will be off then. What with this rain. Nadia feels a spiteful pleasure that he will be thwarted. Simon is not suicidal. Why, he is to be a father! He has everything to live for. 'It should have been you,' he said. Now she sees, now she understands. She wishes he *would* go and that he would die.

Soon he will be home. Bastard man. He will park his car on the road outside. She will hear the door slam. She will hear his key in the door. She will hear his footsteps on the stairs and then he will be in. Will his hair be just a little wet from the rain? Will he kiss her? He will walk into the kitchen in his bloody beautiful traitor's body and somehow she will have to speak to him. Air will travel back past her larynx to be formed by her throat, her soft palate, her tongue and her lips into words. And what will they be? The flames leap within her and she groans at the scorching pain.

Does she really wish that he would die? Those clumped tea-leaves against the white china of the cup said that he would. But he won't go. Death seems the only possible remedy for the anger she feels. Murder. The shock of absolute cold to quench the flames. But Simon's death? Or Celia's? Or, somehow, the baby's? Or even her own? Nadia grasps her hair roughly and pulls hard for the shock of pain. A tangle comes away in her fingers. To think of killing a baby! The hair is warm. She looks at its dry crinkles. She can understand murder, crimes of passion. It must be an irresistible urge, like the stupid scratching of an unbearable itch which you know will lead to pain, make things worse, but it is just not possible to resist. A temporary madness. She understands this.

In her studio she kneads a lump of clay into ugly shapes, into gaping mouths, malformed fish, mutations. She forms it into a phallus: slick fat grey bulbous. She pinches a nose upon it, pokes eyes and a mouth. It has a look of Simon. Ugly monster thing. She makes the Simon-phallus smile, bow, rubs its face on the rough surface of the bench and then she thumps it, grinds her fist into it until it is nothing.

She cannot be here when Simon returns, that much is clear. She cannot. She cannot be held responsible. She will go out, must go out. Now, quick, before he returns. She will go out now and spend some of the dreadful energy that is in her limbs. She will not be here for Simon when he returns. Because she cannot speak to him, not now, or she might ... well, anything

102

might happen. And she cannot *not* speak to him either. Not when he is here, cooking, eating, chatting, washing. Making love to her? What would he expect them to do tonight since he will not be caving? The cinema perhaps? So she could sit like a boiling cauldron beside him.

No, she must go. Not to a friend's, no, not somewhere she will have to be normal. It must be somewhere she can be anonymous, where she can pay to be alone. A hotel. She will take her bicycle, which she hasn't used for months, not for the whole of the winter, and she will just go. Just temporarily disappear. Simon can worry. She will leave no word. Doubtless Celia will telephone and he will know why she has gone. Let Celia tell him then. Let them try and sort it out between them. Let him sweat.

Nadia throws some make-up and a pair of clean knickers into a bag. She ties her hair back with a scarf. She glances at herself in the mirror and hesitates, surprised by the small whiteness of her face. She puts on her cagoule and goes out into the muddy gloom to the communal shed to dig out her bicycle. It is behind a tangled pile of gardening equipment and she steps over this ruthlessly, feeling bamboo canes snap beneath her feet. She hauls the bike over the heap, out into the rain. It is cobwebbed and the chain is dry. The rear light doesn't work. Swearing, she goes back upstairs to search for some batteries. She feels the panic of rush. Simon must not catch her. The batteries in the torch are almost flat. Those in her cassette player are too small. She casts around, panicking, almost crying, and then she thinks of Simon's stuff. He has batteries. Which he won't need. He won't miss them. And serve him bloody right if he does. He can sit and stew. When he knows that she knows ... There is a terrible searing inside her and a monstrous painful glee. She finds the ugly cusp of a smile on her face. Get out of this one, Simon. And she will simply be gone.

She runs downstairs, puts the batteries in her light and wheels the bicycle round to the front of the house. There is a banging at the downstairs window. Nadia looks up impatiently. It is Iris. Is it? Iris has a pile of impressive raven—crow—black hair upon her head. Where has it all come from? Nadia lets out a foolish bleat of laughter. She returns Iris's wave. Her back tyre is flat. She takes the pump off the frame, fumbles with the valve, screws on the adaptor. She will pump only a bit, only enough to get going. She must go. What if Simon arrives now? She pumps hard, catches Iris's eyes still upon her. She is waving something and gesticulating. The rain lashes Nadia's face, it is turning to hail, sharp spiteful grit. Nadia finishes pumping, screws up the valve, her fingers giant and fumbling. The hail skitters and bounces on her bicycle frame. She ignores Iris, who is still trying to attract her attention. Terribly rude but there is no time.

104

She gets on her bike and wobbles away. She has to hold her cagoule hood up with one hand or it will blow off. It is hard to pedal. The stiff chain clanks and complains, the tyres are still too soft, but still, it is good to be moving through the darkening afternoon. Good to be *doing* something. It is spring. It should be warm and light but the stubborn army-blanket of cloud and the hail that is turning back to rain seem fitting somehow, more fitting for this flight. She rides head-down, eyes narrowed against the wet, the hood obscuring her vision, so she doesn't see Simon's white car rounding the corner, never realises quite how narrowly she missed him.

Nadia rides out of town, past the park and the rows of shops, through streets of terraced houses, past an empty school. She rides on to where the road widens, where sulphurous daffodils flinch in the long grass verges and the expensive houses are set further and further back from the road. She hears the rubbery sigh of cars arriving home at the end of the day. Is he back yet? The road is slick with reflections and slithering car lights. Cars swooshing past splash her with muddy water. Rain finds its way in at the neck seams of her cagoule, the cold trickles mingle with hot beads of perspiration. Damn Simon, damn Simon, damn Simon is the sound her pedals make clanking against the chainguard.

Nadia puts her foot down and stops for a

moment. She has left the houses behind now, ridden through the leafy rhododendrons of the valley. How long has she been riding? Her legs are wobbly with the effort. She breathes hard, her lungs hurt and her heart pounds. She realises that the rain has ceased and ahead of her she sees an oblique slant of powdery light illuminate the top of a hill, turning it a shimmering silver-green, turning a drystone wall to pewter. She looks back. The road slopes darkly away towards the town. She has reached the top of a long slope. It is not so cold now. There is a scent in the air like squashed buds, the sappy smell of spring. She sits back on her bike and freewheels down the hill, tyres sizzling through wetness. She lets her hood blow down and the moist air rushes against her face. It is almost all downhill to The Hawk, a pub on the edge of the Peaks where she will stay. She has stayed here before, but not with Simon. And probably never with Simon, never ever now.

She feels—not pleasure exactly—what? Some sort of satisfaction. She whizzes, daring to go too fast, tempting fate. The bumping of the saddle is almost pleasurable, the green edges of the road are a jumping blur, but the hills are still and clear. There are sheep and there are lambs, some straying onto the edge of the road. The light is like an illustration from a Bible story. She takes some confused comfort from it, sits back on her bicycle, closes her eyes for a moment. And then there is a violent jolt and her thoughts flash—What if I die? What if I break my neck?—before she crashes onto the road. The bike grates past and stops, one wheel spinning almost gaily. She lies motionless for a moment, waiting for pain. What is it that she's done? Tentatively she moves her limbs. And then she hears a car and gets up rapidly, drags the stupid bike off the road. Her hands are hurting, that's all. The palms are skinned, and her knees are bumped. Impatiently, she wipes tears of pain from her eyes. It's a miracle she's not more badly hurt, for there are crystals of windscreen glass scattered on the road. When she was little she used to collect these—they were her jewels.

Simon, she thinks. She wants him to make her better. Or her mother. This thought she tries to snuff out, but it is there. However, she is all alone at the side of the road. And she is all right. No bones broken, that's what Mum would have said. Where did her childhood come from, crowding in so suddenly? Mum would have washed her hands and rubbed in Savlon cream and made her a cup of cocoa. There was a green tartan blanket that came out in emergencies when Nadia or Michael were ill or hurt and needed snuggling on the sofa.

She sniffs, remembering the rough texture of the rug, its comforting smell, its fringe which she plaited into stiff tufts. She picks up her bike. The front wheel is twisted right round.

She straightens it and notices that the chain is broken. It trails like some segmented thing, a fossil worm. Useless. 'Shit,' Nadia says. 'Shit, shit, shit.' She picks the chain up gingerly between her fingers and pulls the rest of it off. She puts it in the saddle bag and, hobbling a little, begins to wheel the bike the rest of the way to the pub.

*   *   *

'You must be joking, mate,' Miles says. 'It's been pissing down all week.'

'Yes, well.'

'Maybe next month?'

'Maybe.'

'How about a pint?'

'No ... Nadia, you know.'

'She OK?'

'OK.'

'See you then.'

'See you.' Simon puts down the telephone. Miles is right. What is the matter with him, he wonders, that he could have seriously contemplated ...? And where the bloody hell is Nadia?

He might as well eat since she's not here. He's ravenous. Eat what? Should he cook for her? He puts on the kettle and surveys what's in the fridge. There is all the stuff he bought yesterday, the food he'd be eating if he was going caving. Well, why not? It is the food associated with caving that is one of its pleasures for Simon. As many calories as possible, hot, greasy comfort foods before and after. He eats bread and jam while his bacon and sausages sizzle in the pan. When they're nearly done he breaks in a couple of eggs. Nadia will be angry. She'll have planned something else, no doubt, realising that he's not going. Of course she's realised that, otherwise she'd be here, nagging and whinging. The voice of doom. He turns the eggs over and breaks both yolks. He swears, squeezes the bacon and sausages over to one side, slaps some more fat into the pan and adds a slice of bread.

While he's waiting he takes a stack of exercise books from his bag. He's planned badly this weekend. Thirty essays on Demographic Problems in the Third World to plough through, and a batch of badly drawn maps of the shopping arcade near the school. However did he come to be a geography teacher? What is Celia's definition of geography? The reduction of the fascinating and particular into the tedious and general. Cutting the world down to size the size of a curriculum. But then she gave up teaching for something far more lucrative. Perhaps it's time for a change.

He tips the frying pan so that the hot greasy mass of food slithers onto his plate. He pours brown sauce on top, hitting the base of the

bottle with the heel of his hand. If he *were*
going ... as he swallows he feels a lump rise in
his throat as if to meet the food, so he has to
swallow hard to get it down. It is a strange
sensation—reminiscent of he doesn't know
what. He eats all the food, speeding up,
drinking great gulps of tea hot enough to scald
his mouth.

Bloody Nadia. He'll give her a fright. He'll
go out, take his stuff as if he's gone. And then
what? He'll go for a drive, he's too restless
anyway to stick around this evening. Nadia
will be so smug. What would they do? The
cinema? Most likely she's planned a meal. Well
tough luck. He finds that he's blaming Nadia
for his disappointment. Illogical. But still.

Resolved to go out, he washes quickly and
dresses as if for caving, putting his jeans and
shirt over his thermal undersuit. He picks up
the rest of his gear, even stopping to fill his
water bottle. If Nadia returns now, he'll feel a
berk. He leaves a note. Nothing specific. *See
you soon, sleep well, love Simon.* Leave her
wondering. Silly cow. He hurries downstairs
looking this way and that—she is not in sight.
He gets into his car and drives away.

*   *   *

The single room that Nadia is shown into faces
the road and the bleak darkening hills beyond.
The pub is on a bend, an accident blackspot;

cars veer dangerously past, headlamps swinging past the window.

'Thanks,' says Nadia. 'This is fine.'

'Well, I'll leave you to it, dear,' says the landlady. She is a big smart woman with a hairdo as stiff and snowy as a meringue. Nadia's teeth grit against the pungency of her lacquer. She goes out, giving Nadia a doubtful look. No wonder. Nadia is wet, shivering, pathetic. It is chilly in the cramped room, which has a damp unaired feel, as if it has been empty and unheated all winter. Nadia hangs her cagoule on the back of a chair. She pulls her woollen jumper over her head and squeezes it over the sink. She hangs it on the radiator. Her jeans are soaked too, and ripped at the knees. She didn't notice before, they were so muddy and stuck to her skin. She peels them off her goosepimpled bluish legs, cursing herself for her stupidity in not bringing a change of clothes. She is effectively imprisoned in this room now until her things are dry. It is a miserable room. Just right, she thinks, looking at the limp olive curtains and the tin waste-paper bin with its pattern of racehorses. On a squat table is a kettle, at least, and some sachets of coffee, powdered milk and teabags.

Nadia fills the kettle, awkwardly twisting it to fit the straight spout under the twisty little tap. She turns the lukewarm radiator up and is startled by its fierce clanking. The back of her T-shirt is damp but she keeps it on. In her rush

111

she didn't even think to bring a nightdress. She wraps a starchy towel round her shoulders and climbs into bed with her cup of tea. Yellowish blobs of undissolved milkpowder float on the surface. She wonders what Iris could read into these. She has nothing to read—didn't think to bring a book. There is nothing here but a Gideon Bible and a pile of pamphlets advertising local attractions: a tram museum, a sculpture park, a stately home, illuminated show caves. Fun for the tourist. She begins to cry.

*   *   *

As Simon's car swooshes along the wet road, he reflects on how many rules he would be breaking if he was actually to go underground tonight. No sane caver would attempt it in this weather. Suicide, some would call it, if they didn't appreciate how well Simon knows the cave system, didn't realise the extent of his skill. Never venture underground alone—well, that is a rule made to be broken. A rule for the uninitiated. Always inform others of your whereabouts. Nadia knows, or will when she returns and reads his note. If he *was* going to do it, he would be covered in that way. As it is, all he is doing is driving. He might stop and look at the entrance to Curlew since he's going that way. Rehearsing, one might say, enacting the possibility. He switches on the radio and music swells, a voice urges him to tie a yellow ribbon round the old oak tree and he laughs and joins in, feeling suddenly idiotic and free. He drives very fast, on the edge of danger, turns up the music. It *is* almost freedom. He swallows and recognises now the lump in his throat: once he played truant, flagrantly walking past the school, flaunting the rules. Then, as now, he had this difficulty swallowing. He laughs at himself, a grown man, a teacher now himself, a deputy head possibly, before long, if he sticks with it. He swings past a pub on a dangerous bend. Its windows are dull rectangles of light. He considers stopping for a pint but the pub is behind him before he's decided. He doesn't want to turn back, this rushing forward is thrilling.

No alcohol for twenty-four hours before a caving expedition, that is the strict—largely ignored—rule. It is good to be alone—but if only he could be going underground this evening. Though, of course, if he was going underground he wouldn't be alone. Miles and Celia would be in the car. Or Miles, at least. And they would talk trivially, laugh, find humour in the slightest thing in the suppressed excitement of their anticipation.

It is another planet underground. There are places where no human foot has ever trodden, which no human eye has ever seen. Cave exploration is pioneering. The idea makes him feel grand. There is dignity in discovery.

Roland must have felt this on his last journey, driving on this road. Not in this weather, of course, and not in the evening. Afterwards his movements had been pieced together: he'd set out on an early morning in June—the longest day. Simon imagines the tender pearly blue of the sky, the trembling newness. How Roland's heart must have thudded at this adventure. The ultimate challenge of a solo descent. What fineness! What pride he must have felt. And fear perhaps—for Roland knew the risk he was taking. For glory, Nadia would say, a sneer in her voice, as if glory was a petty thing, a paper rosette to pin on your chest. But Nadia is simply wrong. There *would* be a sort of glory in a solo discovery—once it was known—but glory wouldn't be the main thing. Not the nub of the achievement. That would be personal. That would be private, would be ... oh what would it be? There would be a growth, an inner growth, a spiritual growth. Simon is uncomfortable in the realms of the metaphysical. He changes gear unnecessarily and shifts in his seat. But it *would* be something beyond the physical. It would be an expansion, a new knowledge of self, of the limits of endurance ... the pitting of self against nature ... he squirms, imagining Nadia's hilarity if only she could hear his thoughts. However. There *is* something, something he hasn't the vocabulary for, which is worth the risk of life.

114

For Roland this had to be undertaken alone, it could not be a shared experience, for a shared experience is—however extraordinary—rendered common by the sharing. Simon understands this now. Forgives Roland for leaving him out.

*   *   *

Nadia holds the bedclothes up to her chest. Headlamps flit across the room. She has left it too late to murder Simon. She should have done it immediately. She should have waited for him in the kitchen, a smile on her face, a knife behind her back. The anger was there, and the strength. Now the strength has gone. The impulse to flee, then, was what made the difference between herself and a killer. Now the moment has gone. But one iota less resolve—a hesitation; the telephone ringing; stopping to find out what Iris wanted—any of these things and Simon would be a dead man. Might be. Oh so melodramatic! But all the same, it happens. She picks up the little plastic-covered New Testament and Psalms. At the beginning it has a list of topics for guidance. Where to find help when: Afraid, Attacked, Bereaved, Bitter, Choosing a Career, Conscious of Sin, Contemplating Marriage, Contemplating Revenge—she pauses at this one—Desperate, Distressed. So much to choose from, right through the alphabet to

'You Have Left Home'. There is nothing beginning with Z to suffer from, it seems. She cannot choose from the headings, so she opens the book randomly, lets her fingers pick a verse from a psalm and reads:

My companion attacks his friends;
he violates his covenant.
His speech is smooth as butter,
Yet war is in his heart;
His words are more soothing than oil,
yet they are drawn swords.

Ha! Some comfort! She throws the book across the room where it hits the radiator and falls, open, on the floor.

What is he doing now, her oily companion? Missing her, pacing the flat? Or, more likely, waiting, unconcerned, feet up in front of the television, a can of beer beside him. Perhaps he is cooking her a meal. Or perhaps Celia has rung and told him that Nadia knows his secret. Perhaps they are together, fair heads touching, regretting the past, pitying Nadia. She grits her teeth. There's nothing to stop the two of them getting together. Now there's the baby, the future baby. Perhaps they'll fall in love again. How *could* Simon? How *could* he fuck Celia and then come home to Nadia with never a word or a sign? Did he come home and fuck her too? Did he hope to score twice, two successful impregnations in one night? Oh, what a stud he

116

must have felt!

Again she feels the urge to stab. Interesting that it doesn't give 'Contemplating Murder' as an option in the Bible.

She realises what Iris must have been waving at her—her Amazon eyeshadow. She snorts at the perfect irrelevance, typical somehow of Iris. There is the smell of cooking, the sizzling fatty odour of chips. Her room is directly above the kitchen, and occasionally a puff of steam wafts up from the small window beneath and clouds her own. Even if she was hungry she could not go and eat, not yet, not with her clothes all wet. Even if they were dry she could not face the thought of eating in a public place alone. She cannot face the thought of food at all, not with the embers in her belly still glowing.

Someone beginning with J will have a lump, Iris said. Suddenly it comes to her that her mother begins with J—she is called June. How curious that this hasn't occurred to her before. She thinks back to the last time she saw June. It was after her father had died, quite shortly after, at her mother's wedding. June had married an Australian called Pierre. They married in England before they flew away to set up home in Sydney, near Pierre's daughters and grandchildren. Nadia recalls the hurried little ceremony, her mother in an unlikely flowered hat strangling some freesias, the few embarrassed relatives eating vol-au-vents and

117

searching for topics of conversation that avoided Nadia's father or the funeral only nine months before—where they had unfortunately been treated to an almost identical repast. Now June is widowed again and back in England, and, if Iris is to be believed, developing a lump.

Nadia lies down, curls her knees up to her chest. She is cold despite the radiator and the blankets. Her hair is still damp. Her skin feels chapped. The fatty kitchen odour mingles with the smell of drying clothes. Her palms and her knees sting. She doesn't know where Simon is or what he is doing or thinking. She has cut herself off. She cannot even telephone. Tears that feel surprisingly hot leak from her eyes. All she can do now is try to sleep. But how can she when the anger still lurks? It comes in waves, like labour, she supposes, a rhythm. That is how it works. No one can be angry every second. It ebbs and flows. When it ebbs she is engulfed in self-pity, but when she thinks about her predicament and why she is in it and how she has been betrayed it flows, it flashes, it flames.

There is a knock at her door. She shrinks into herself, curls tighter under the covers. It cannot be meant for her. Why should anyone be knocking at her door? She cannot see anyone. She is peeled, maskless. In this room she has stripped down to raw, flinching nerve. But the knock is repeated and there is a voice too—the landlady's. 'Miss Crowley? Miss

Crowley? Are you there?'

Nadia squeezes her eyes shut. What should she do? Could it be something urgent? A fire perhaps. But there is no panic in the voice, there are no alarm bells or charging feet. Simon? But there is no way, not unless he's trying every hotel in a ten-mile radius. She snorts at the ridiculous thought. More likely he hasn't even noticed that she's missing yet. He is probably sipping beer with Celia in a snug bar somewhere, red velvet seats, fair heads glowing in the lamplight.

'Miss Crowley!' The woman is not going to give up. Nadia gets out of bed, shivering, and goes to the door.

'What is it?' she asks.

'Ah, good. Could I speak to you for a moment dear?' She pauses. 'I wouldn't dream, normally, but we're in a spot.'

'What?' Nadia's voice is croaky.

'Could I come in? Only I never like to talk through doors.'

'I'm not decent.'

'I'll give you a moment.'

'No, you don't understand ... all my clothes are wet. I've nothing else ...'

'Hold on then.' There is the creak of floorboards under carpet and then silence for a minute. Nadia stands by the radiator. It is too hot to lean against with her bare legs, but doesn't seem to be giving off any warmth into the room. Steam rises from her sweater with a

119

wet woolly smell. It is beaded with white, like soft frost. What can the woman want? Curiosity has awoken within her, unfurled a tentacle.

'Miss Crowley?'

'Yes?'

'I've got some things for you here. Open the door, dear, and I'll pass them in.'

Nadia fumbles with the lock. She receives a neatly folded pile of clothes round the edge of the door.

'They should fit—pop them on and then come down to the lobby. I won't enquire about your predicament. Ask no questions hear no lies.'

'What is it that you want?'

'A favour I'm afraid, *not* our normal policy to ask favours of our guests, but ...'

'Well I don't know ...' Nadia is not in the mood for doing favours. But it seems that the landlady has gone. She looks at the clothes. There is a velour tracksuit—horrible blancmange pink—some sparkling nylon socks and a pair of fluffy pink mules. The clothes are slightly warm, as if from an airing cupboard, and they smell strongly of an unfamiliar detergent. They are soft and cosy like baby clothes. As she dresses, Nadia remembers a sensation, a swaddling in warm towels, slippery cold limbs, safety and comfort, someone big to hold her tight. She looks in the mirror and grins. She looks grotesque, white-

120

faced, red-eyed, wild-haired, blancmange-clad. She brushes her hair and ties it back. She puts on lipstick—quite the wrong colour for the suit, it should be frosted pink, like cake icing. She hesitates, wondering what is to be required of her. Perhaps she should take it on, whatever it is. There's nothing for her in the room but chilliness and misery between the waves of rage. It is actually a relief to have been dragged out of it, even if the relief is temporary and artificial. It will pass time and the more time passes, perhaps, the better things will be. Time heals all. What a rotten lie. It might make a scab, time, but this it will never heal. Simon will always have betrayed her. Oh she can just imagine his defence! His wounded eyes, his pretended incomprehension at her reaction. She could even end up seeming to be in the wrong ... She takes her key and leaves the room quickly before she is engulfed again.

'That looks nice. Flattering colour, pink. I'm Ruby, by the way.'

'Nadia.' Nadia follows Ruby out of the hotel reception area through the bar, through a door marked PRIVATE and into a living room which screams with roses—trellised on the wallpaper, puddled on the carpet, stretched in neon nylon on the three-piece suite. She is so dazzled that she does not at first see the carry-cot.

'What?' Nadia asks again.

'This is kind of you,' Ruby says. 'Of course, we'll make a reduction for your room.'

'Yes?'

'You see George and Liz have left Paula with us for the night—our granddaughter you know, our first.' She indicates the carry-cot. 'Usually no problem, we think the world of her, but tonight Barry and Anna have let us down—bar staff! Hopeless!—and I simply have to go out. Obligated. No two ways about it. Cancel, Stan says!'

'Stan?' Nadia asks weakly.

'Husband. Flat out he is. Busiest night, Fridays. He'll cope with the bar but Paula's due for a feed at ten. Like clockwork she is, not like George, he was a terror—but she's hard to settle, colic. I'd take her with me if I could, but it's not on—Old Time Music Hall tonight—I do a bit of the theatricals, you know. So could you possibly, dear? I'll tell you what, room and breakfast on the house. How's that?' She pauses, confidently anticipating Nadia's agreement.

'All right,' says Nadia. She hasn't the strength to refuse. It is warm in here. The gas fire glows a cosy orange. 'That's no problem.'

'An angel of mercy.' Ruby smiles and pats her arm. 'Now ...' She leads Nadia into the kitchen and points out the baby's things. 'She's actually breast-fed normally, of all inconvenient things, but she'll take a bottle if coaxed. Now, bottle made up, there. Needs warming in pan, there.' She points to each item, which increases Nadia's feeling that she's

122

just arrived from another planet. 'More formula here, if you should need it. Gripe water here.' There is the faint bass thud of the jukebox starting up in the bar. Back in the sitting room she hears a snuffling from the carry-cot.

'How old is she?' Nadia asks.

'Nine—no—ten weeks. Bless her.' Ruby pauses and lets her face go soft for a moment. 'Now. Drink? I'll fetch you something from the bar. What'll it be?' Nadia hesitates. 'Port and lemon,' suggests Ruby, 'to warm you up? As I say, I won't ask what you're doing here with no luggage.' Nadia gives a wan smile. 'TV, videos, all mod cons. Make yourself at home. I won't be back till the early hours—Stan should be finished by midnight or half-past. Regulars stay late on Fridays. All right, dear?' She flaps through the heavy door into the bar and comes back with a large brimming glass. 'Got you a double. Help yourself from the fridge if you're peckish.' She puts the glass down on a beer-mat on the tiled coffee table. 'All right then. By the way, any experience with . . . ?' she gestures at the carry-cot.

'Oh yes.'

'An angel of mercy,' Ruby says again, flicking open a powder-compact and dusting her nose. She fetches her coat, buttons it and smooths her hands down her portly suede body. 'I'll be off then. Bye-bye, darling,' she coos into the carry-cot. 'And cheerio, dear. See

123

you at breakfast.' And she leaves.

Nadia sinks back onto the sofa and feels her hair crackle with static from the nylon. There is the smart clacking of high-heels past the window, the starting up of an expensive engine and a soft purring as the car drives away.

She sips from the glass. The drink is sweet and sticky. A red-stained slice of lemon floats on top. She sits very still, listening to the nibbling sound of a carriage clock on the mantelpiece. This and all the other shelves are crammed with framed photographs and the stiff frills of china roses. The drink begins to warm her, her limbs relax; she had not noticed she was holding them so tensely. An occasional flame leaps against her ribs, but she quenches it with port-and-lemon. She finishes half the glass and then she gets up, unsteadily: it is the drink on an empty stomach. She goes over to the carry-cot and kneels down to look inside. She breathes in the smell of baby lotion and sweet breath. She cannot see much of the baby; she is lying on her side with her back to Nadia. There is a puff of dark hair, a smooth cheek. She makes such a tiny hump under the blankets. Nadia lays her hand lightly on the baby's back and feels the movement of her ribs, thinks she can feel the tiny beating of her heart.

*　　　*　　　*

The wind that blows is full of the smell of rain,

124

although the rain itself has stopped and the sky is clearing. It is a sweetish night, the wind is mild and full of the scent of spring. Simon throws his head back and inhales. He is invigorated by the sappy, peaty smell. The clouds have broken to reveal the ink of the sky, hard points of stars, the skinny conspiratorial grin of the moon. Right above him is the Plough, the simplest most childish constellation. He attempts to focus his eyes beyond the stars and his eyes ache with the strain of the emptiness. But it is *not* emptiness. The unknown is far from empty. If he lived in another age, another life entirely, Simon might have been able to explore those reaches. He has an explorer's heart and it beats loud enough to hear at the thought of all that space. Unknown but not unknowable. A soft bank of cloud drifts across the stars, blotting them from his sight. The wind blows, a soft sound, a mumble in the hills, a sibilance in the grass, and his heart beats steadily: a muffled drum. Above him are the taunting heavens which will never be his: but below his feet is a kingdom that is. Below him is a labyrinth. The earth is laced with secrets and they are his to know. Nobody else quite comprehends his feeling. Perhaps Roland felt it, but nobody else. Even Miles and Celia see the caves as sport and challenge rather than as understanding. He cannot, of course, say the things he feels to anyone. '*Boys' Own* adventure', Nadia would scoff, and the others ... well there is no need for him to say. The feelings are his own business and they are serious and real.

He walks down from the road where his car is parked towards the entrance to the cave. There is a cross flurry by his feet, a sleeping bird or animal disturbed. He imagines Nadia at home. By now she will have read his note, telephoned Miles. Miles will be out and she will assume they are together. If Miles *is* out. If not, what will they think? Miles wouldn't believe he would undertake the trip alone. Miles will know he's having Nadia on. Will he? Is Simon not capable, then? Capable, yes, but not stupid. Is that true? The stars are so bright out here away from the lights of town; they are layered above him like the scattered atoms of some solid object.

When Simon was a boy he used to wonder if the world was just a tiny fragment, a molecule of a larger world. It seemed to him that looking through the lens of a telescope took you one way into the massive spaces, while looking though a microscope lens took you the other way towards the minute ones. He would wonder about this until his head felt ready to burst with the ungraspable idea of infinity. Did it go on for ever, then, both ways?

Why shouldn't he, tiny, complex, enormous creature that he is, go where he wishes to go? He stumbles and nearly falls. The ground is drenched. Nadia would be furious. It hurts him

126

that she does not value what he considers the best part of him, that part that marks him out. If he'd been born earlier, in the middle of the nineteenth century, say, he'd have been an explorer—the jungles and deserts of Africa would have been his, the Arctic wastes. But now, in the late twentieth century, what is he, what is his discoverer's spirit reduced to? Teaching geography in a comprehensive. Apart from *this*. Apart from this way of reaching the so-far unreached. Of being the first to set his foot in the unknown places of the earth.

Above him on the road a car sweeps by, its headlamps two long cones of powdered light flicking across him. It seems to slow down and he holds his breath. Catches himself almost ducking. For if Nadia *has* telephoned Miles and he *was* in, they might between them decide that he has flipped his lid. They might come after him. He imagines them slamming the car doors, leaping out, shouting his name into the darkness. How stupid he would look! He relaxes. This car has driven on, its red eyes receding into the darkness. But eventually it will happen. He will be missed.

Simon walks back to the car. He is not thinking about anything deeper than his immediate actions. He takes off his jeans and sweater and puts on his wetsuit and helmet. He takes his emergency food pack and water bottle out of the car. He locks the door and

127

stands beside it for a moment. It is a white Datsun, a car he loves. He shines his torch on its rain-beaded surface, feeling absurdly fond, almost as if it is the last bit of his material life he is going to see. But he cannot be thinking that, of course, for if he was he would never go underground, and certainly not now, on his own, deliberately into danger.

*   *   *

The baby sleeps. Nadia has moved the carry-cot round in front of the sofa and put the hood down so that she can see Paula's face more clearly. Her mouth is slightly open and a trail of clear dribble has made a wet patch on the sheet under her cheek. In the bottom of the carry-cot is a folded changing bag and mat, which Nadia has unrolled and discovered to contain some clean clothes, disposable nappies and baby wipes. The nappies have an edging of pink and yellow bunnies. Nadia sniffs one of them; it has a clean, comforting, hygienic smell. She touches Paula's cheek with her fingertip. The skin is so soft she can hardly feel anything at all, but the baby stirs and makes a little whinnying sound.

Nadia decides to play a game. In the game this is her own house and her own baby. Not Paula—she can't bear male diminutives for girls—but ... she will choose a name she might give a girl child if ever she was to have one:

Sophia. But that is too grand for the little scrap in the carry-cot; it would certainly be shortened to Sophie. But 'Sophia' is beautiful for a woman. Wisdom, it means, and it makes Nadia think of powerful women and also, for some reason, of long necks and sapphires.

During the five-month pregnancy, Nadia and Simon discussed names. Simon disliked Sophie—too much like sofa, too comfortable—but had half accepted Sophia. He'd preferred something flowery like Rosie or Lily. It had been a wonderful squabble while it lasted. That grief has emerged in Nadia's mind again and become tangled with her anger. Will Simon have a say in naming Celia's child? Will it have one of *their* names? The fire has gone out. Inside her now is coldness, a deep well of icy water, thoughts nudge and circle like dark fish. But she concentrates on the surface, on the flash and glitter of dragonfly reflections: the game of let's-pretend.

Nadia goes into the kitchen and looks in the refrigerator. She takes a slice of ham and butters bread. She slices a tomato and spoons mayonnaise from a jar. There is only ready-ground pepper, like dust in its plastic pot. Put peppercorns on the list, she thinks. In the supermarket there are special trolleys for tiny babies too young to sit up. Little wire-mesh eye-level cots on top of the groceries. Sophie can go in one of these tomorrow, and if she times it properly, between feeds, she will sleep

129

all the way round or she will watch the bright packages and bottles flicking past her on the shelves. And if Sophie cries, other mothers will meet her eyes with sympathy, knowing just how it feels, trying to shop with a baby.

She puts the bottle on to warm, for surely Sophie will wake soon. She sits down in front of her and eats a mouthful of the sandwich, but something has happened to her appetite. The food tastes like pretend food, a plastic picnic. She finishes the drink. It is good, sweet and unfamiliar. She'd like more, it's relaxing, a way to unwind. No one could blame a mother for having a drink in her own home at the end of a tiring day. No, wait a minute, this isn't *her* home. She would never have such dreadful wallpaper. She is a single mother and this is her mother's house and she is staying until she gets herself sorted out. That's it. She unlocks and opens the heavy door into the bar. The grandfather—her father?, no, he is just some man, it doesn't matter—is serving someone. When he's finished, he grins. 'How do,' he says amicably. He is a hefty, upright man, white-moustached. He wears a maroon cravat tucked into the collar of his shirt.

'I'm afraid I spilt my drink,' she says.

'Like a refill? What's your poison?'

'I had port and lemon.'

'Same again? I'll give you a double. How's the nipper?'

'Sound asleep.' Nadia looks round the bar.

130

It is full of people, standing at the bar with pints of beer, or sitting at the flimsy tables eating chicken or scampi or chips from baskets.

'Glad to hear it. Anything else? Crisps? Nuts?' says the man, handing her a brimming glass.

Nadia shakes her head. 'No thanks.' She takes her glass and goes back to Sophie. She swigs the drink and then she leans down and picks up the sleeping baby. She cradles her in her arms and sits back on the sofa to examine her. She isn't the prettiest of babies. She has a longish face, pale. There is a tiny red birthmark on her forehead and a scattering of spots on her cheeks. Patches of her fluffy hair have worn away. One of her cheeks is imprinted with a crumple from the sheet. She is still *so* new. She has little whorls of hair growing on her temples, and fine down on her ears. Lanugo, Nadia recalls. Robin was covered in this, she remembers. There was a day when she held him in her arms, light scrap. She had not spoken but Sue had known what she was feeling, had looked away, had hugged her fiercely when she left, tears in her own eyes. Nadia has forgotten that newborn downiness until now, studying the face of her own baby girl. She runs her finger wonderingly over the eyebrows, two perfect, invisible lines of colourless hairs like the stitches of a skilful embroiderer. The baby screws up her eyes. She is dressed in a pink

131

sleep-suit with a lamb appliquéd on the front, underneath which is embroidered *Mummy's pet*. Not Nadia's choice for Sophie, of course, but a grandparent's gift. It doesn't suit her. Too pretty-pretty for the stern little face.

Nadia picks up one of Sophie's hands. She has very long fingers, limp in sleep, with translucent nails. They are artistic hands, more artistic than Nadia's own, which are square and capable. She turns the palm over and looks at the little lines etched so clearly: life, head, heart, fate, all there already, written clear. The fingers curl in Nadia's palm. Such a perfect thing. The baby wriggles. Her sleep-suit is too short in the legs, taut against the minute feet. Nadia can see the shape of the toes straining against it. She kisses Sophie's head, noticing under the fluff a little yellow crust on her scalp. 'Cradle-cap,' she murmurs, recognising this from one of Sue's children. What is it Sue rubs on? Something or other, she will have to ask.

A trail of dribble runs from the baby's mouth and then she wakes, squirms, pulls a few experimental faces—surprise, outrage, disapproval—and then the decision is made, her bottom lip turns down and she begins to cry. It is a high, musical sound. Nadia hushes her, rocks her in her arms, but it is no good. Sophie becomes more upset, her mouth opens into a square, and she is like a pair of bellows, all breath and crying and the effort of crying, her little arms and legs waving in time with her cries. Nadia looks into her mouth at the furled tongue, the serrated surfaces of the gums where the teeth will be. She puts her finger in Sophie's mouth and the baby sucks for a moment, looking feverishly up at Nadia, gasping between futile sucks. And then she spits the finger out disgustedly and begins to yell more loudly. 'All right, Sophie,' Nadia says, 'let's go and get your bottle.' She carries the baby into the kitchen. She does not seem to like being cradled but struggles to be upright. Nadia holds her up against her shoulder and she stops crying for a moment, her tummy gurgles and she belches. 'Good girl,' Nadia murmurs, 'nasty wind.'

The bottle is far too hot. She has left it too long and the water in the pan is nearly boiling. She splashes it on her wrist and is scalded by a thin stream of white formula. 'Oooh,' she says, 'silly Mum.' She turns on the cold tap and holds the bottle under it. Sophie waits for a moment, her attention caught by the sound of the running water, and then begins to cry again. Nadia jiggles her and pats her back. She turns the tap on harder and the water runs brown. It is from the peat that stains the reservoir water, from the water running down from the hills. Sophie's crying is becoming increasingly piercing. Nadia finds herself losing her composure already. Well, it's been a hard day, she reminds herself; looking after a colicky baby is no joke. She carries Sophie through into the sitting room again and has another swig of her drink. She squirts some of the milk into her own mouth but it is still hot enough to sting her tongue. She begins to sing the song that is Sophie's favourite and she is quiet for a moment, listening.

'Hush little baby, don't say a word,
Papa's gonna buy you a mocking bird,
And if that mocking bird don't sing,
Papa's gonna buy you a diamond ring,
and if that diamond ring turns to brass ...
then what?'

Nadia has forgotten and Sophie has lost interest anyway and her desperate wailing is making her mother desperate. 'I'm drunk,' she says. 'Naughty Mum.' She embarrasses herself, the way she is talking to Sophie like some parody of a mother, but it is the way of talking that comes naturally while she's holding the baby. She sits down on the sofa and tries to cradle her in her arms but Sophie will not relax, she claws at Nadia's front, nuzzles her face against her breasts, making little animal noises. Of course, Sophie is a breast-fed baby. What has got into Nadia tonight? Breast is best. Nadia would never dream of bottle-feeding, not if it wasn't absolutely necessary.

'All right, Sophie,' she says. She lifts up the pink top. The baby waves her limbs frantically, recognising the action. Nadia rests her on her

134

lap while she reaches back to unfasten her bra. Her breasts loll heavily down. One of Sophie's hands, icy cold and sharp as a little claw, clutches a handful of her flesh. It can't do any harm, can it? It might soothe the baby. She looks at the door. It is locked. No reason for the man to come through. The curtains are drawn. She lifts Sophie towards her left breast, and she butts her head against it, her neck powerful, her mouth open, searching for the nipple. Nadia has to pinch her nipple between her finger and thumb and introduce it into Sophie's mouth. Just until the bottle cools, she promises, and then Sophie latches on with an expert flick of her baby tongue and Nadia gasps at the sudden sensation, feels as if her hair is standing on end. It is as if she is being pulled inside-out, all of her streaming from the end of her nipple into the voracious child. There is a sparkling tingle deep in her breast, a feeling of flow, as if she is really lactating. The baby seems happy enough. There are tight fizzy strings inside Nadia which reach inside her with each powerful suck, right into the pit of her belly, startling, unexpected, sensual, even sexual tugs. She closes her eyes, becoming accustomed to the shocking power of the baby's suck. Only till the bottle cools, she thinks weakly. There are a few moments while Sophie is quiet, except for her snuffling breath. Her face is as serious as a businesswoman's; her hands flex and relax in rhythm with her suck,

135

one of them opening and closing on Nadia's finger. Then after a few moments she stops and relaxes, her lower lip flutters and she almost lets the nipple slip from her mouth. Her mouth is wet and a trickle runs from it before she latches back on again. When Nadia sees the trickle, startled tears come into her eyes and she wails. Sophie opens her eyes and looks up at her sharply, for it is not a motherly sound. Nadia wails because the trickle that runs from Sophie's mouth is bluish white. She dips her fingers in it and tastes a slight sweetness. It is real milk.

*　　*　　*

Simon knows the way, would know the way in utter darkness, but there is the beam from his lamp, a shrill bugle of light, illuminating the glistening passages. He breathes in the smell of inner earth, a mossy, mushroomy dankness. It is the first time he has been here entirely alone. The rope drop down the short pot was easy, routine, something he has done a hundred times, has taught others to do. Then the squeeze through the muddy slot, one shoulder first with his head, and the rest of his body slithering through the tight rictus of rock into a comfortable, walkable passage. It is faster alone, no waiting. The darkness seems more intense, crowding up behind him, an odd experience. He was afraid of the dark as a child. But it was never really dark then. There was always the line of light under the door, or the leak round the curtain edges. There was always the knowledge of light downstairs, only a panicky dash away. The darkness he was afraid of then was only a partial blotting of the light. Temporary. But here it is really dark. For ever.

He is testing himself. That is it. He has no intention of going far. Of going into danger. Here it is safe. Under the sheltering rock and the thickly padded heather and peat above. Where safer? He is taking no risks. The corridor slopes downwards, but gently, imperceptibly in parts, a safe floor. Here, when the cave was first explored, were found the skulls of dogs and sheep and, incongruously, a tortoise-shell. It is dry in this corridor, the walls are fluted. There is a floor of dog's-tooth spar, and long stalactites hang down like vegetable roots. There is talk of lighting this stretch of cave, fixing a permanent ladder down the entrance pot, making it a show cave, a tourist attraction. It would be ideal—easy, comfortable, quite spectacular—especially when flooded with light to make an exciting mineral glitter of the formations. Simon hates the thought of the echoing clamour and litter of sightseers. Tourists—in his own kingdom. But it would only be the entrance, after all, the gateway. They would not penetrate the depths.

He reaches the end of the easy stretch, a

137

boulder floor which is harder going, an unsteady scramble over the huge jammed surfaces. There are bats here; the rocks are thick and slippery with guano; the smell is sweetish and cloying. He flicks the beam of his torch upwards into the scoop above him, and senses rather than sees movement, as if the surface of the rock itself is ruffling and shuffling.

This junction is where the system ended for a long time. It took the shifting of a boulder, a laborious job, to find the entrance to the branched passage above. He climbs. He knows the crevices in the rock, the ledges, with his eyes closed. At the top he perches, listening to his own breathing. There is blackness behind him. He has never minded the darkness before—but before there have always been companions. The blackness seems a solid thing. Not an absence of light, but a thing in itself. Is light just an absence of dark? The darkness itself is now his companion. Surely he is not afraid? He grins at the foolishness, a small lonely grin, buried beneath tons of rock and moor. He turns and makes his way along the low passage; Hesitation Way, this has been christened, for there are so many choices to be made. It is like a child's maze of dead ends and culs-de-sac. But Simon knows the way.

The passage he chooses is the one that looks the least promising. It is narrow and dank, with a low uneven roof. It is still walkable, just, bent almost double, in an excruciating monkey-shamble. He pauses after a time, wincing with the strain in his back and calves. He rests, his hands braced against his thighs. This part is a sheer bloody slog. It is a miserable passage, a long downward-sloping tube that leads into the lower cave system. The walls are muddy and there are strange wet growths. Water trickles down the walls and soon he is following the path of a small stream. This is no surprise, there is usually a trickle here, and with all the rain it's only surprising that it isn't worse. He is not worried about the water. Lower down, the system opens out into a keyhole-shaped corridor, a huge channel, which he estimates will contain the flow, will more than contain it, with a narrow slot above, narrow enough to straddle, high enough never to be flooded at the top. There is only the short duck at the end of this that is a worry. But he will stop there. He should stop now. He might just as well. Why press on with this slog only to turn round and come back? His neck aches with the effort of holding his head, heavy with helmet and lamp, at such an awkward angle. Occasionally his boots slither on the wet rock.

One day he will bring his child down here, introduce him to the kingdom which is his father's, and can be his own. Or her own. But somehow he imagines a son. He imagines him at about eleven years old, like the first-years at school, a strong boy, long-legged, bright-eyed.

An adventurer. He experiences a ridiculous swell of pride at the thought, warmth at the trust between them. A girl would be delicious too, of course, his daughter. He would be just as proud. It is just that the child of his imagination is a boy. The first child.

Now he has to sink onto his hands and knees. Despite the padding on his knees it is a painful crawl, for the ground is uneven and sharp under the flowing water which has risen to several inches deep. He'll stop after this in the Ballroom. Roland gave this grotto its name. He has a sudden rush of memory, Roland's laugh, the dark glister of his beard, the constant stream of profanities thrown good-humouredly over his shoulder. He will stop there, rest, replenish himself, and then he will go back. He will be out of the cave and home while Nadia still sleeps. He'll creep into her warmth and in her sleepiness she'll enfold him. She forgets her anger in her sleep and he has tricked his way inside her that way many times, so that her body has woken and received him, responded to him, before her mind is awake, and by that time, by the time she's remembered her complaint, it is too late, he is too close, she cannot resist him and he is loved and forgiven. He hopes she hasn't rung Miles. He curses himself for leaving the note. What will she have done? She *will* have rung Miles, or even Celia, to check what he's doing. She isn't stupid. She isn't stupid, but she can be spiteful.

He likes that about her, sometimes, the piquancy of her spite. It can be childishly, näively, transparent. It is endearing. But what, in this case, is spite likely to lead her to do: leave him to it, or chase after him and try and spoil his fun? Make a fool of him. He doesn't know. He cannot imagine her perspective. She is in another world. He forces back the cuff of his wetsuit and looks at his watch. The figures glow dim green. It is only eleven o'clock. She'll be watching TV still, sulking, drinking wine. Or maybe she's gone round to Sue's to moan.

That other world is going on up there, like another dimension of reality, all that buzzing crucial life balanced on the thin crust of this ball. The thought of the buildings clinging to the thin surface skin of the earth, the tall impudent constructions stretching their tops into the sky, straining at their foundations, makes him feel a momentary panic. What if they were to topple like trees, their foundations ripped from the earth like roots? He jerks his head too swiftly at the thought, and bangs his helmet on a sharp projection on the roof. The crack is sharp enough to jar his teeth. It stops the wild train of his thoughts. He pauses and listens. It is the solid silence he loves. Not utter silence of course, for there are the workings of the earth just like the workings of any machine. There is the trickle of the stream and the louder rush of the river he is approaching. There is the sound of dripping, the sound of his own breath

141

and, when he moves, the echo of his own progress.

*   *   *

Sophie sleeps in Nadia's arms. It is an uneasy sleep and Nadia can hear the bubbles moving in her tummy. She lifts the baby against her shoulder and rubs her back to send the bubbles upwards. Her breasts are pressed against her ribcage by the baby. They are damp and raw, and her nipples sting. She puts Sophie down for a moment and reaches back to fasten her bra and pull down her top. She has a mouthful of drink to try and rid herself of the sickly milkish taste in her own mouth. She does feel sick. She holds Sophie up again and nuzzles her face into the comforting warmth of her neck. The clock on the mantelpiece gives a tinny chime. It is eleven o'clock. The jukebox is turned off abruptly. Nadia hadn't realised how much noise it had been making; now that the bassy thud has stopped it seems oddly quiet. The clock nibbles away at the minutes; there is the occasional sound of a raised voice from the bar. But the walls are thick. There is also the smell of beer and smoke which drifts through whenever the door into the bar is opened. Not a good atmosphere for a baby. Nadia feels a mother's indignation. Not good for her tiny lungs to breathe in smoke.

Sophie wakes and is quite violently sick, a

sour yellow froth all down her front. Then she begins to cry again, a miserable weak cry. Nadia wipes away the worst of the sick with tissues. There is an acrid smell now, and Sophie feels cold. She should be changed out of the dirty sleep-suit. But perhaps she is still hungry. Nadia picks up the bottle, which has cooled now to blood heat. 'Let's top you up,' she says. Sophie accepts the clear rubber teat happily, almost with relief. She looks earnestly up into Nadia's eyes as she sucks, a little puzzled frown on her brow. Occasionally she relaxes her mouth around the teat for long enough to answer Nadia's smile and then resumes her sucking more fervently than before, as if to make up for lost time. Nadia marvels at her purpose, the way she is so much *here*, so definite a person, so dignified even. She is more relaxed with the bottle than with Nadia's breast. There is less struggle, not so hungry now, Nadia thinks, proudly, guiltily. She looks at the steady beat of Sophie's fontanelle. The softness of her head is terrifying, the precious brain protected only by the soft pulsing membrane. Sophie flexes her toes against the tight material of her suit. Nadia holds her hand against them so they have something to push against. Sophie pauses in her sucking to give an appreciative gurgle.

'Good girl,' Nadia says. 'Clever Sophie.' She bends down her head and kisses the baby. How could any mother ever leave her baby for even an instant? She would never leave Sophie with another person, not with a grandparent, not even with ... her father.

But her mind stops when it comes to Simon, for he is not part of the game. He is somewhere outside. The cold fish butts her in the belly with its blunt nose. No. Simon is not in the game. Or the hurt or the anger. No, that is the other thing. And she would not leave Sophie with anyone. Not trust anyone. Ever. Not Sophie's granny, not even if she begged. It is another presence now that nudges, another memory that rises to the surface. 'You won't know what it's like till you're a mother yourself.' It is her own mother. Perhaps it is because she has this baby now that the memory of June is becoming so irresistible, emerging so irrepressibly. All the clichés that are always there on the tip of her tongue are her mother's clichés, they are what will bring her mother back unwelcome to her mind. All her adult life, Nadia has flinched away from the sayings and the clichés. But they are woven into the fabric of her own mind, together with her flinching, like a fault. And she has to admit there is truth in them, a depressing aptness, a truth that trivialises rather than dignifies her experience of life—but truth nevertheless.

Although she isn't dead, Nadia has pushed her mother into the area of her mind reserved for the dead or those gone for ever from her life. Sophie has fallen asleep. One of her eyes has not closed properly and Nadia pushes the lid firmly shut, as if Sophie is a doll. The bottle is empty and she has been sucking in her sleep on thin air. Nadia removes the bottle from her mouth, looks at the swollen lips, the little sucking blister on the top lip, then cradles Sophie close.

Once June must have held her like this, close and warm, her own tummy distended with milk. She reaches forward and drains her glass. She feels quite nauseous and fuzzy. She remembers a conversation. It took place in her first flat, shortly after she'd left home to begin art college. It was a huge flat, one wing of a mansion house which had been left stranded incongruously on the edge of a dual-carriageway. She shared it with several other students. She was proud of the flat, ignoring its seediness and focusing instead on the elegant windows that reached the floor, the long tasselled velvet curtains, the Persian carpets. 'Persian *type*,' June had insisted, 'and on their last legs at that.' Nadia's own room was a slice of another, so that the ornate coving on the ceiling was cut off at a sudden angle and almost one whole wall was taken up with a marble fireplace of surreal proportions. Nadia had spent her first few weeks concentrating on her room. She'd painted the walls dark blue and stencilled golden stars on them. She'd dyed sheets dark blue and appliquéd them with moons and stars for a bed cover, and curtains that were only slightly too short. She had been proud of it, longing for her mother to visit so that she could show her how grown-up she was, how capable of making her own home. She'd spent an afternoon shopping, skipping a lecture to do so, and bought all her mother's favourite things, shrimps, flaky-pastry sausage rolls, Battenburg and chocolate éclairs.

Sophie wakes and cries. She is cold. Nadia reaches for a shawl from the carry-cot and wraps her up. She smells horrible in the sicky sleep-suit. 'I'll change you in a minute,' Nadia promises. She turns up the gas fire and walks round with Sophie looking over her shoulder, holding her little fingers out stiffly, gazing sleepily at the garish roses.

June hadn't said a thing about the room. And it was not the sort of décor that could possibly pass unnoticed. If she'd wanted approval she should have chosen magnolia or muffin, she had thought bitterly, and flowery cushions and scatter rugs. June approved of the tea, though, and munched her way through it as they sat side by side on the edge of Nadia's sagging bed, talking about people Nadia had left behind in her home town. Nadia felt disgruntled that June didn't seem more interested in her, more regretful that she'd left. She didn't bring food like some of the other students' mothers did. She didn't ask to meet Nadia's new friends, or look around the rest of the flat. She didn't even ask about Nadia's course. Nadia felt that June had washed her hands of her and the crumbs of Battenburg dried in her mouth and she'd felt on the brink of self-pitying tears.

'I want to talk to you,' June said then, not noticing Nadia's unhappiness. 'There's no one else I can have a real heart-to-heart with.'

'All right,' Nadia said unwillingly, and then she had been irritated when June started procrastinating, insisting on another cup of tea, which entailed a trip down to the kitchen.

'Go on then,' Nadia said when they were eventually settled back on the bed.

June cleared her throat. Her cheeks were pink, her eyes behind the lenses of her glasses bright and shifty. 'I'm in a bit of a spot,' she said eventually, 'well more than a spot, a ... a *crisis.*'

Nadia was startled to hear June rising from euphemism to a real serious word.

'*Crisis?* What? Is it Dad?'

'No, not Dad. Not really.'

'What then? Money?'

'No.' June sipped her tea, put her cup down on the floor and wiped her mouth with a handkerchief. 'Nadia, I'm expecting.'

Nadia put her own cup down and there was a pause. She felt cold prickles travel all down her spine—Someone is walking on my grave, she thought and then shook her head, impatient at the way her imagination was so ensnared. She didn't know what to say. What does a

147

nineteen-year-old say to her pregnant mother?

'But you're fifty!' she said.

'Forty-nine.'

'I didn't think it was possible at your age.'

'Well now you know,' June snapped. She picked up her cup again. 'I found out last week. I'd been feeling off. Periods stopped. Assumed it was the change, well you would, wouldn't you, at my time of life ...'

'What does Dad think?' Nadia asked.

June blushed, a dark mottled flush on her neck, her crêpey ageing neck, Nadia noticed spitefully.

'Your father doesn't know.'

'Well you'd better tell him then, hadn't you? Unless you're planning to keep it a lovely surprise.'

'Sarcasm is the lowest form of wit,' June retorted, nettled.

'I think you'll find it's the pun actually.'

'I'm confiding in you because I thought I might get a bit of sympathy.'

'Sympathy!'

'You see, I'm not keeping it. I'm having it ... seen to.'

'An abortion you mean?'

'Horrible word.'

'But still, that's what it is.'

'All right, Nadia, abortion. I'm having an abortion. Satisfied?'

'I suppose that's the best thing,' Nadia said. The idea repelled her, the whole idea: her

148

mother—sex—abortion—blood. And the most sickening thing was that she had to know. She didn't need to know.

'I didn't think Daddy was up to it,' she said cruelly.

'Well, you see, it isn't his.' June said this quickly, looking down at her knees. Nadia looked down with her at the plump knees, white pleated skirt, sheer tights, thick ankles and black patent-leather shoes, high-heeled and pointed. She'd dressed up for this meeting in the scruffy student flat. How pathetic.

'What do you mean?' She wondered if her mother's thick legs were sexy then, to men of a certain age. Her mother! Men!

'I thought you'd have realised,' Jean continued quietly. 'Your dad hasn't been ... well, not capable, for years and years, not since his illness.'

'I hadn't thought,' Nadia said honestly.

They sat without speaking for a short time, listening to the window rattle as traffic roared by on the road outside. Someone upstairs put Genesis on loudly in the room above. 'So you had affairs?' she asked weakly. 'Couldn't you have just ... not?'

'Not *affairs*, Nadia,' June said. 'And for years and years I did "just not". But then I met John last year at my French evening class and we got on like a house on fire. Introduced him to your father, him and his wife.'

'Oh, so he's married too, this John.'

149

'Oh don't worry, it was all above-board then. Just good friends. Daddy liked him very much. Likes. But then his wife went off last Christmas. Left him high and dry. On the cards apparently, but he's such a nice man, so discreet—and loyal. But it all poured out one night in the pub after French. She'd given him the run-around all their married life apparently. And ...'

'And?'

'We started to go out. The pictures, that sort of thing. All quite innocent. Daddy didn't mind. Encouraged me. Well, he couldn't come to the cinema, could he, not with his wheelchair, not without a great song and dance and you know how he feels about a fuss.'

'And now you're up the spout.'

'Nadia!' The telephone rang; someone answered it and shouted Nadia's name but she didn't answer.

'I don't know why you're telling me all this,' she said.

'I thought ... oh I was wrong, I can see that now, I thought you'd be a help. A trouble shared ...'

'You didn't think about *my* feelings. Poor Dad. Whatever will he say?'

'Your dad would understand. He knows I'm still ... well, still a sensual woman.' Nadia winced and picked at a loose thread in her skirt. 'It doesn't stop when you're thirty, you know, madam. Sex. It gets better.' June stood

150

up. The embarrassment in the air was almost tangible. They did not look at one another again. 'I'm sorry if I've offended you,' June said, and she tried to say something else but her voice came out as a sob. She went out of the room. Nadia listened to her hard heels clacking on the uncarpeted stairs, feeling only glad that she had gone. She had been left thinking that she had been wronged. For twenty years she has held that against her mother. Held what against her? Her sexiness? Her unfaithfulness? But was it that? Perhaps her father had colluded. The abortion? Looking at it now, Nadia can see that was the only thing she could do. None of it was as simple as it had seemed then. Holding Sophie in her arms has unexpectedly wrenched her perspective. She flounders. Sees herself suddenly, her nineteen-year-old self, as heartless. All her mother had asked for was friendship. Light pours back over the years, cruelly illuminating her cruelty. She blinks.

And then what happened? She never knew. Presumably her mother had had the abortion, there was no more mention of the subject. There was her father's death only months after that—he had been crippled with multiple sclerosis for years. And then the embarrassing wedding. And that had been the last she'd seen of June. They had exchanged Christmas cards each year. June has tried for years to communicate with Nadia, written, phoned, but Nadia has been uniformly cold and unresponsive. Stupid cow! she thinks now. So heartless? And now there is this lump—well might be—the lump that Iris read in her own palm.

Sophie gives a small expert burp and Nadia smiles. Did June feel such tenderness for her? She holds Sophie out at arm's length and plays with her, lifts her up and down, until she laughs—perhaps her first laugh—and goes cross-eyed with surprise at the noise. Nadia is overwhelmed by a wave of love. What if Sophie rejected—for that is what she had done—rejected her mother when she came to her for help? How could she bear that?

'Oh my God,' she sighs. Sophie grins at her and then goes red in the face and fills her nappy.

*   *   *

The crawl narrows to a short squeeze, just one long squirm through, the rock pressing. He exhales to narrow his girth and pushes through. The tightness is only a body's length, and soon he is able to haul himself out into the Ballroom. Roland christened this the Ballroom because from the ceiling hang thousands of fine straw-like stalactites which when lit from below glitter like an enormous crystal chandelier; and because of the stalagmite columns, three pairs of them, that

152

look for all the world like dancers frozen in time, turned to stone in the midst of a waltz. Simon stands and stretches. His knees are bruised and his back aches. He is sticky and white with the soft calcite—moonmilk—that coats the walls of the squeeze. He and Roland, in their delight at discovering the Ballroom, had danced together, a clownish parody of a waltz, la-la-ing the 'Blue Danube', their loud jubilant voices vibrating the straws on the ceiling until they shivered and clinked.

'No one has ever set foot in this place before,' Roland had said when they stopped, his voice reverent. 'No human being.'

They had stood together then, the echo of their voices still reverberating, light from their lamps skittering over the points of the rustling straws and casting long swaying shadows from the dancers. And now Simon is startled by the memory of their loud foolish voices, like an echo trace sounding from the walls, or is it in his ears? Faint concentric circles of sound.

Roland had stood, a big man, bearded, bluff, and in his eyes Simon had thought he had seen tears. Roland had been moved by the beauty. Changed perhaps? He'd turned to Simon and his eyes had been naked, and Simon had understood, would have understood even if Roland had not blundered with words: 'Makes you wonder, man, what it all means. Is it all just ... chance? Christ! All this down here, this fucking beauty, man. Makes you realise ...'

Simon breathes in sharply. He feels as if he has been winded by this sudden vivid memory of Roland, the very sound of his voice. Roland, whose last hours alive had been spent in this place, in this quest to make a link. Who had stood in this very spot, moonmilk glimmering on his back and thighs, and thought, no doubt, about Simon and known that he would feel betrayed by the exclusion. For it should have been the two of them. Roland had deceived him. Simon feels cold for the first time. This is what he has always assumed, but it may not have been a deliberate deception. Perhaps whatever has come over Simon, seduced him down here alone, came over Roland too. Simon cannot ignore the terrible sensation that someone is beside him. This feeling has been growing, it is as if someone is there just at the corner of his eye, just out of his field of vision, and because of the slow sweep of his light as he turns, they are always just out of sight. But there is the sense of a presence. Of course there is no one. That is something you can be sure of underground, so very far underground. The interior of the cave glitters. Last time it glittered so, it had been the rescue party's torches that illuminated it, their voices that set the straws rustling. Simon had been one of that party. But they never found Roland. Some of his equipment, but not a sign of the man.

This is where he will stop. He can hear the

rush of the river. No louder than the sound he remembers, surprisingly. Underground water is unpredictable. The torrents of spring rain may have found another way, may not have altered this river more than slightly. He hears a gurgle below him, near his feet. He steps back and looks down. There is a small but rising pool of water, a perfect swelling circle in a hollow on the floor. As he watches, it swells to the size of a child's paddling pool and stops. It seems to tense—as if the surface skin has tensed with anticipation—and then there is a sucking sound as it diminishes, shrinks back through a tiny aperture like a plughole in the floor. He smiles, his momentary fear at the sight of the rising water evaporating. Strange he doesn't remember this. It is an ebb and flow pool. Sure enough there is another gurgle, almost as if the rock itself is chuckling, and the water rises again. On his previous expeditions the weather has always been dry, that is why he's never seen it before. The limestone is gorged with water. It is a magical thing, the slow regular pulse of crystal water.

Simon is cold. He should eat and then turn back. He is tired, his legs are trembling. There is this terrible sensation that he is not alone, which is so ridiculous. He turns sharply, the beam of his lamp jerking over the walls, making the dancers and their shadows judder and sway. The gurgle of the rock is like Roland's laugh. No it is not. That is ridiculous.

Oh so stupid. Pure fancy. His mind is playing tricks. 'Get a grip on yourself,' he says, and his voice is frightful in the cave, breathy and intimate.

He unscrews his water bottle and takes a swig. He unzips his rubber pouch and takes out a barley-sugar tablet to suck. He needs something. The sugar might give him strength. The sweetness is a comfort, strangely a female sort of comfort. Is sugar female then? And what is male? Cheese? Beef? Slugs and snails? Again the feeling—almost breath on his cheek this time—and he jerks round and sends the shadows chasing, glitters skittering over the mineral points and planes. The water disappears with a sigh.

He should go back, but there is this presence now behind him. It is not imagination. Simon prides himself on his lack of imagination. There is something made up of darkness behind him and beside him and he knows he must go on. There is no real choice here. The darkness is his companion. There is not far to go. Out of here there is a short descent into the entrance to the roaring river passage. His legs are weak. No, no, they are not weak. He takes a bite of oatcake and swigs water to wash the dry crumbs down. He has done this before. There is just the keyhole passage, just a matter of perseverance, back pressed against one side by the strength of his legs. And then there is the duck, the place where he will have to go under

156

the water. But it is only short, one comfortably held breath, no obstacles. He has done it before. Followed by the burst out into fresh air. And it is the fact that it *is* fresh air that is significant. There is even a draught. He and Roland experienced a definite draught against their faces, which can mean only that there is an opening into the Boss System. And they had ascertained that there must be a way through, via a small tube that they had spotted.

He will find his way through. He will achieve what Roland set out to achieve. He must finish what has been started. He thinks briefly of Nadia, asleep now surely, snuggled warm and soft in the softness of the bed. To get back there he must go on. He does not dare turn round and face the darkness behind him, which is, he has almost convinced himself, only the fear of failure made manifest. Strange things take on edges in this kingdom of dislocation.

The water rises again, more forcefully this time, a little spray like spit first, and then a chuckle and then the clear swelling flow. He'll watch it rise and fall once more and then he'll go on.

LIMESTONE

Nadia lays Sophie on her changing mat in front of the fire and begins to unfasten her sleep-suit. The baby is filthy. An onlooker might suppose

157

her neglected. Her front is covered in slimy drying vomit; yellow shit escapes from the legs of her nappy and oozes down her legs, soiling the pretty pink velour. It has also leaked upwards, Nadia discovers, dirtying her vest. She manages to get the sleep-suit off, but the vest fastens with poppers between Sophie's legs, so that pulling it over her head is bound to dirty her face and hair. The only thing to do is to bath her. She picks up the squirming, stinking child and carries her—at arm's length—upstairs to find the bathroom. There is no baby bath, but the washbasin is big enough to serve. She runs the water, testing it with her elbow, and then kneels on the floor and takes off Sophie's vest and nappy. Nadia is horrified by the acidic pool inside the nappy, and by the redness of Sophie's bottom. Perhaps she was dirty before, she thinks. Perhaps it is my fault. But she smelt so sweet before, only a clean sweet smell. Nadia wipes the worst away, and then lifts Sophie into the basin. At first she struggles and flails her arms, but then she relaxes. Nadia supports her head with her hand and Sophie floats, pushing her toes against the side of the basin and gazing into Nadia's eyes. Her thighs have creases in them, gorgeous silky folds; her tummy is as round and fat as a puppy's, her sex a tiny split almond.

'I love you,' Nadia says. 'I will never let you go.' Sophie smiles at her, a wide-open smile of such purity that it makes Nadia hurt. Sophie

158

doesn't know it's a game. To Sophie it is real. Nadia is her mother and that is all right. More than all right. It is perfect. Nadia's breasts ache with love. She wonders if June could ever have looked at *her* with such amazed love. The emotion is surely unique. No one else has ever ached with such love for a baby. Nobody who ached so much, who felt about to burst so full was she of love, could leave their baby in a pub to be looked after by God knows whom. By any lunatic who happened to be there. Lucky that Nadia was. Nadia soaps the baby, her fingers slipping on the perfect skin. Her grazed palms sting with the soapy water. It seems another life ago now, that cycle ride out of the city. And what it was that she was fleeing from.

Nadia closes her eyes for a moment as a wave of nausea sweeps her. She should eat. She is drunk. She cannot think straight, her thoughts are all rough and scribbled. But the important thing is this baby. She opens her eyes and sloshes water over the round tummy. Sophie kicks her legs with glee. But the water is cooling. Babies can die quickly of cold, she thinks, panicking. There is something about that she remembers. They cannot shiver, that is it. Nadia reaches for a towel from the radiator. It is almost impossible to manage the slippery slithery baby in one hand. The radiator is too far away. Nadia stretches and slips. How does she slip? She bangs her head on the radiator, there is a terrible clang that reverberates

159

through all the pipes in the house and at the same time there is the more terrible quiet thud of the baby hitting the floor.

Nadia cannot understand this. What is going on? The baby is lying still and quiet on the hard scratchy carpet tiles. What a stupid floor to have when there is a baby to bathe. Her head is clattering, pain bounces off the planes of her skull, lights flash. She reaches for Sophie, who is limp and cold and wet. She pulls the towel from the radiator and swaddles her. She gets unsteadily up, feels herself sway, holds Sophie tight against her chest. The baby whimpers and Nadia breathes. She had not noticed that she had stopped breathing. Did she really think that the baby was dead? The moment is branded in her mind. It hisses and steams. Sophie wriggles inside the towel. Nadia can hardly bear to look at her. She carries Sophie carefully downstairs, putting both feet on each step and holding tightly to the banister. The pain in her head swoops nauseatingly at each movement. She thinks of a trapped bird in there beating its filthy wings.

Nadia sits by the fire and cradles Sophie for a long time before she dares to open the towel and look at what she has done. The baby's eyes are closed and she looks pale. Does she look pale? Wasn't she always a pale baby? Don't they have rosy cheeks? Wouldn't Nadia's baby have rosy cheeks? The birthmarks on her forehead are livid. They are only tiny, a

160

sprinkling of ink. 'They will fade,' Nadia says. She finds her tongue is thick in her mouth like a slab of cooked meat. She swallows away the awful taste. There is no more drink in her glass. She'd like more. Perhaps she should have coffee to clear her head. But it is perfectly clear, it clangs like a bell with pain, at each throb Nadia's sight is squeezed, so that Sophie seems to pulse like some sea-creature. There is nothing else wrong with her, nothing obviously wrong. There is a graze on the side of her head, a tiny pattern of scratches from the hairy carpet. Oh, they have such tender heads! Such a tender space where the soft bones are not yet fused and the throb of the brain is visible. It must be so easy, so pathetically easy, to kill a baby. Is she asleep, or is she unconscious? Nadia's heart scrambles. But babies do sleep a lot. Most of the time. Didn't someone say that to her once, didn't Sue complain about how boring babies are? She pleads with her memory to reassure her. And it is, after all, late at night. It is time she was asleep.

She puts Sophie down by the fire and finds some clean clothes in the carry-cot. As she leans over her head swims again, and she holds it in her hands. She might be sick. She does not want to be sick. How do mothers manage when they are sick? She staggers into the kitchen and drinks a glass of water. It is hard to swallow, as if it has edges that stick in her throat. And then she returns to Sophie to dress her. The baby is

161

still sleeping, and she is cool. She fastens the nappy round her and then struggles with the white baby-gro. It is a stupid garment that has to be stretched to get it on, with endless poppers to get confused. She puts Sophie's feet in first and gets the legs done up and then picks her up to get the arms in, but when she bends Sophie's arm back to get it in the sleeve, the baby wakes and screams. It is not like her earlier cry, it is a scream of pain. Mothers know these things, recognise different cries. The arm looks odd. The baby flinches and screams again when Nadia touches it.

'I have to dress you,' Nadia says. 'You're cold.'

But she cannot bend Sophie's arm back. She takes off the garment and starts again, this time easing it over the arm first and fumbling with the stupid fiddly poppers that flash in her eyes like sparks. Sophie is wide awake now. She struggles and squirms and kicks. Each time Nadia gets one foot in, Sophie kicks the other one out. At least she is awake, not unconscious; alive and kicking. But it is impossible to dress her and time is getting on.

'All right, Sophie,' she soothes, but the baby's cries become wilder, and high-pitched, so that they hurt Nadia's head like fingernails in her brain. She holds one foot firmly with one hand and the other under her chin so that she can manipulate the garment. She gets both feet in but then the baby falls again and bangs her

162

head on the floor. 'Oh stupid baby!' Nadia shouts. The sound of her voice shocks her. Pulled you up short, says her mother from somewhere. She picks Sophie up. She, also, looks shocked. She stops crying and widens her eyes at Nadia. 'Sorry,' Nadia says, but Sophie turns down her lip as if she has realised that Nadia isn't her mother, just some incompetent stranger who has hurt her, broken her arm perhaps? Damaged her brain? As if Nadia is an impostor.

At last Nadia finishes dressing the baby and wraps her in a shawl. Sophie calms down. She is, after all, tired. It has been a tiring evening. She drifts off to sleep. Nadia is sure her cheeks are rosier. She is sweet and clean again, a sleepy fragrant girl.

'Time to go home,' Nadia whispers. She tucks the slumbering baby in her carry-cot, then she telephones for a taxi. Half an hour, the woman promises. 'Fine,' Nadia says. 'Tell the driver to sound the horn outside. I'll be waiting.'

* * *

Simon is braced above the river which rushes under him, glittering in the light of his lamp like licorice-water. Its breath is cold and raw, the breath of January down here where the season is always the same. The roar of the water is deafening, deep, continuous,

163

exhilarating. It's like daring to stay in a tunnel with a train roaring past, the wind cold in your face. The water splashes up the sides of the walls, which have been worn into cusps by the torrents of millennia roaring through the channel of dissolving stone. It reaches up for him, long watery tentacles thrown up to splash hard and cold against his legs.

He laughs out loud at the power he has, at his own presumption. He has dared to do this thing. Alone he has dared to do it. He has cocked a snook at nature and at human caution and there is quicksilver in his veins. This is what he craved. Himself against the elements. And Simon will be victorious. He will worm out of the earth its secret ways. But he does not think, tries not to think of anything but this immediate moment, which is the inching-along of a body inside stone, over water. The water is high, but has recently been higher. Above the surface, caught in the flow cusps, are bits of twig, heathery sprigs that have been tumbled along with the water and then left stranded when the level fell.

The beam in his lamp is weakening. But he has more batteries. After this, after the rest of this slog and the duck, he will rest again. He will eat and drink and change his batteries. There is no question of turning back now; the water roars its challenge, and there is still something beside him, behind him, which prevents him looking round.

He slips a little, shocks himself, braces himself harder. He must not get cocky. Maybe Roland slipped. Perhaps he tumbled into the river, into the black roaring rush. It must be so utterly bone cold. But such a relief to let go ... The water lashes up at him again. He is shocked suddenly by a trail across his face. He gasps. It is something against his face like string. He cannot jerk away as he would naturally do, he has to control his response, stiffen the muscles that panic, jam them against the rock. He cannot think in the rush. He opens his eyes and fingers the thing. It is like a soft stalactite. No, it is a root. The thin tenuous string of a root. It cannot be. How far below the surface? Two hundred and fifty foot, at least. It must be the root of a tree probing down through the earth in search of the water that rushes below. The roar of the water is like endless applause, but not for Simon. Simon is irrelevant in this drama of inner earth. He drops the root, and braces himself harder against the rock.

*   *   *

Nadia opens the door through into the bar.

'How's it going?' the man asks. 'Nipper asleep?'

'Nearly,' says Nadia. 'I'm just getting something from my room.'

He nods and goes back to his conversation.

165

The pub is almost empty now. It has gone closing-time and the diners have all gone, leaving only a handful of chosen regulars in the thick, rosy, lamplit smoke.

Nadia's room is steamy, the curtains are open and condensation mists the black glass. The room is like a place in her head, a horrible memory, a scrap from a nightmare. She can hardly believe she was really here such a short time before—but there are her clothes on the radiators, her own wash-bag, her bed crumpled like a sickbed. There is her empty cup, and there the Bible lying splayed upon the floor.

She looks in the mirror at the bump on her forehead. She fingers it tentatively, and then pulls her hair down to cover it. She takes off the pink clothes and puts on her jeans. They are dry now, and the denim is hot; a metal button scorches the soft skin of her belly. The sweater is still damp but she pulls it over her head. Her hair has dried frizzily; she tries to run her fingers through it but they catch in the tangles and she winces at the pain. Even the skin on her scalp hurts. She straightens the bed and folds the borrowed clothes. The nylon cagoule has dried. She stuffs it in her bag and leaves the room. In her own clothes she feels stiff and reconstructed.

The man gives no sign of noticing that she has changed. He leans across the bar, laughing with someone, and only dips his head at her in acknowledgement as she passes. Nadia lets herself back into the bright rose-garden of a room. The clock is tickling the air, Sophie is breathing smoothly. Nadia picks up her bottle and the tin of formula. She puts the soiled baby clothes in a plastic bag and tucks it in the bottom of the carry-cot. Upstairs, she wipes the sink and folds the towel. There is a faint wet mark on the carpet. Nothing more.

She catches sight of herself on the mirrored wall. The bathroom is lined with mirror tiles. She is reflected many times. Strange she didn't notice before—but then she was focused entirely on Sophie. Now she sees herself repeated. She puts her hand to her mouth. In her black jeans and scarlet sweater she is Nadia again, the real Nadia. All the hands have gone to all the mouths. She is scattered, split. She sits on the edge of the bath and holds her poor head. The game is over.

Still, she tries to pretend. Downstairs she puts on her cagoule and fastens the waterproof cover over the carrycot. She is ready. But when she peers into the cot at the sleeping face she sees not Sophie but a stranger's baby. A baby called Paula. And she is in a stranger's house, nothing more than a babysitter. The nausea rises in her throat and this time there is nothing she can do but stagger upstairs to the bathroom and vomit, averting her eyes from the bright reflected figures on the walls.

She comes unsteadily downstairs. In the

kitchen she puts on the kettle for coffee. It has all been make-believe. What is real is the anger that is still there. What is real is that she has no baby, but that Celia has *her* baby, the baby that should have been Nadia's. And somehow, the stranger's baby has got hurt. The pretend-mother Nadia, the bad, drunken, pretend-mother has hurt the stranger's baby.

Outside a car hoots. Nadia listens as it hoots again. And then she realises it is for her. It is her taxi. It should never have *really* come. It was only part of the game. Nadia stands perfectly still. There is the sound of a car door slamming, footsteps, a hammering on the door of the pub. A pause. The feet again, angry, scuffing steps. The slam of the car door, the engine starting up and driving away. Nadia takes off her cagoule and carries her coffee back into the sitting room. She sits on the sofa. The stranger's baby begins to cry. Nadia picks her up. She can see her mistake now. This baby's face is wrong altogether, her head is the wrong shape. There is nothing familiar about her. She's quite a nice baby, but not Nadia's. Nothing like Nadia's.

The graze on the baby's head is only slight, a faint crosshatching of scratches. If only she had more hair it wouldn't be noticeable at all. And there is another even fainter bump, just a reddening. It is her arm that Nadia is anxious about. What if it is broken? She has a choice now. She could wait for the man—the grandfather—and explain. Or she could just

168

leave the baby, who has found her thumb and is sucking at it, her eyes closing again. Not say anything. Hope they never notice.

Holding the cup awkwardly away from her so she doesn't spill any on Paula, she sips her coffee. Of course she will have to own up. What can they say? She has done nothing wrong. The baby was dirty, she washed her. Accidentally, she dropped her. It could have happened to anyone—even the real mother. The coffee is bitter, but it is doing her good. It is taking the taste of sick away. She sips it, grimacing. I did nothing wrong, she thinks again, but there is an unhealthy feeling of guilt hanging around her. Her nipples are a raw reminder of something that is wrong. That feels as if it was a sort of perversion—involving a baby in her game. In her fantasy. But was it wrong? It may have been a game but it really comforted Sophie. Paula. And where is the harm in that?

*   *   *

Simon shivers. He shakes his head and the drips of water fly from him, lit by the faint electric beam of his lamp. That was the worst of it. The duck under the water, his legs almost carried from him by the flow, his lungs burning. But it was all right. He made it. Burst through into the air and felt his lungs expand like the crumpled wings of a butterfly freed from its chrysalis. And now he is in the small

169

grotto above the water looking up at the narrow aperture through which he must climb.

There are no batteries in his pouch. There were batteries when he made his preparations. He would swear there were. Surely Nadia wouldn't have taken them? No. Nadia would never do such a stupid thing, a thing so far beyond forgivable spite.

He unscrews the top of his water bottle and swigs from it. He sucks another barley-sugar tablet. There is no going back. He has light enough, faint though it may be, for another hour perhaps. And that may be all that is needed. And if it is not? Well, then, it is not.

He leaves his stuff on the floor. The tube ahead is tight. The floor in this grotto is curious, soft white sand, sand that would sparkle silver in the light of the sun. There are stumpy red formations projecting from it. He is careful with his feet. It would be desecration to destroy these mineral statues, so shockingly red against the soft white floor. He hoists himself up. It is so easy. He rises as easily as if someone is giving him a leg-up.

At first the tube is easy, far easier than he had anticipated. A simple crawl, the tunnel slopes upwards, low, but comfortably wide. He crawls some distance before it tightens. The roof seems to be scaled with overlapping ridges like slate roofing. He reaches his hand up and feels the sharp edges. They are the fossils of oyster shells. Once this tube of rock was part of the soft sea bed. He closes his eyes and experiences a wave of something like elation. This is discovery. 'Neptune's Crawl' he christens it—and will anyone ever know? And then he is washed over with the sudden sensation of the earth as an unformed ball of matter, a vision of shifting, sliding, crumpling plates of rock, pits opening, ridges rearing, lava tumbling, watery expanses lapping and splashing and the whole thing tumbling through the space that is out there, outside the rock, outside the capsule of air. He feels a sort of helpless vertigo. He is out of control. It is all out of control. All he can do is go on.

The crawl has tightened and seems unaccountably to be sloping downwards now. And turning upon itself. This is not what he imagined. He stops for a moment, gathering his thoughts. What does it mean? He tries to make a diagram of the passage in his head, but it will not translate. If the bend continues, where will it lead? Maybe it will straighten again. He can only hope. He goes on, inching forward. The passage is becoming uncomfortably tight. The oysters are sharp against his back. Just what is round the bend, that is all he wants to know. It could be an opening-out, a cavern, an easy stroll. It could be a dead-end. No one on the earth knows.

'Go on, Si,' he hears. It is Roland's voice.

'No,' Simon says. He closes his eyes. He will have to go back. Whatever is behind him. No.

171

There was no voice. He is alone. Roland is five years dead. The squeeze is too tight and sharp. It is icy cold. Suddenly he is icy, although there is sweat running down his brow, drops of sweat that harden like frosty beads.

Hallucination, disorientation, dislocation, he thinks. These are enemies underground, that is all it is, the mind playing tricks. Or is it the air? These could be symptoms of CO_2 poisoning. He should move back to the main airflow. There is a clean draught back there, in the grotto of the white sand. Is it poisoning or is it only fear? Whatever it is, get out. Whatever is behind him or ahead of him he must get out. Go back. He squirms back forcibly, but he cannot budge his body. His back is caught on the sharp scales. He is squeezed by the walls, which surely are tightening? No. It is not possible. He is psychologically stuck, that is all, not physically. Not. He has seen this happen to others and has talked them through it. But he has never been stuck himself before, never felt the panic that he holds at bay now, only just. Never felt the mineral clamp of the earth.

Stress causes expansion. He knows this. The minute expansion of the body caused by stress can be enough in a narrow space to make the difference between movement and not. And what of Roland's voice? What of that? He cannot see behind him. He cannot see much ahead of him. In the dimness of his lamp there is the glimmer of a round white rock. That is all. How can he go back against the serrated edges of the shells? He tries to breathe deeply in order to relax before he attempts the gradual worming back, the serpentine wriggle that will save him. But he cannot breathe deeply, there is not room. His ribs are held clamped, ribs against stone. They will not expand. There is not room for breath. Not room. His heart scrambles and tumbles against the stone of his ribs. Not stone: living bone, warm, flexible, but unable to flex.

There is a sound again. A voice. Or voices. Is it Roland? It is like a sort of song, or chant. Ahead or behind? And then at once he realises what it is, recognises the rhythm. It is not voices and there is no one. The sound is his own heart beating through his ribs against the walls of the cave and amplified by the tube. He almost laughs—would laugh if there was room enough for inhalation—with relief that it is only the chant of his heart that he can hear. There is nothing supernatural to fear. Only the natural. All he has to do is free himself. Oysters are biting through the rubber of his wetsuit into the flesh of his back. He cannot go back against their edges. He will have to go forward. One arm is ahead of him, the other pinned to his side. There is not room for both arms and his head. All he has to do is move forward. The light is growing fainter. It illuminates weakly the wall ahead of him, glimmers on the white ovoid stone. Soon it will be dark. He will be entirely in the dark.

When the light is gone there will be utter, choking dark. Even in the womb there is no such darkness. Nadia's womb is empty but Celia's contains the first beat of life. His. Only now does the deep stupidity of this wash over him in a wave that leaves him breathless, tightens the stone against his ribs. Utter bloody stupidity. He never thought, never followed it through. All the implications. Easy enough to fuck Celia, eyes shut, thinking of Nadia. Stud. Father. Only *not* father. Father means things: a deep voice, a bristly cheek, a smell of tobacco. It means the grip of a big hand, the lighting of fireworks, the filling of stockings. It does not mean just a squirt of white. He is not, will not now ever be, a father. But perhaps they will come. Perhaps they will make it right, make everything all right. Perhaps someone will come and there will be light. This is not worth dying for. Mother, oh Mother, switch on the light. Tears squeeze from his eyes—which he finds are shut.

*　　　*　　　*

The grandfather, Stan, comes through the door in a waft of beery smoke.

'All right, my dear?' he asks. Nadia looks down at the baby in her arms and nods. 'Can I get you anything? I always have a coffee and a sandwich at this hour. Very reviving.'

'No thanks.' Nadia sits holding the baby stiffly like a pretend baby in a Nativity play, a bundle of shawls.

Stan goes through into the kitchen to put the kettle on and then comes back. 'I should get off to bed then,' he advises. 'Comfortable beds in those single rooms. Tolerably new mattresses. We sleep in each room at least once, doncha know. Quality control.'

'Oh?'

Stan leans over and looks down at Paula's face. 'Land of Nod,' he says approvingly. 'First grandchild, you know. We think the world of her.' His smell reminds Nadia of her father's smell after his snifter on Sunday mornings.

'I dropped her,' she says.

Stan pauses, still half bent over, his breath whisky warm on Nadia's face. 'Dropped?'

'You see, she was filthy. She needed a wash … I dropped her in the bathroom—on that scratchy carpet. I …' Nadia's voice clogs with tears and she cannot finish.

'There, there,' Stan says awkwardly. 'No call for that.' He sits heavily down beside Nadia and pats her knee. 'No damage done by the look of it.'

Nadia sniffs and wipes her eyes on her sleeve. She pulls back the shawl. 'Look,' she points at the faint graze.

Stan looks at it, and then at Nadia, curiously. 'Can't see it myself,' he says. 'Dropped her on the carpet you say? Like India

175

rubber, nippers, aren't they? Bounce.'

'And there's her arm ... it looks funny. She cried when I dressed her. I think ... I think it might be broken.'

'This arm?' Stan says, touching Paula's right one.

Nadia nods and tears are tipped from her eyes. Stan takes Paula from her arms. 'I'll tuck her up,' he says. He gives a grunt of effort as he kneels. His big belly stretches his pullover out of shape. He has big hands, big and red as a butcher's hands, but they are tender as he puts the baby down and arranges her covers.

'Nerve damage,' he says as he stands up.

'What?' Nadia is startled. Fresh tears stand in her eyes and she is dazzled by prisms.

'Difficult birth, doncha know, a shame but it could have been worse ...'

'Ah ...' Nadia blinks.

'The wife should have said ... You look pale, my dear, let me get you a brandy.'

'She *was* in a rush,' Nadia says.

'What'll it be?'

'Oh nothing, thank you.' Nadia stands up. 'I'm tired. I'll get off to bed now.'

'Well good-night, my dear. Thanks for your help.'

'No trouble,' Nadia says weakly. She walks through the deserted pub where smoke hangs in ghostly wreathes over the empty tables. She pauses at the foot of the stairs. She cannot bear the thought of entering that miserable room

176

again. She wants only to go home. Perhaps she'll be able to think straight at home. There is no need to go back up there. She has all her things in her bag. There is no need to stay. Quietly, she opens the door and steps outside. It is a fine, dry, cold night. Would she really have taken the baby? No. It was only a game. In games things are easy, you can do anything, you can break the rules. There are no implications. Because in a game you can stop playing whenever you want, whenever you have had enough. If the cold fishy pain that is Simon's treachery was only a game, Nadia would stop playing. But it is real.

She finds her bicycle and begins to wheel it along the road. She switches on the lights— bright thanks to Simon's batteries. A rabbit skitters in front of her, stops, sits up on its haunches, paws dangling, dazzled. She smiles at the stupid thing. God, I'm tired, she thinks. The cold air presses like stainless steel against her face. Her head throbs in time with her footsteps. It is a long road home.

*　　　*　　　*

The light has gone. There is nothing but a phosphorescent glimmer on the cave wall. Or is it in the eyes, a memory of the light?

Has the earth got him then? There will be a search. There is his car outside, his stuff on the sandy floor below this squeeze. But the earth

177

has hold of him now and it feels a greedy thing. He never thought this would be the way he'd go. Nadia said. Nadia feared. Nadia. Nadia. Nadia. Sleeping now, in the warm hollow of the mattress.

The earth got Roland. Now they are joined in failure. It is utterly black. There is no blackness like it on the earth, only inside in the secret windings.

His eyes are useless in the blackness. Useless orbs. He tries again to wriggle forward. The fretted oysters slice his back. Have they cut through the rubber and the skin? Is there blood? There is not room to bleed. In the utter darkness it is difficult to think, to grasp hold of a thought. He is dislocated. Thoughts are like strings dangling just out of reach. If he could catch one with a loop of his mind he could think. For a moment he would be out of the crush. He could be anywhere in his mind, put himself anywhere. Only in imagination, but imagination is all he has. His only faculty. He can hardly feel now, wedged into the rock. He has lost the boundary between himself and the stone. The flesh is turning to stone. He loops a memory, a tenuous string, but it is only an old story and no comfort. There is a face on the end of the string with writhing scaly hair, a blur of flickering tongues. A stone stare turning flesh to stone. The string slips away. The feet can move. The toes wiggle. If the toes wiggle it means blood must be flowing. He thinks they are wiggling. Somewhere far away.

It is the Nadia string he wants. He wants to see her. Wants her. Wants Nadia and light to see her by. Wants to breathe in light. Oh if only the lungs could fill. They are screwed like fists. He wants his head on the soft, friendly loll of Nadia's breast. Or to watch her reading. Or to see her standing on her head, her hair a fuzzy corolla on the floor around her, her face red, her legs swaying, her shirt falling away so that he can see her stomach, the smudge of her belly-button through her nylon tights. Colour and light and warmth. And room to breathe. But that is only imagination. The string falls away. All that is real is dark and cold and stone. There is no connection.

The greatest freedom is the freedom of the ribs to move, the lungs to bloat like wings. That is all he wants. If only the lungs could swell. The thirst for air and for the room to spread is the main thing now. The only thing. Panic is there just ahead. It glimmers ahead of him in the dark, a round white stone. No, there is nothing. It cannot be real. It cannot be a real sight. For the eyes are useless. Like a switch when the power has gone, he cannot tell whether they are open or shut.

He cannot believe in light that travels freely through the air. In sound. He can hear, muffled, something. There was something before. Sound. What is it? Particles, dust-motes sparkling. No, ribbons, unfurling, dissolving as they travel, firework trails. But not here. Here, sound is only the muffled mineral tick of time, concentric circles in the stone. The pulsing sea-beat of his own heart. It is ... there is ... something more, something that makes him think of fur; of the intimate smell of flesh. But it is not smell. It is sound. Before there was not this sound. Was there? Is it sound, or is it feeling? It is a sort of rushing. A watery sound, but confused in the babble of his own heart. Babble, babble, babel. Tongues of Babel. His heart is like the tongue of a bell striking the stone. The rushing is the sound of a train, or the wind buffeting trees. It is the rushing to be heard inside a seashell—a memory of the sea. It is water, the rushing of the water that made this press of blackness, this taste of stone in the mouth, this coldness, these icy seams of blood. There are silly flaps of skin, cold leaves, whorls stuffed with sea-sand, soft silly appendages. They are the ears with which he is supposed to hear. But it is his skin that hears; through the planes of his squeezed body he hears, feels, tastes the echo of his own sea-salt, sea-cold blood. And what is it that the blood is singing? Mother will come. Mother. To switch on the light. Night-night. Oh the rock so lovingly tight. Sleep tight.

CHAMPAGNE

Celia holds a heavy strip of pasted paper across her arms. Carefully she climbs the step-ladder. She has the air of bearing something precious—a gift for a king. At the top of the ladder, she stretches up, lets the paper unfold, presses the top against the wall, eases the edges together, butts them with her deft fingers. Celia is the decorator. Dan brings her tea, makes helpful comments, admires the way her fingers smooth the paper. It is her efficiency he loves, her sexy capability. She drives fast, changes her job regularly and rises swiftly to the top like cream, converses wittily, cooks like a professional. Even conception. Once, it took, thank Christ, only once. And now she stretches her long limbs, her buttocks tensed under her black leggings. He climbs up the ladder and presses his face against her bottom.

'Oi!' Celia objects, half laughing.

He climbs down. 'Don't overdo it.'

'I'll just finish this wall.'

'You should take it easy.'

'Would you like to take over?' She looks down at him over her shoulder. There are hairs stuck to her cheek with a smear of wallpaper paste, and she shrugs her cheek against her shoulder to remove them. Dan steps back and watches. She wears her body like a perfectly

181

fitting suit. No odd corners, no clumsy or sagging bits. It is lovely to see her move, she should have been a gymnast or a dancer. Soon she will begin to swell. He cannot wait to feel the curve, to slide his lips down the white hill. It is odd that the memory of the birth of his daughter, Lucy, is so dim. At twenty-two he had taken it all for granted. The pregnancy, the thick gracelessness of Ellen. He had been there at the birth, a spare part, clutching Ellen's hand and looking away. He must have been moved, he supposes. Isn't it supposed to be the most moving experience on earth? Why can he only remember the bloody slime on the baby's head and the ugly twisted cord? He had fallen out of love with Ellen before the birth. Perhaps he was distancing himself strategically, to minimise his own loss when he left.

Lucy is ten now. He hasn't seen her since she was five. The photographs show a stolid, toothy little girl, a miniature Ellen, whom he might one day like to meet again.

'Pass me the cutter,' Celia says. He does so and watches as she trims a tiny strip from the top so that it is perfectly level with the coving round the ceiling. She climbs down the ladder to attend to the lower wall. She squats, her legs apart, the black fabric stretched impossibly tight like the skin of a ripe fruit, ripe to bursting.

'I love you,' he says.

'Hmmm.' She frowns over a minute nick on

182

the edge of the paper.

'I want to fuck you now, on the pasteboard, all slithery with paste. I want ...'

'Give me a break, Dan!' She stands up and grins at him. 'Half done.' She unrolls more paper and cuts across it with large scrunching snips. 'Anyway it's full of fungicide.'

'When you've finished I've got something to tell you.'

'What?'

'When you've finished.'

'You tantalising sod. I thought you had work to do.'

Dan groans and goes off to unpack his briefcase.

Celia relaxes now he's no longer watching. She loves decorating, wallpapering particularly. It is such an easy transformation. This paper has a leafy nineteenth-century print and it takes concentration to match the strips. There is no pleasure in being watched. She fumbles when he stares at her like that, comments on what she's doing as if she needs encouragement or advice when she's been decorating perfectly well without his help for years. She needs to be alone to concentrate, and when she concentrates it goes well. She gets lost in the rhythm of it, measuring, cutting, pasting, matching, sticking, trimming. And it looks *so* good. This is the dining room, which has been white-walled and Scandinavian for five years. It is time for a change. The baby will be born into a house with thick curtains and wallpaper with flowers, birds and leaves and rugs full of pattern and colour so that it can lie on its tummy and trace the patterns with its fingers, just like Celia did as a child, weaving stories into the carpets with her imagination. It will be an intricate house full of pictures and patterns and mirrors, full of things to hook memory on.

She will take up knitting. She'll make many-coloured jumpers and jackets and leggings with spots and stars. She'll make hats with tassels and mittens with strings. Dan's study is going to be the baby's room. She has seen wallpaper with ducks and balloons, matching fabric for curtains, a frieze, a lampshade. She is impatient to begin. But she will wait until she's very pregnant. Until the baby is big and safe and squirming reassuringly inside her.

Unwillingly, she remembers Nadia's miscarriage. Nadia had felt the baby move before it died. They had all been at a dinner party and Celia had seen the look of astonished absorption on her face. She had watched Nadia take Simon's hand and press it against her belly so that he could feel it too—but he could not detect such a faint flutter through Nadia's flesh. Celia had hated Nadia at that moment, the moment when Simon's hand had been against her, when his face had been intent with the effort of feeling the sensation. She had hated her for carrying Simon's child, for being the one to give Simon a child. Not that *she* wanted Simon. Oh no. But Nadia wasn't welcome to him, not then. Of course, he was bound to have other lovers—she slaps paste on the paper and spreads it to the edges with the sticky brush—but Nadia? Of course, she was sorry when Nadia lost the baby. Sorry for her and for Simon. Amazed at the bleakness on his face, as if the end of the world had really come. She was amazed that Simon could care so much, this Simon who'd refused to even contemplate a baby when he was *her* lover.

And now Celia has Si's child inside her. One day she will let him feel its movement. She wishes she had not told Nadia, that she could untell her somehow, unsay the words. Nadia will tell Simon, of course, and Simon will be angry. 'You, me and Dan,' he'd said, 'are the only ones who'll know. As far as the world's concerned, it'll be Dan's kid.' This he had said before insemination, before conception, before the confirmation of pregnancy. It had been his only condition. She hasn't spoken to him since the positive test. Not properly. He was brusque on the telephone—well, Nadia was probably there. She'd wanted to meet him but he'd refused. She only wanted to celebrate with him a little. Shouldn't they celebrate their success?

She matches the paper at the top. There's a wasted strip, Dan's fault for distracting her. She matches twining stems, joins leaf to stalk. Something has occurred to her that she should

185

discuss with Simon. Shouldn't they tell the child who its real father is? Would it be better to lie? Oh, what possessed her to tell Nadia? She strokes a soft brush over the paper, eases out crumples and bubbles. Simon will be angry with her; Dan furious. Nadia will probably never speak to her again and so it will be harder to see Simon. It was a ridiculous, irrational, un-Celia-like thing to do. It was cruel to Nadia. It was reckless, like tinkering with an experiment, shoving an extra element into a test-tube and then regretting the fizzy coloured flare.

She climbs off the ladder and crouches to trim the bottom edge—only just long enough. Her back is beginning to ache. What if Dan is so angry that he leaves her? What then?

She can hear him singing in the shower, some inane pop song. So, he is not working, which means he'll be preoccupied all weekend when she wanted him to come shopping for carpets. He's showering and shaving so that he will be ready and waiting for her when she gets into bed. But she is tired. She doesn't want him inside her. It is so delicate in there, so early, so precarious, even in the first few weeks. He can stroke her if he likes, rub her back perhaps until she sleeps, but he is not welcome inside her in the place which has become newly sacred.

She has never felt so weary, as if all her limbs have doubled in weight. She cuts the last piece of paper, an awkward piece which has to fit

186

round a light switch and over the top of the door. And when she's done that, she'll finish, soak in an orchid-scented bath, perhaps watch the beginning of the late film in bed—she'll never last till the end. What is it that Dan wants to tell her? It is her birthday soon—perhaps he's planning something for that, a weekend in the country in a cosy hotel would be nice, roast beef and languid sunny walks—nothing strenuous. How lovely it is to have a reason to feel spoilt. Thank God she didn't go caving tonight—well, there was no chance because of the weather—but if it hadn't rained ... She shudders at the thought. How quickly her desire for that has diminished. It is the last thing in the world she feels like now.

It's an awkward door, not perfectly square at the top, so she must pay attention. It's expensive wallpaper. A mistake above the door might not show, but Celia would know. And Celia likes to get things straight.

That's why she told, to make it straight. Even. Nadia had to know, otherwise it wasn't symmetrical. And after all, she was only being honest. More honest than the rest of them. Why should she feel guilty? And why should Nadia mind so much when Dan didn't? But Dan might mind her telling Nadia when she promised not to, and without even discussing it with him first. Dan is a great one for discussions. Well, so am I usually, she admits, biting her lip, coaxing the paper to stick to the uneven plaster above the doorframe. What if Dan leaves? A single parent, she thinks, and the idea is not entirely unappealing. And after all, there's Simon. If Dan left he would give her some support, surely. Once he saw the baby, his baby, and held it in his arms ... then who knows what might happen?

She frowns, remembering the perfunctoriness of Simon's love-making. She had been surprised. He was clearly aroused by her—but it was over so quickly. He touched her just enough to make her moist, and then entered her and very quickly finished. He hadn't touched her breasts or even kissed her on the lips. She had felt let down. What did I expect? she asks herself. Roses? A golden ring? He had done what she had asked him to do: a favour, a service, something mechanical that she couldn't manage herself. Like a bloody plumber. Except that she had never paid him. She had been left feeling unsatisfied, stirred and bothered by the special smell of him that she had forgotten, the smooth muscles of his back and the abrupt manner of his departure. He had rested for a moment on top of her and then left, saying nothing, only brushing her hair with his lips. And then Dan had returned and taken his turn, pounding so hard that it hurt, as if trying to drive the memory of Simon out of her, mixing his useless semen with Simon's, shouting so loudly when he came that it hurt her eardrum. She had been irritated by him. She was tired. He made her sore. She felt dirty, brimming with the cocktail of their juices, confused by her contrary emotions.

She eases the diagonal slits in the paper over the light switch, trims away the excess paper. She flicks the light off. There is still lightness in the sky, a rim of it round the rooftops. The waning moon is visible. The clouds have lifted then, at last. Perhaps tomorrow it will really be spring.

*　　*　　*

Celia watches the bubbles cluster round the plughole as the last of the bathwater gurgles away. She cannot see herself in the steamy mirror, but she stands before it anyway, and runs her hands over her slim body, her perfectly flat tummy. She doesn't really believe that there is anything in there. There is nothing to show, and hardly a symptom, except for this tiredness and a ravenous, insatiable hunger. She dries herself and puts on her dressing gown, planning a thick sandwich with cheese, ham, pickle and tomato.

Dan watches her kneeling on the floor in front of the wardrobe mirror, drying her hair and eating the sandwich. The hair dryer whines like a mosquito.

'Hurry,' he says.

Celia looks at him in the mirror, a diminished figure above her left shoulder, propped up on pillows. There are computer spreadsheets scattered all over the bed and he has a pen behind his ear. He looks ridiculous, bare-chested, bespectacled, with the pen.

'What is it then?' she asks. Her hair is almost dry. She brushes it back from her face and climbs into bed with the remains of her sandwich. She takes off her dressing gown and her clean silky hair tickles her shoulders.

'I want to celebrate,' Dan says.

'Well yes, so do I.'

'No, you don't understand. I've got something to tell you.' Celia crams the last lump of sandwich in her mouth. She looks at him quizzically as she chews.

'I had a test done today.'

'Test?' She swallows and puts the plate down beside the bed.

'Celia,' he says. 'You're not going to believe this, but ...'

'Go on.'

'This is going to sound daft ... but I had a sperm test today.'

'Sperm test? But why?'

'I don't know ... I just felt, feel in my bones, that this is *my* kid. I know it's not logical, but ...'

'*And?*'

'And there is sperm—not a full complement, but some.' Celia licks her finger and picks up some breadcrumbs from the quilt cover. Her mouth has gone dry. She feels nauseous now,

190

cold too.

'How?'

'Spontaneous regeneration of the vas deferens.'

'After all this *time*? I know vasectomies fail sometimes, but ...'

'It does happen,' Dan says. 'Well of course it does. It *has*.' He beams at her. He looks heartbreakingly proud. Under the quilt he finds her hand and squeezes it. 'You're chilly. Come here.' He pulls her closer and puts his arm round her shoulder. She lets her head rest on his chest and feels the fast beat of his heart, watches her light hair tumble on the olive skin of his belly. 'Very rare,' he says. 'A bloody miracle.'

'Yes,' says Celia. 'So ...'

'So this baby,' he continues, his hand resting flat on her belly, 'could very well be mine. Ours. So ...' With a flourish he produces from beside the bed a bottle of champagne.

Celia makes herself smile. Dan pops the cork and she watches the little spray of gas, a tiny champagne-scented ghost, rise from the bottle before the froth overflows down Dan's arm and onto the quilt.

'Mind,' she says. He catches the froth in a glass. 'Just a little, Dan. I'm more in the mood for cocoa.'

'Spoilsport,' he says. 'Don't you think it's worth a celebration?'

'Of course.' Celia accepts the glass and his

kiss.

'To us and our kid,' Dan says, and clinks his glass against hers.

Celia sips. There is quiet. They are both reflected in the mirror now, side by side, his dark hair and her fair against the wicker headboard. A loving couple engaged in celebration, champagne in bed—they look like an advertisement for something, Celia thinks, but what? Insurance? Cornflakes? The NHS?

'Dan,' Celia watches her small image say. 'I want to say two things. I don't want to burst your bubble, but ...'

'I *know*, it's OK.'

'No, let me just say this and then I'll shut up.' Dan shrugs. 'First, of course, it's wonderful about your ... your ... well your sperm. Welcome back. And it is, does seem, miraculous. But that doesn't necessarily mean that this child *is* yours. It could still be Simon's.'

'But I fucked you hundreds of times last month—Simon only once. So the chances ...'

'I don't want to get into that. The point is that it doesn't matter. It's our child anyway. It made no difference to you before, that's what you said, otherwise we'd never have done it like this. It makes no difference to me.'

'Wouldn't you rather it was mine?'

'Well yes,' Celia says, her heart sinking uneasily. 'But it doesn't, shouldn't matter.'

'No,' Dan says. 'But this makes it seem more

like mine. I want you to tell Simon that it might be mine, tell him that you think it probably is—and nobody else will ever know about the … business … with Simon.'

They are quiet for a moment. 'Simon will feel a fool,' she says. 'Feel used.'

'Ha!' Dan swigs his champagne and refills his glass. 'In fact once the baby's born you could tell Simon we did a blood test and that it *is* mine.'

'Even if it isn't?'

'Why not?'

'Don't know,' Celia says. Her lips are dry. 'Sorry,' I can't drink this.' She hands her glass to Dan and lies down.

'I thought you'd be pleased,' Dan says.

'Oh I am, Dan, really I am, just … well, confused.' Her voice sounds unconvincing even to herself, smudged by the pillow and her tiredness.

Dan snuggles down beside her and begins to caress her. His fingers play between her legs, stroking and opening, but she is dry. She squeezes her thighs together. 'Sorry,' she says. 'I'm utterly knackered.'

Dan grunts crossly and flops against her. He fits himself round the curve of her back, keeping one hand tucked obstinately between her legs, as if bagging it for later, she thinks, wondering if it is just hormones that are making her feel so irritated. Full of champagne, he falls quickly asleep, his breath

193

hot on her neck. She doesn't want to be touched, *clutched* like this. She wants to lie flat. She stiffens herself into an uncuddlable shape until his sleeping self gets the message, sighs and turns over.

Celia lies with her eyes open in the dark, looking at the glowing red figures on the digital clock. The minutes change so slowly, her eyes hurt waiting for the change. Eventually she turns over and hides them in the pillow.

She thinks about Simon and how he has changed. Living with him five years ago for a few months had been like living with a cheerful, sexy boy. He had seemed almost to lack a dimension, and she had moved in with him to try and discover it; to try to move their relationship on a stage from its sibling casualness. And she had failed. Si had remained resolutely unserious, unprepared for her idea of an adult relationship. When she had mentioned her wish for a child he had shuddered. 'Never-ever-ever,' he'd said. 'Too much a child yourself,' she'd retorted and he hadn't minded, had agreed with her. And so she'd given up and left him. He must have been hurt but had disguised it well. They had continued their friendship—caving expeditions, occasional drinks—almost as if there had never been anything between them. When Celia had met Dan and found in him all the things missing in Si she had fallen gratefully into his arms and in with his plans. And Si had seemed completely unperturbed. Even at her wedding, he had been his usual light-hearted self.

And then he'd met Nadia. At first, Celia hadn't taken her seriously as a partner for Si. She was so unlikely, so serious and arty and intense. She had been amazed when Si said, quite casually, that he'd asked her to move in with him. And he has changed since then. Nadia has found in him the dimension that Celia failed to find. It was the despair in his eyes when Nadia lost her baby that told Celia that.

Dan stirs in his sleep and his heavy arm falls across her back. She feels trapped, pinned to the bed by its weight. The bed is too hot and smelly with Dan's alcoholic breath. She feels she'll suffocate, she cannot breathe with the arm on her back like a heavy branch, her face pressed into the pillow. She eases herself out of bed. It is cold. She puts on her dressing gown and goes to the window to look out at the night. The stars are scattered like granulated sugar in the clear black sky. Dan murmurs something in his sleep. Quietly, Celia finds her sleeping bag in the bottom of the wardrobe and takes it downstairs. She lies on the sofa where at least it is cool and she is free from the weight of Dan's arm and the sickly, celebratory smell of champagne. She closes her eyes and imagines a perfect scenario. It is all nonsense, of course, and quite impossible. She wouldn't *want* it necessarily. But there is no harm in dreaming. Nobody has ever been hurt by a dream.

It is Christmas. She is with Si. He holds the baby, a girl, blonde of course, with hair like dandelion seed-fluff. Si's face is the very epitome of pride. He holds the baby up to see the Christmas-tree lights and she smiles. Her first smile. That is the way it could be. Or it could be Dan holding the baby, she thinks, guiltily amending the scene. And they could be happy, would be happy, *will* be happy. Because it is Dan she loves. Celia feels weak with misery and an intense weariness, a tiredness that makes her bones feel soft. She goes back upstairs to bed and clings on to the slumbering Dan.

*   *   *

'I hate it when you do things like that,' Celia says. 'What a stupid thing to do!' She has discovered that Dan unplugged the telephone the previous evening.

'I didn't want us to be disturbed,' he says. He sits at the table with his chin in his hands. He is bleary and stubbly, hungover from the champagne.

'It's just bloody stupid! What if somebody wanted us? What if something happened?'

'Like what?'

'I don't know. Just don't bloody do it again.' Celia frowns at him and bites into a piece of toast. She is feeling queasy and trying to pretend she isn't. 'I hate feeling cut off.'

'Sorry,' Dan mumbles. She shrugs. 'You all right?' he asks.

'All right,' she says grumpily. And then, looking at his crumpled face, feeling guilty about her night thoughts and suddenly tender: 'Really all right. Sorry I snapped. Feeling bloody awful, actually.'

'You look it.'

'Thanks a million.'

'No, I just mean washed out ... pale. Why not go back to bed for an hour?'

Celia shakes her head. 'That wouldn't help. I thought we might go shopping this morning. *Do* come, *do*. Help me choose some carpets. Then we could have lunch in the Grapes.'

'OK.' He stretches and grins. The telephone rings and Dan reaches out to answer it. 'Hello!' he says. His voice is surprised, and Celia's interest is caught. 'Oh ...' his voice sinks, 'oh no, Christ almighty, Nadia. No.' He looks sharply at Celia and then away. She had been getting up but she sits down again, her knees suddenly weak as if they will buckle and bend the wrong way.

'What?' she asks, but Dan frowns at her and cups his hand over the receiver. She has gone cold right through. She notices that the tulips on the table are beginning to flag, their lovely scarlet petals turning soft and dark. There are speckles of black pollen on the table-top.

'I will. Yes, of course, we will. We'll be here. See you, Nadia. Chin up, eh?'

He replaces the receiver.

'What?' says Celia calmly. If she can be calm, then nothing can be very wrong. Dan doesn't look at her immediately. In the sunshine she notices that his glasses are filthy. She is surprised that he can see. But at least there is sunshine.

'It's Simon,' Dan says. 'Looks as if the silly bugger went off last night ...'

'Off?'

'Curlew Cavern.'

'No.' Celia holds on to the edge of the table. She swallows. 'And Miles?'

'Not Miles, no.'

'On his own?... Si?' Celia presses her fist into her belly. 'I don't believe it.' Dan grimaces and shrugs. 'And is he ... all right?' she asks, as if the very act of asking makes it a possibility.

'Don't know yet,' Dan says. 'Nadia was ringing from the cave. Rescue under way.' Celia's tongue has stuck like rice-paper to the roof of her mouth. 'Are you all right?' Dan says. 'You've gone green. Are you going to faint? Oh Christ, Celia, don't faint. Oh Christ.' He fetches her a glass of water.

She sips it. 'Of course I won't faint,' she says. 'We must go.' When she stands up she does feel faint, there is no denying the fizzing in her ears, the fuzziness around the edges of her eyes.

'I'll make some sweet tea,' Dan says. 'Put

your head between your knees.'

'No.' Celia smiles at him, feeling fond, forgetting for a flickering instant. 'Some tea would be nice though.' And then it comes back to her, a swinging fist in her gut. 'That stupid bloody pillock,' she gasps. 'Oh Dan, what if he's ... remember Roland?'

'I said we'd be here. They'll ring if ... well, when there's some news.'

'But we must go ...'

'No point, Celie. What could we do?'

'I don't care! We can't just sit here, waiting.'

'I'm not sure ...'

'Well *I'm* going ... I'll go mad here. If you hadn't unplugged the phone ...'

'What difference?' Dan sighs. 'Poor bloody cow.'

'What?'

'Nadia ... sounded half out of her mind.'

'Yes,' says Celia. She remembers Nadia's face yesterday when she told her about Si, about the baby, how pinched it looked, how her lips had whitened. Her hand goes protectively to her belly, she sees Dan see and his own face tighten. It *is* Si's child, whatever Dan says, she knows it. 'Poor Nadia,' she agrees.

Dan hands her her tea. She cradles the cup in her hands, puts her face over it to feel the heat rise, closes her eyes. 'Please,' she whispers, 'please let him be all right. Please.'

*   *   *

Simon's car is parked just off the road on a patch of gravel. There are other cars parked behind it. They look like cars parked for a picnic, the sunshine glinting on their roofs. The ling is still brown but the long rough grass stirring in the wind has the sheen of healthy dogs' hair. Clouds skitter across the pale blue sky like lambs, dappling the hills with shadow, flickering over Simon's car and all the other cars. Some vehicles have driven down the slope to be as near as possible to the entrance of the cave.

There is an ambulance, three more cars—among them Miles's—and a Land Rover. There are several people standing about—a man and a woman by the ambulance, smoking; a row of onlookers standing at a respectful distance, gaudy in their bright jackets, pink and purple and fluorescent yellow. Onlookers got here first, Celia thinks.

Dan parks the car and Celia gets out immediately and runs down the slope. Wet jewels splash up around her feet. There is a man standing by the cave entrance holding a portable telephone. 'What's happening?' Celia demands breathlessly, steadying herself for a moment on his arm. He frowns and pulls his arm away, and then recognises her and smiles. 'Sarah, isn't it?'

'Celia.'

200

'That's it—didn't you and—' he jerks his phone towards the cave, 'used to have a thing going...?'

'Yes. What's happening?'

'They've reached him, matter of prising the bugger out now.'

'Is he ...'

'In a bad way.' He doesn't meet her eyes. She looks nervously at the dark hole which has been festooned with official-looking orange tape.

The man speaks into his phone. Celia recognises the weak crackly voice of Miles. 'May I?' she asks.

'Handing you over to Sarah,' the man says.

'Miles, it's me, Celia,' she says.

Miles's voice on the other end of the line is reassuring. 'Wotcha mate,' he says. 'Si's jammed in down here, clear of the water, thank Christ.'

'Can I help? I could come down.'

'Oh no you don't,' says Dan, reaching her and putting his arms round her as if to stop her bolting. The man takes his phone back.

'He said to look after Nadia,' he says before moving off to speak to the ambulance crew.

'And anyway you're in no condition...' scolds Dan, and Celia smiles bleakly at this old line which is so perfectly apt. Her legs feel rubbery again. She wants to sit down.

She looks up and sees Nadia. She is standing some distance away on the slope above the cave entrance. She is alone, a small figure in a green duffel coat, arms wrapped around herself, hair tumbling wildly in the wind.

'Oh God,' Celia says. She lifts her hand, but Nadia does not see, or at least does not respond.

'Poor kid,' Dan says. He stands behind Celia and she leans back against him, grateful for his steadiness in all the shifting and flickering and unruly glistening of the April day.

'She looks lonely,' Celia says.

'Shit-scared, more like.'

'Yes, but ...' Celia gazes at the small figure, motionless but for the writhing of her hair. Nadia's misery communicates itself to her; she feels it as something separate from, beyond, her own. Si is Nadia's. And he is below their feet, squeezed in there, sandwiched in the rock.

'I'll go and talk to her,' Celia says.

'I'd leave her be,' Dan advises.

'No, I must just ... you wait here.' Celia walks down and then up the slope towards Nadia. The plastic tape across the cave entrance rattles in the wind.

Nadia does not acknowledge Celia. She is like a little stone statue. Her face is white and set and her lashes are wet with wind-blown tears. There is a bruise on her forehead which shows when the wind lifts her hair. Celia has no idea what to say. They stand for some time without speaking, the blustery moaning wind the only sound. A strand of Nadia's hair lashes

202

Celia's cheek. The man, whose name Celia cannot remember, speaks intermittently on his phone. The ambulance crew cup their hands round fresh cigarettes. Dan looks up at them, his glasses glinting in the sun. The bright row of onlookers fidget. One of them pours a cup of something from a thermos flask and passes it round. Another car draws up and two people dash out of it, one with a camera slung round her neck. A cloud passes across the valley, dimming the scene suddenly.

'Nadia,' Celia says. She puts out her hand and touches the rough cloth of Nadia's coat.

'Piss off,' Nadia says through clenched teeth.

'Nadia, please.'

'Remember yesterday?' Nadia says. 'Just fuck off, Celia.'

'Yes.' Celia withdraws her hand. Tears come to her own eyes.

'*You're* all right,' Nadia says, glancing her fury at Celia. 'He might be dead.'

'No . . .'

'He might die,' Nadia continues. 'You have a part of him. I have nothing.'

'Nadia . . .'

'No one. My arms are empty.'

Celia closes her eyes for a moment. She opens them to find the sun is shining again. She sees the tiny figure of Dan below her. She is confused. Her head is clogged. She does not know what is true or what is the best thing to

203

say. I was wrong, the baby isn't Si's, she could say. Would that be the kindest thing? She doesn't know. She needs advice. It is too complex for this panicky day with the blustery wind and the skittish sunshine, and the dread of what is happening under the earth. What if what she said caused this—caused a row—caused Si to flee into such uncharacteristic foolhardiness? And what if it wasn't even true? Is all this for nothing then? She cannot bear to know.

'Just let him be all right,' she whispers.

Nadia breathes in a long shuddering breath. Celia sees that her hands are screwed into fists, the knobs of the knuckles shine like ivory. Nadia is holding herself together in the wind, in the gusting misery.

Celia tries to imagine Simon, tries to visualise his face. Are his eyes open or closed? Is he conscious? Who is in his head as he lies there?

'I'll never go underground again,' she says, and Nadia darts her a look of pure contempt. 'No, I didn't mean...' she says, realising too late how selfish and irrelevant this remark seems.

Nadia breathes out. A long controlled exhalation. Yoga breathing, Celia realises. Nadia is controlling herself with the rhythm of her breath. She is unwillingly impressed at Nadia's strength. There is the long looping liquid song of a skylark somewhere far above them. Celia breathes deeply too, and realises she needs to pee.

There is a sudden burst of activity below them. Dan raises his arm to Celia in some sort of signal and the ambulance crew begin moving towards the cave, their yellow tunics flashing in the sun. There is the glinting of binoculars from the onlookers. Celia looks at Nadia, at the startled hugeness of the pupils of her eyes. 'Come on,' she says, and tries to take her arm. But Nadia stays put. She is like someone in a dream. Her lips move but she makes no sound. 'You can't stay here,' Celia says. 'Come on, Nadia, please. Si will want ...'

But Nadia will not move or respond. So Celia, unable to bear the not-knowing any longer, runs bumpily down the hill, twists her ankle on a tussock, stumbles down to the mouth of the cave, to Dan, who puts an arm around her shoulder. Two of the rescue team emerge first.

'Move back, please,' cries the telephone man. The photographer begins to work, darting around to get different angles. Then Miles emerges, and a stranger, and between them a stretcher on which lies Simon. His hair is wet and he is smeared with blood. His face is the colour of rock. One hand trails down, strangely soft and heavy, the loose fingers grazing the ground.

Dan holds her tight. The faces are grim, exhausted, depressed. Miles does not appear to recognise her. The ambulance crew take over. There is oxygen, blankets, bright optimistic movement. It is only minutes before the ambulance has driven away, lights flashing, siren intermittently wailing.

Celia looks for Nadia. She has walked down in her dream towards the place where the ambulance was parked. Her face is ashen and her mouth is open, as if she has got stuck in a gasp, and wisps of hair cling to her lips. She moves like a sleepwalker.

'Christ,' Dan says, 'we ought to take the poor kid home.' But Miles approaches her. He is wearing a wetsuit, which, Nadia notices, is ripped on the back as if he's been savaged by terrible teeth, and there is blood.

'Miles needs help,' Celia says, stepping forward, but Miles reaches Nadia first and puts his arms around her and Nadia sags. All the stony strength leaves her and she is small and shuddering and soft. Miles holds her against him.

'Shock,' Celia says. 'She should have gone in the ambulance—Miles too.'

'We're driving them in,' the telephone man says. 'Ironic that it wasn't the water,' he adds. 'Lucky bastard was high and dry.'

'He knew what he was doing,' Celia says, and the man looks at her as if she's mad.

People have surrounded Nadia and Miles and there are blankets and thermos flasks. 'Be seeing you,' the man says and he goes over to take charge, to bundle Miles and Nadia into the Land Rover and drive them away.

Celia and Dan stand looking after it for a moment. The onlookers disperse. 'Thank Christ he's alive, at least,' Dan says.

'Yes,' Celia agrees doubtfully, remembering the awful blue-greyness of Si's unconscious face. She has no confidence.

'Now it's you that needs looking after,' Dan says. 'Let's get you home.'

'We could follow them to the hospital and see how Si ...'

'We'll phone,' says Dan firmly. He takes her hand and leads her back to the car.

'I'm dying for a pee,' Celia says.

'Can you wait?'

'Well I'm not doing it here.' The road is full of traffic now. It is an ordinary sunny Saturday. People are streaming out of the city to enjoy the air, the change of weather after weeks of greyness and rain. Celia has no idea how much time has passed. Her ankle begins to throb. 'I'll wait till we get home.'

LIGHT

Simon opens his eyes and is blinded by the bright, ridiculous, blaring light. It is like the shriek of angels. Even inside his lids the dark is diluted. There is no mineral tick and no roar. But there is sound. He concentrates on it, his

207

brow furrowed in stiff ridges. Through all his memories of sound he searches until he finds it. It is the stuffy bustle of a woman's legs inside her skirt. That is it. He opens his eyes a slit and this time the light retreats, shrinks back through the square window until it is appropriately daylight. A sunny morning in a hospital ward. The woman is a nurse. She holds his wrist between her fingers; he feels the pads of them against his skin, perfect little cushions of flesh. 'Simon?' she says. 'Back with us at last.' The flesh of her face seems to fall forward away from her bones as she leans over him. Under her eyes are shiny grey hollows. There is orange powder clogged in the fluff on her upper lip. She is technicolour and warm and beautiful. She smiles at him. He smiles back but there is a time lag between his thought smile and the stretching of his muscles. He shifts slightly and there is pain in his back as if seams are splitting. There is a tight wiry stinging in his arm.

'Mind your drip,' the nurse says. He tries to speak but his lips are as stiff as parchment and he is afraid that they will rip. His tongue is a loose parched thing, a curled leaf in the dry cavern of his mouth. He closes his eyes.

*   *   *

When he wakes he is somewhere else. The light is coming from another direction. There is no single square window as surely there was before. Was there? He opens his eyes gradually, letting in the ward by degrees—the squares on the ceiling, which are a white-painted corky stuff, the frosted-glass light set into the ceiling asymmetrically, annoyingly not in the centre of the squares. There are long windows with blinds pulled up, fat radiators. He can see, in the bed opposite, a man with a shiny bald head and closed eyes. Floral curtains are drawn around the other beds.

'Simon?' says a voice. 'I'm Doctor Rani.' She has black hair pulled back from her face. 'Can you remember what happened, Simon?' This time he dares to smile and runs the dry tip of his tongue around his lips, feeling the flakiness, the sharp spikes of skin. 'Water,' the doctor says, 'just a sip.' She helps him. The water has the taste and temperature of the ward. She speaks in an exquisite, doctorly way, with exact measured doses of words. He could easily love her.

'I remember,' he croaks.

'Good. Good. Now, we have stitched your back. Very nasty lacerations. Dehydration. Hypothermia. You were in a bad way. You're lucky.' She starts to move away. Her hair is long, a loose plait down to the small of her back, a flat bluish shine.

She looks over her shoulder. 'I'll return later. Nurse will freshen you up. Maybe a cup of tea later, eh?' She leaves him and her walk is silent almost, just a faint cottony rustle and the peeling sounds of her soles lifting off the floor. His heart rises and flutters, a loose light thing in the enormous freedom of his chest.

*   *   *

Nadia holds his fingers in her hand. She looks at his closed face, closed like a bud, his eyes, his lips sealed as if with wax. A terrible dread and tenderness and anger battle within her.

'Simon,' she tries again. She has been watching him sleep and willing and fearing his awakening. Now he stirs. Opens his eyes. She starts, seeing how bloodshot they are, the grey irises standing out shockingly against the red.

'Nadia?' he whispers.

'Fool,' she says, smoothing his hair back from his eyes.

'Don't say ... I told you so,' he says with difficulty, his dry lips stretching into a sort of smile.

'Hmmm.' Nadia plays with his fingers. They are limp and warm. The nails are broken as if he has been clawing at the rock. So, he is alive. She is glad. She loves him. If only it was as simple as that. She is the only one with him inside the flowered cubicle, but inside her head she is not the only one. Celia flickers there like a pale film between them. She has told herself she must wait until he is strong before she tackles him. But how can she wait? She needs Simon to know that she knows what he is, what he has done. If he doesn't know, then he will be operating in a different place from Nadia, a place with different premises and different rules. And how can they communicate then?

'Simon. I saw Celia,' she begins, watching his face for the slightest sign. He gives none. 'Celia told me . . .' she says experimentally, and from the little electric twitch of his muscles, the flinching of his eyes, she knows that it is all true. He does not ask, What?, and she does not tell him. The minute hope she had that it was a lie or Celia's fantasy falls away. He does not reply. His fingers splay uselessly open.

Nadia grasps his fingers and twists them in her own. 'What can I do?' she says and her voice is thick with despair. 'Simon. How am I supposed to bear it?'

'Sorry,' he mumbles, and the insulting inadequacy of this word makes her snort. But what other words are there? Oh yes. 'I love you,' he adds.

Nadia drops his hand. It lies crumpled on the white sheet like a dead flower. She stands up, walks around, pours herself a glass of tepid water from his jug.

Simon gives a weak cough and groans with the pain of it. A nurse sweeps the curtain aside. 'All right?' she says. 'Shall I help you turn?' She lumps Simon, groaning, onto his side. She smells of cigarettes. She puts a hand on Simon's forehead and frowns. Nadia notices a tattoo on her wrist, half hidden by her cuff. Despite her despair she finds herself grinning at this incongruity. 'I'll get Doctor to pop in ...' the nurse says. She frowns again, feeling his pulse and squinting at her watch. 'Five minutes,' she says to Nadia.

Nadia nods and the nurse leaves, whisking the curtain shut again.

'Oh Christ, Nadia, I hurt,' Simon groans. 'It hurts in my chest.'

'Bruising,' Nadia snaps. She will not feel sorry for him. Easy for him to evade the problem now, to retreat into pain. Oh, there is real pain. He is not putting it on, it isn't that she thinks that. His cheeks have suddenly paled. The tenderness rises again, flickering through her anger like weak sun through gathering clouds. She strokes his forehead. It is hot. 'Simon,' she sighs. 'You know I love you too. But how can I stand this?' She puts her knuckle in her mouth and bites, the hard pain preventing her tears. It is not fair to do this to Simon now. He is in *real* pain, real *physical* pain. Which after all may be easier to bear.

'I'd better go,' she says. 'I'll be back.'

'Don't go,' Simon says. He grips her hand, but his is slippery with sweat, easy to pull away from. 'Oh my head aches,' he mutters. 'Nadia, why am I hurting more and more?'

'I don't know. I'll tell the nurse you've got a headache on my way out.' Nadia kisses him on his mouth and feels a shock of angry desire.

212

She picks up her bag. 'Bye-bye. Try and sleep.'
Her own head is swimming. She has lost track
of time. She has not eaten or slept. Her head
throbs still and her nipples sting. She frowns,
remembering Sophie's voracious sucking. It is
like a dream now, that, the greedy lips, the
garish roses, the sticky drink, the game, the
horrible sour milky mess and the terrible fright
when at last she got home, of finding the flat
empty, of finding Simon's note. Miles had
answered the phone and organised everything.
She cannot remember much more than the
blackness thinning over the edges of the hills,
the pale lemon of the dawn discovering the
dewy huddles of sheep, the gnawing of anxiety.
People had spoken to her one after another,
urged her to do this or that, eat this, drink that,
go home. But she had stood frozen while the
dawn turned to day, while under the earth
people risked their own lives to prise out her
lover.

'Wait,' Simon says. His eyes are closed now.
'What?'
'It should be yours,' he whispers. His voice
has lost its colour, it is a paper voice.
Nadia cannot answer. She presses her lips
together hard until she can feel the edges of her
teeth against them. She squeezes his hand, and
then she leaves.

*　　　*　　　*

213

Simon opens his eyes. There is the flowered material. What are the flowers supposed to be? They are very bright. Orange and brown. Are there brown flowers? The word 'nasturtiums' comes from somewhere. Nadia has gone. When did she go? He can feel her finger stroking his palm, potter's fingers stroking as if he is clay, as if she is smoothing him out. He frowns and feels the rising furrows like the ridges on the wall of a cave, flow lines. Or like, more like, the lines on a clay mask, just made, soft glistening furrows. Wet corduroy. His father had lines that arched like a rainbow on his brow when he was surprised. There is a sound above the rustling clanging hospital sounds, a constant sound, high-pitched. Is it the light? His mother had soft arms. If you pinched the skin above her elbows it held the mark like dough. Made her laugh crossly, slap him away. Yes, it is the light that is high-pitched. What? Buzz. This is discovery. He should tell someone. He is in the world and he can hear the light. Humming. And Nadia's thighs are like silk. Her buttocks are coarse-skinned but the insides of her thighs ... Sound and light are one. They are part of the same continuum. Is this not known? Has he not demonstrated it on the blackboard? It is so plainly true. Sound is low, from a mumble to a hum, light high, from a song to a whine to a scream which becomes ... phosphorescence, moon shimmer, the scream of the sun which is pain too. What was it his mother said? The sun is heat and it is light and it is pain. There is the smell of heat and the taste of sun-baked stone. Surely he has tasted sun-baked stone? Or is it just the orange curtain. Marigolds? Chrysanthemums? He never paid attention. And his mother would always say ... something ... something about light, was it? He wants to shout. Why is it so bloody cold and why is he shuddering? What was it in the cave that he cannot remember? Something seen. Surely there is limestone in his eyes. 'Nadia,' he says, and his voice is a real thing, a clear thing that rises from him, separate like a balloon. It will float out and somebody will see it, nudging between the curtains. Nadia.

He is filling with pain like a vessel, like a bladder swelling. His ribs are stretched now. No longer squeezed, they blossom out like fans, like wings. He is a balloon tight with pain and it is beyond white ... what is it called, the colour beyond white? There was something he saw that he should remember, that he should tell. Nadia is not there. His eyes are closed, he thinks, but what is the dazzle? And his mother said switch off the light. Is that it?

*　　　*　　　*

Simon has a hazy notion that people are working on him, hauling in the thread of his life on the end of which he floats, loosely. After

215

the bursting in his chest he floated into a place where the taste and the light were like sweet butter and where he slithered warmly, quite contentedly, but they are pulling him back, reeling him in as surely as if he was a fish.

*   *   *

When she gets home, Nadia lies on the floor, her hands loosely open, her knees rolled apart. She draws in smooth breath, focusing her mind on the way it flows. From Iris's flat downstairs comes the sound of the television. There is a comedy on, the laughter comes in stupid blurts. Nadia closes her mind to it. Tries to imagine the colour gold, to concentrate on drawing golden breaths inside to suffuse her muscles and her heart with well-being, but the colour of her breath remains resolutely grey. She pushes up her back to make a bridge, cupping her hands under her back, walking her feet out, pressing her shoulders and her soles flat on the floor. Then with a grunt of effort she moves her hands behind her head and pushes up into the Wheel. Her body arches. Outside a car door slams, someone is whistling. We should get double glazing to shut out the noises, she thinks. She'll suggest it to Simon, she pretends. For it all depends. Simon and Nadia, their future. It all depends. On what, she isn't sure. She lets herself down onto the floor and tries to relax. But she cannot. There is too much in her mind. See the mind as a river rushing past, she tells herself in the soothing voice of her yoga teacher. You are on the bank watching it all rush past, all the flotsam of your life, all tumbled together in the rushing flow. But it is no good; she cannot remove herself from its splashes, she cannot pull herself out of it, is instead swept into the flow.

There was a time when Simon caught lice from school and they both had to treat themselves. The lotion was dark and oily and they had to rub it into their hair and leave it on overnight. They had treated each other. Nadia remembers rubbing Simon's head, the lotion darkening his hair, rubbing with tiny deft circular motions every inch of his skull, discovering bumps and dips in the bone. That night they had lain together stiffly, their sticky heads on towels to protect the pillows. They had talked about work and about money and lay with a space between them as if the delousing treatment demanded this formality. Later, Nadia had dreamt about Simon, an oily, foul-tasting dream, dreamt he was making love to her on a garage floor and woken to find him really inside her. She had given no sign that she was awake. The taste of the lotion was in her mouth. He fucked her silently, hotly, tightly, and then rolled off, rolled right away from her. She had lain awake for ages afterwards listening to his breathing slowing, feeling sore and wet, cross and confused. They had never

217

spoken of it. She didn't even know if he had been awake. It had been nothing to do with her, she was sure of that. She could have been anyone or anything. There had been something disgusting about it, the anonymity, the reek of the poison lotion. And yet she had not resisted or even blamed him. She gets up quickly. Why remember that now? She has a filthy taste in her mouth.

In the kitchen it is as if time has stood still. And indeed it is only a day since Simon sat at the table, eating his meal. His greasy plate is half submerged in the bowl of cold scummy water. Tomato pips and a sliver of egg white float on the surface. Nadia's own cup is there too. And the tap still drips sluggishly, shivering the greasy surface. She tips out the cold water and with hot water and detergent cleans away every trace of grease.

Simon's note is still on the table. She picks it up, crumples it, and then smooths it out. The ink runs with the wetness of her hands. His name is smeared, and his love. The telephone rings.

*　　　*　　　*

'Out of danger,' the woman is saying, 'no need to come ... sleeping soundly.'

'But I didn't know he was *in* danger...' objects Nadia. 'I thought he was safe... in hospital.'

218

'We did try to ring... massive infection... cardiac arrest. Unexpected, but can happen... all over now though, sleeping soundly.'

'But...'

'Try and get a good night's sleep yourself, dear, I should. Visiting from ten tomorrow.'

Nadia puts down the phone and catches sight of herself reflected in the dark window. She looks like one of her own masks, her eyebrows raised crazily, her mouth open. Simon's had a cardiac arrest? *Simon.* A heart attack. But he's all right. Sleeping soundly.

*   *   *

She wanders about the flat vaguely. What is it she should do? It is night but she is not tired. She should be tired. It is thirty-eight hours since she last slept. At least Simon is sleeping soundly. It is Saturday night. What can she do? There was a song they sang at school, a stupid repetitive song, the point of which was that each verse was in another language. '*Tout le monde aime samedi nuit.*' She finds herself humming it as she wanders around. In her studio she lifts the cloth from her sculpture, strange, damp, strong thing. She could work. She notices the pile of clay she left yesterday, scrunched by her angry fist on the board. No, she cannot work.

Iris and Derek have turned the television up downstairs. It sounds like a film now, she can hear shots being fired, the roar of a speeding car. She could go down and see them. Iris would listen to her, welcome her. She remembers Iris trying to attract her attention last night. Was her hair really black and piled up like a bonfire? She closes the door of her studio, thinking of Iris's room downstairs with the filthy crow feathers everywhere. She was right about Simon anyway, about the danger. Probably just coincidence. Easier to think that. If not, how to make sense of it?

A heart attack. Simon. She cannot connect the two ideas in her mind. Heart attacks aren't for fit young men. She remembers the sensation of Simon's heart beating against her own, or against her ear when she lay with her head on his chest. The comforting regularity. And it stumbled, stopped. Arrested. No. But it's all right. It *is* all right.

Iris told her to contact her mother. A mother alone, she said she saw. Well that is wrong, for her mother is living with Michael in Eastbourne. And Iris talked about a lump. Nadia has the phone number in her diary. She picks the receiver up and puts it down several times. It is rather late—nearly eleven—to be ringing, out of the blue like this. But she needs someone. Just someone to talk to.

She finds she has dialled the number before she is really ready. She listens, discomforted, to the sound of it ringing in that unknown house. Luxurious, June said on her Christmas card.

220

That's all the contact they've had for years, Christmas cards, birthday greetings, cowardly scrawls on cards full of ready-made words. What if Michael answers? He's angry with her for neglecting their mother. There is a spider's web on the paper lampshade. She remembers a dark-painted room with stars and moons and the lorries roaring by, rattling the windows. How dreadful and dark and sordid it must have seemed to June, and yet she never said. The soul of tact, that is the sort of thing she would have inwardly said. The phone is still ringing. No one there. Nadia is relieved. She stands on tiptoes and bats the lampshade. Dust showers onto her head and scatters on the striped rug. And then a woman answers. It is Donna, Michael's wife.

'Could I speak to June please,' Nadia says. She winces, waiting to be asked for her name, but Donna doesn't ask.

'Hang on,' is all she says and bangs the receiver down unnecessarily hard. No wonder she is cross, disturbed by a stranger at this time on a Saturday night—at the climax of a film perhaps. She can hear the muted sounds of television. Maybe they are watching the same film as Iris and Derek. Maybe I should watch it, she thinks, if everyone else is. Not a stranger though, part of the family. A selfish cow, Michael once said Donna considered her.

'Mum,' Nadia can hear her calling. She is a long time coming to the telephone. Nadia is cold. She thinks of Simon sleeping soundly, his heart restored. What if he had died? Dreadfully, dreadfully, she finds herself thinking that at least it would be simple then. She would simply be without him. Does she mean it? It's the sort of thing it's easy to think when everything's all right. She hears a rustle and then her mother's voice, 'Hello. June Samson speaking. Who is this please?'

Nadia's mouth is dry. She swallows. June Samson, of course, her new married— widowed—name. 'Mum?'

'Pardon. You'll have to speak up ...' The voice is firm, it sounds no older than before, and is there an Australian twang? Surely not.

'It's Nadia,' Nadia says.

There is silence, a seashell sound in the cupped plastic, two hundred miles of surprise transmitted down a wire.

'Nadia,' June says at last. 'Well...'

'Mum, I...' What on earth can she say? Suddenly she *is* tired. Too tired to think.

'Well, this is a surprise. I was thinking about cocoa.'

'It's late. Sorry.'

'Not at all. Well, this is nice. After all this time.'

'Yes... I...' Even Nadia's mouth is tired. She is puzzled, starts as if from a dream of telephoning her mother to find herself telephoning her mother.

'Are you well?'

'Oh ... fine. You?'

'Well you know.'

'I'm sorry about ... Pierre. Sorry I didn't write or anything.'

'Didn't expect it, dear.' There is the faintest frosty edge to the voice.

'I know, Mum. I *am* sorry ... for everything.' This wasn't why I rang, Nadia thinks. It was for *me*, to talk about *me*. And Simon is sleeping peacefully; not peacefully, that is for dead people, sleeping soundly.

'And your young man, Simon is it? Is he all right?'

'Fine.' Nadia shakes her head disbelievingly to hear herself say this, watches the walls slide past her sleepy eyes. 'How's Michael? And the family?' she asks, obedient to convention. It is getting out of her control, all these platitudes, ready-written lines. She panics, waves her hand, finds her voice rising, interrupts her mother's response. 'I wanted to say sorry.'

'Well I should think so, after fifteen years ...'

'No, I mean ... I was remembering that time, the last time we really spoke.'

'Daddy's funeral?'

'No Mum, before that ... don't you remember? You came to see me. You needed to talk.'

'Did I dear? About Daddy?'

'No. You must remember. The room with the moons and the stars. You came for tea, we had shrimps and Battenburg ... you needed to

223

talk, you said you had no one else, no other friends.'

There is a rustling at the other end as if June is leafing through the pages of her memory. 'Well I had your father, before he died of course, and Pierre...'

'No *women*. No one to confide in...'

'Don't be silly, dear. I had you, and Auntie Betty.'

'But you *didn't*, that's the point. Don't you see? You didn't have me, I failed you. I let you down.'

There is quiet for a moment. 'I'm sorry dear, you've lost me. Of course I've been upset that we've ... well, gone our separate ways, but now you've rung...' Nadia holds the telephone away from her as her mother talks, looking at the inscrutable grey plastic, slick with the sweat from her palm, the miniature familiar voice issuing from the daisy pattern of holes. Plans spin out of her mother like the filaments of a web to draw Nadia back. Visits, parties, holidays together. She must meet Simon. Nadia must meet Michael's children. It will all be so normal, and so much fun.

'Yes,' Nadia says. The stripes on the rug writhe like snakes. She blinks her eyes firmly to stop them and finds that they want to stay shut. There are bright fuzzy shapes inside her eyelids like amoebas.

'Mustn't forget your phone bill,' her mother is saying.

'No,' Nadia agrees, and her voice is sluggish in her mouth. It does not want to come out.

'But you will visit soon? I'll speak to Donna and ring you tomorrow.'

'Good,' Nadia says. 'I'll have to go, Mum. Nice to speak to you.'

'Good-night darling.'

'Bye.'

Nadia crawls into bed. She didn't say the things she meant to say, her mother didn't say the things she ought to have said. They have skirted around a reconciliation. It is in there somewhere among the rules that governed their conversation. There is real meaning, real feeling. She has to assume that there is. It is just that it does not do to make a song and dance about things. There are some pages of memory that it is better to rip out. And there is comfort, somehow, in that. It was always so. Never an exact connection between them, between what they said and what they meant. And all that guilt seems like a joke now, a silly fancy on Nadia's part. So that is all right. Everything is all right. Except Celia. Except the baby. Inside her somewhere below the thick cloudiness of sleep she feels the cold fish of her anger nudging, but even this has not the power to keep her awake.

*   *   *

She is woken by a knocking on the door. She

225

opens her eyes, finds herself alone, adrift across the bed, bright sunshine spilling through undrawn curtains. She lies puzzled for an instant, groping to make sense of the day and the time. And then there is the knocking again. And a voice calling her name. It is Iris. And then she remembers everything.

'Anyone home?' Iris calls. Nadia staggers from the bed. She is still half dressed, having had the energy only to pull off her jeans and sweater before she slept.

'Hello,' she replies. She struggles into her dressing gown. The room is full of bright, sharp, tricky light.

'Everything all right?' Iris asks. Nadia goes to meet her in the hall.

'Wow,' she says, remembering the glimpse of Iris through the window through the rain. Before. It feels like weeks ago. Iris's hair is piled in a glistening lopsided mound. She wears her red and black shawl, giant gold hoop earrings and scarlet lipstick.

'The door was open,' Iris says. 'Thought you'd been burgularised. Thought I'd look in, make sure nothing was up. Do you like it?' She touches her lips. 'Bee-Sting, it's called, a sample actually, but no bugger was interested.'

Nadia laughs weakly. 'I'll make coffee,' she says. Her eyes will not focus properly. The texture of Iris's hair is complex, and glistens fuzzily like black candy-floss. 'Your hair,' she says.

'Oh not mine, sweetheart,' Iris says. 'Polyester. Look.' She whips it off. Her own grey hair is flattened to her head with a gold net. 'Debenhams sale,' she says, putting it on the kitchen table.

'Lovely,' Nadia says and finds herself giggling feebly at the sight of Iris with her hairnet and lipstick and ear-rings.

'Part of the new image,' Iris says. 'I'll just leave it off for a mo.' She scrabbles her fingers scratchily over her scalp.

Nadia's eyes leak from the laughter and the sunshine. She wipes them on her dressing-gown sleeve. 'Sorry to laugh,' she says. 'It's not you really, it's ...'

'Amazon,' Iris says, indicating the flat package that she's also put on the table, '£3.75 but no hurry. So, what's been going off?' She sits down. Nadia spoons coffee into two cups.

'Well,' she says, and flounders. Where can she possibly start?

'I saw you rushing away,' Iris prompts, 'on your bike. "Like a bat out of hell," I said to Derek. Thought you might need your eyeshadow, that's why I waved.'

'No,' Nadia says. 'I didn't need it.'

'Have you done your sculpture?'

'Well, yes, sort of.' Iris looks expectant. 'Want to see?'

'I'd like to see what you made of me.'

'It's not *you* exactly,' Nadia warns, leading Iris through into her studio. She pulls the cloth

227

off the object. Iris screws up her nose. 'It's not directly representational,' Nadia says, 'I mean …'

'I know what you mean.'

'Sorry.'

'God,' Iris says. 'Looks like it's about to jump right off that bench. It's got, something. Energy or something.'

Nadia is delighted. 'Really? Do you really think so?'

'What d'you call it?'

'I don't know. I hadn't thought.'

'So will you be wanting me again? To model.'

'Oh … not just now though. I'm feeling … it's been a rough couple of days.' Rough! She laughs at her own understatement. She is full of laughter today, silly bubbles of it like pressure escaping.

In the kitchen, Nadia hands Iris her coffee and sits down. For an instant she thinks Iris is Simon, preposterously, and shakes her head. Soon she will see him, in his hospital bed with his vulnerable heart beating. She is afraid to see him. If she had waited to confront him, waited until he was strong … but she cannot think about that now, not with Iris in her glistening hairnet sitting there, waiting.

Looking not at Iris but at the light dancing on the surface of her coffee and at the elliptical reflection flittering across the ceiling when she moves her cup, she tells Iris about Simon,

228

about the rescue, about the heart attack. Iris listens with her mouth open. 'Bleeding hell, Nadia,' she says intermittently.

'So you were right,' Nadia finishes.

'Right? Me? In what way?'

'You saw danger in the tea-leaves.'

'Listen,' Iris says, leaning forward urgently. 'It's a load of cobblers. Really. This fortune business. I make it all up.' Nadia frowns, disbelievingly. 'Oh I'm quite telepathic. I pick things up. But otherwise ...'

'You're a fraud,' Nadia says, sitting back.

'Not a fraud, no. I wouldn't say a fraud.'

'But if it's all lies ...'

'Intuition. But sometimes—if I can't, well, intuit anything, then I make it up. It's what the punters want.'

'So you made it up about Simon's danger?'

'Well no. I mean the sign *was* there, and near the rim of the cup—that means the near future. Anyone can do that, you only have to look it up in a book. But I don't believe it myself. I mean, how can it be related to anything? How can it?'

'I know,' Nadia says. 'That's what I think, but ... well, how can you do it then? Take people in?'

Iris laces her hands together and clicks her knuckles. 'It's a service,' she says. 'People only come if they want to be taken in.' Nadia opens her mouth to object. 'And it's a job,' Iris continues. 'I'm going for it now—new image,

229

see. Given up the selling. "You have to believe in your product," that's what the silly bitch area sales manager said, reeking of bleeding Addiction, sneering at my "so-called sales record". So I packed it in. Kept the samples though.' She smears her lips together, tasting the Bee-Sting.

'What about Leonard?' Nadia says. 'You said you saw in his palm that he'd die young.'

'And then he went and got himself killed by a load of haddock.'

'Cod, you said.'

'Never was sure of the species. That's true. But I didn't see it, not before. Good story though.'

'So it's all stories, lies?' Nadia touches the bruise on her head and winces.

'Not lies. Things come to me, or they don't. Not a lot to do with the tea-leaves, or whatever ... can't pick and choose.' Iris narrows her eyes, and Nadia notices again the odd intensity that their different colours gives her. With her hair flattened to her head she has a witchy look. 'I *can* tell,' she says, 'that something's wrong. Something apart from—before—last night. Have you lost a child?'

Nadia gasps. It is as if someone has stroked a raw nerve. She bites the rough corner of her thumbnail.

'It hurts, I know,' Iris says.

'You don't know ...' Nadia wails. She half stands but Iris continues, 'When I was twenty I

230

had my first baby. A boy. Stillborn.'

Nadia sits down.

'And since then I've had three more, full-term still births. No explanation. And over twenty miscarriages.'

'My God,' Nadia says. 'Twenty.'

'So how many little souls is that who trail behind me?'

Nadia gasps. 'Iris ... I'm sorry.' She squeezes her eyes against the vision of a cloud of little filmy wraiths around Iris's head.

Iris shrugs. She picks up her wig and puts it on, becoming at once grand. 'You survive,' she says. 'It's a case of having to.'

Nadia watches Iris get up to leave. 'I'm sorry I was so ... I just didn't think.'

'Why *should* you, my duck? Old fart like me.' Her eyes shine, she whisks her shawl dramatically over her shoulders: '£3.75 for the eye-compact, remember. But no rush.'

Nadia follows her to the door. 'I'll drop it in later. I'm going to see Simon.'

'Send him my best,' Iris says. 'Poor sod. He'll be all right. I feel *that*, for definite.'

'Thanks.'

Iris opens the door and then turns back. 'Listen,' she says. 'If you want my advice, don't give up hope of a baby but don't *pin* your hopes on it either. Understand? There's more to life ... talented girl like you.'

When she has left, Nadia goes back into the kitchen. She must eat something and then she

231

must go to the hospital. Why does her heart sink at the thought? On the chair where Iris has been sitting there is something dark. She picks it up. It is the feather of a crow. She shudders as she drops it in the bin.

BITTER

Simon is sleeping. Since the accident he has slept deeply, almost dreamlessly he claims, although Nadia, lying awake beside him, hears him groan and feels him struggle and sometimes clutch her as if to save himself.

Nadia puts on a short flowery dress, a gesture to summer, and then she stands beside the bed, looking down at Simon's sleeping face. He is peaceful now, flushed; the sunshine falls across his face, lighting the filaments of stubble so that they glitter like fuse wire. He is so pink and gold and alive that it is impossible to believe that he nearly died. He stirs in his sleep, turns over, and the quilt falls away from his shoulders, revealing the angry red ridges of his scars. She runs a fingertip very gently along the length of one, stretched like a grin across his shoulderblade. The scars will fade to white but they will never disappear. Apart from the scars he is better, *physically* he is better.

He wakes with a start. This is the way he wakes now, always, his body stiffening, his eyes wide with fear. She watches the flaring of his pupils as he turns over. When he sees past whatever is in his head, sees her, his face relaxes and he smiles.

'Morning,' Nadia says. He reaches up for her hand but she moves away before he can touch her. 'I'll make some tea.'

While the kettle boils, she goes into her studio. The light is pure and grey in the mornings in this room, no silly sunbeams, a clear, uniform light. The sculptures are grey, bits of Iris, bits of herself, of Simon, transmuted by her fingers and imagination into strange solid forms. The first sculpture, the foot, she has not let dry. It is not finished somehow; it remains under a damp cloth while she works on the others. Simon stared at these shapes uncomprehendingly. 'Good,' he said, surprised by the work, as Nadia too is surprised. But she knows that this is what she's been waiting for. It has been shocked into germination by the accident perhaps. 'Accident' is what they call it—Nadia and Simon, Celia and Dan and Iris.

'What?' Simon asked, with the grey forms before him. 'I can't quite make out ...'

'That's the point,' Nadia explained, smiling at the puzzled dip of his eyebrows.

Simon gets up before Nadia has made the tea. He follows her into her studio. He is naked. 'Watch your feet,' Nadia warns. The floor is littered with little blobs and curls of dried clay. 'I really must sweep up.'

Simon puts his arms around her. 'Come back to bed,' he says, nuzzling his bristly face into her neck, pressing his pelvis, his soft penis against her.

'Not now,' she says. 'I've got to go out.'

'You haven't got to.'

She pulls away from him. He smells fusty, of sleepy anxious sweat. 'Why not shower and shave?' she says. She leaves the studio and he follows her into the kitchen, watches her make the tea.

'I do love you,' he says.

'I know.' The love on his face bothers her, and the wistful, almost yearning look in his eyes. Now he is up he looks less rosy. He seems to have aged in just a few weeks, so that occasionally she catches glimpses of the old man he will become in the slanted set of his head on his shoulders, the lines that stretch from his nose to the corners of his mouth.

'Do have a shower,' she urges. 'Why don't you go out? You can't stay in on such a lovely day.' Simon's eyes flicker nervously towards the window. He nods unconvincingly. 'See you later,' Nadia says.

'Aren't you having breakfast?'

'Had it.' She gestures at her empty cereal bowl.

'You should have woken me. Where are you going?'

'Just to see someone.' She hangs around in the kitchen until she can hear the shower and

234

then, relieved, hurries down the stairs, out past Iris's door into the sweet sunshine. It is mid-May. The air is like warm scented sheets against her face. She stops to bury her nose in some voluptuous purple lilac. Rampant early-summer growth burgeons out through the park railings, trespassing onto the footpath, catching at her ankles as she brushes past. She hesitates at the corner of the road. She has nowhere to go but out. Soon Simon will return to work and then at least she will feel free during the day, free of his constant neediness which hangs around the flat like a cloying smell; and free of her own guilt for feeling like this. She walks past the shops, stops to buy an apple from the greengrocer's, crunches it as she walks, watching herself flicker past shop windows, running her hand through her hair. The sun is warm on her winter-white arms, an almost forgotten sensation. She feels sexy walking through the streets, damp in her armpits, conscious of the warm bell of air inside her dress. She is chafed from Simon's never-ending screwing. If she doesn't get pregnant the way they are going, she never will. She is awash with opportunities.

The trouble is, it does not feel like love that drives him into her morning and night, not even desire, but desperation. If it was not for her desire for a baby she would not tolerate it. She throws her apple core into a litter bin and wipes her juicy fingers on her skirt.

Through the streaming water, Simon hears the
door bang, gets out of the shower and goes to
the kitchen window to watch Nadia leave. He
shivers. She has a loose bouncy walk as if she is
relieved to be free. Her hair glints red in the
sun. Yesterday she hennacd it and there are
still clots of henna on the bathroom rug and
greenish grains leaking brown around the taps.
He does not like the colour. It is a false red. It is
not Nadia's colour and the wiriness of her hair
snags the light so that it is haloed round her
head, exaggerated. She didn't consult him. The
first he knew was the vegetable stench of the
stuff in the bathroom, the filthy towels, the
splashes she neglected to wipe up. And why the
hell should she consult him? No reason, except
that once she would have done.

The colour is not welcome in the flat. Not
that false, ethnic, vegetable red.

Nadia vanishes round the corner and he
shudders. Perhaps it is over. Perhaps that is
what he has to face. She no longer treasures
this naked body that shivers and catches the
sunshine in slithering drips. Her adoration has
been a constant in his life for five years. Not
always deserved. Taken for granted. Never
deserved? But he does love her. His hand cups
his wet shrunken penis. He is cold right
through. He can see the sun outside glittering
on the roofs of cars. He can see warmth in the

slowness of the people outside, the lazy trail of mothers with push-chairs to the park, but he cannot feel it in himself. Nadia is right, there is no reason why he shouldn't go out. He could take his newspaper to the park, laze on the grass, listen to the wood-pigeons cooing in the trees, the ducks quacking on the pond. He could do that. He could even go out into the countryside. The car is there, parked below him, undriven for weeks, dull with a patina of rained-on dust. All he has to do is take his keys and go. He could drive out to a pub for lunch. If Nadia was here he would suggest it.

Instead he finds the warmth he seeks in bed. Only for a time. He will not spend all day in bed. But there is still warmth there, left in the quilt by his body and by Nadia's. It is good to breathe in her scent. The sheet is rumpled and stained over and over by their love-making. He wants her all the time, wants to burrow into her, the warm softness, the easiness. He cannot get enough of the way she holds him inside her and then lets him go, of the loose loving slip-slide of it. It is such a simple thing, but so profound. It is his only relief.

He closes his eyes against the sunshine that taunts him for being there between the sheets like a sick person. He is bothered by a memory, something that is preventing him from moving forward. It is something he does not tell Nadia, that rises in his dreams, and bobs beneath the surface in the waking time, nudging sometimes

237

almost up into the light, and he yearns to give a name to it. He yearns so hard that he finds his fingers clutching the thinness of air. It bobs below the surface, domed and hollow, a white calcite glimmer in the deep utter darkness; and the white skull grin of recognition which his mind protects him from has remained submerged except in the helpless flailing of his dreams.

But now in the space between sleep and waking he is jerked, as if by a hand in his hair, upright. There is a rearing in his mind, a fusion of memory and dream. The white stone that he saw in the passage before him was Roland's skull. Oh yes, it could have been a stone, it could have been an illusion, some flicker, a memory of light playing on his retina, it could have been many things. But he knows that it was Roland.

*　　*　　*

Nadia walks between people, across roads, only vaguely registering her purpose, so absorbed is she in her feelings. There is the anger, and to her surprise a sort of boredom with the way it grinds on and on, over and over. And there is the longing for a child, which is constant—but even that has become confused. She no longer necessarily sees herself and Simon with a child. The child is as important as ever: Simon, perhaps not. And this thought

238

sets up a dull ache inside her, a guilty throb.

Often she dreams about suckling a child. Sometimes it is Sophie but sometimes another baby, unknown but familiar. Sometimes it is a tiny swaddled Simon. Once she woke sweating and trembling from a dream in which she realised that the baby she was suckling was a crow, its tiny wet rosebud lips protruding from its beak. Her breasts smart when she wakes from these dreams and she lies on her front to squash them against the mattress, squash away the sensation.

Nadia's feet have carried her to Celia's street, a row of red-brick terraces most of which have peeling paintwork and radical posters in their windows. She hesitates outside Celia's, noticing things: the constellation of dandelions amongst the grass, the milkbottles by the front door, clean and wet and bubbly. Celia or Dan must just have put them out. The garden is a mess but this house is painted more smartly than the others in the street and there are tulips in a vase on the windowsill.

How smug she must be feeling in there, how pleased, brewing up the child, filling the house with flowers. Nadia has been here before, been before and looked, not stood and gawped but walked past, shot oblique glances, but now she hesitates outside. There is something she wants to know. Dan might be there, of course, as well as, or instead of, Celia, which would be more awkward. *More* awkward!

The wrought-iron gate grates on the concrete as she pushes it open. She rings the bell and waits, but the house is settled and empty. No Celia or Dan, no sense of any stirring within. Nadia starts to go but turns back. She is fired up now. She wants to get in. Better if the house is empty. It makes it all the easier if she can only get in. She is not entirely sure what it is she needs to know. But it is something contained in Celia's house, some clue that she needs in order to continue: to know *how* to continue. She tries the front door but of course it is locked. She goes down the passage to the back of the house. Here, a yellow nylon tracksuit—Celia's? Dan's?— sways on the washing line above the small weedy lawn. Someone has been half-heartedly gardening. There is a turned-over strip and a seed packet stuck on a twig. The back door is locked, but the key is in the most obvious of places, under a plant pot beside the door.

She has never broken into a house before. But this is not breaking in. Breaking in suggests something smashed, a window, a lock. But it *is* trespass. It is even criminal. And it is thrilling. She could desecrate the place. What is it they do, the breakers and enterers? Shit on the carpet, smear obscenities on the walls. But, of course, she won't do that. She will only snoop. The key sticks in the lock. She has to pull the door towards her to make it turn. And then she is in.

It is not quiet. Washing sloshes sudsily in the machine, the refrigerator hums. There is a strong smell of paint. The kitchen is very clean. There is masses of fruit arranged in a wide china bowl, polished apples, bananas snuggled in a yellow bunch, fat white grapes. So much fruit for two people, and so perfect it looks plastic. Nadia opens the fridge. There is juice, milk, wine, cheese, salad stuff, half a chicken carcass covered in foil. She picks off a shred and chews it. It tastes of nothing. She sucks the grease off her fingers and closes the door. There is no clue.

The dining room and sitting room both have a stiff, newly decorated air. The smell of paint and new carpets is overwhelming. A flowering azalea competes with flowery curtains, and the tulips she noticed from outside stretch their snouts disdainfully upwards. On the sofa is a heap of green and blue wool, needles and a knitting pattern for a baby's hat. There are only a few rows on one needle and the wool is wiggly as if it has been much knitted and unravelled. Nadia is pleased to find that Celia is not as good at knitting as she is at everything else.

She goes upstairs. She looks in the bathroom at Celia's hypoallergenic cleansers and moisturisers, Dan's shaving cream, ointment for a skin condition, the two newish tooth-brushes, their heads resting companionably together. There is no grime. Even the towels are folded. The toilet paper matches the blind. There is a dish of pot-pourri on top of the cistern. Nadia catches sight of her frowning face in the mirror, the unfamiliar red cloud of her hair. She hears a noise downstairs and freezes, her face a comic grimace.

Crazily, she's hardly considered being caught. What on earth could she say? She strains her ears for further sounds, footsteps, doors, voices, but there is nothing. The washing machine begins to spin, a high-pitched whirligig sound. She goes to the top of the stairs and looks down. There is no movement. No sense that anyone is in the house. It was only the washing machine shifting cycles. And anyway, she has rights of sorts. She has the advantage of having been wronged.

Nevertheless she hurries. It is the bedroom that is the important place, and she goes there now. The bed with its wicker headboard is huge and flat, made tidily with a white lace bedspread over the quilt. There are lace curtains at the windows. A pretty room, calm. She approaches the bed, touches the pillows, then pulls back the quilt. The linen is all pale blue and smooth and cool, quite clean except for one long pale Celia hair. On a cupboard on one side of the bed are a clock-radio, a lamp and a pile of motoring magazines. On the other is a glass of water with dust floating on the top, a bottle of vitamin pills and a pile of books— P. D. James, Ruth Rendell, Margery

Allingham. She picks up the top one, which has a shopping list stuck into it as a bookmark. She pulls it out and reads: *deodorant, courgettes, basil, bog cleaner, whipping cream*. She sticks it back, deliberately in the wrong place. She lies down on Celia's side of the bed. This is where Simon's child was conceived.

There's a round glass lampshade on the ceiling. Did they have the light on or off? The bed is firm, she bounces herself a bit. The wicker headboard creaks. That was the sound they will have heard while they were doing it. She opens her legs. Did they do it like this? she wonders. That is what Celia implied, the most efficient, medical sort of position. But who knows? And afterwards Celia lay with her knees up waiting for Dan to come in and fuck her. Reclaim her. And what was Nadia doing at the time, so unaware? She waits for the anger, clenches herself against it, but it fails to hit her, or pokes her only gently, a frayed old fish now, brushing her with its ragged fins. She catches sight of herself in the wardrobe mirror and gets up quickly, feeling absurd. She straightens the bed.

On top of a large chest of drawers there are more books, two about pregnancy and some pamphlets about nutrition. Nadia recognises these, she has some at home—followed their advice during her five-month pregnancy, for all the good it did her. There are also two old toys, a bald eyeless bear and a one-eared rabbit, its pink stuffing leaking from its worn-out paws. The rabbit's eyes are bright glass, round and scoffing. She looks away.

The top drawer is full of underwear, Celia's and Dan's together. So utterly intimate. Celia's underwear is surprising, all white cotton, childish: bras with wide straps, waist-high knickers. All white—true white, like something from an advertisement for washing powder—nothing grey, and all ironed by the look of it. Nadia grimaces, thinking of her own scraggy tumble of colours and shapes, all mended straps and tatty lace. And then there are Dan's boxer shorts, pale blue and dark blue, ironed and folded, nestling against Celia's knickers. So companionable. So, somehow, trusting.

Nadia is moved and repelled. There is a card on top of the chest of drawers, a picture of a koala bear and its cub. Inside is written *To both of you, with all my love for ever*. Nadia winces, at the purity, the näivety, the nakedness of love and hope. All my love for ever, she mouths. For ever. And yes, looking round at the order, the evidence of love, care, co-operation and of anticipation, Nadia can almost believe it. She is an intruder, a violator, a rat in a doll's house: ruiner of order. But no, for there is no ruin. There is only a leaching of secrecy and of privacy, and that will never be known. She looks away from the rabbit to the soft blank eyesockets of the bear. One is Celia's and one Dan's, she guesses, grey snuggling relics of their childhood. She looks again at the bed where Simon came one night when she was unaware and then came home to her. It is only a flat white bed, a slab of upholstery. She leaves the room, looks back. There is nothing of herself here but a smudged reflection, and that she effaces with the closing of the door.

She stops half-way down the stairs, convinced that someone is in the kitchen: someone, Celia or Dan. Or even a burglar, a bona fide burglar. The stair she stands on creaks. She clenches her fists and bites her knuckles, tasting the saltiness of her skin, waiting. But the sounds are only the sounds of a house going about its electrical business. The fridge switches itself off, the washing machine lurches into silence, there is a gurgle in a distant pipe. There is no other movement, no shadows moving on the shiny wooden floor. Nadia dares herself to go down. And there is no one there.

She leaves the house quickly, her fingers clumsy and slippery, fumbling with the key. She stoops to replace it under the flower pot and then straightens and hurries off. The sun is hot on her face and the backs of her legs. As she walks down the street she senses the twitch of curtains, a stir of curiosity and outrage, but when she looks round there is nothing and no one, just the dusty gleam of windows. Truly, there is no one looking. She is just a small woman scurrying and no one is the least bit interested, or cares. And no one will ever know what she has done. How can they know? She has left no trace of her intrusion, but will there be a sense of uneasiness in the air? Surely Celia will feel it when she arrives home, surely she will sense a jarring, a not-quite-rightness? But nothing can be proved. And there is no harm.

Nadia slows her pace, relaxes her shoulders which have been hunched almost up to her ears, lets a slow breath down into her lungs. There *is* no harm. In fact, perhaps there is even good. Perhaps among all that evidence of love there is the clue she needed. *All my love. For ever. Both of you. For ever.* She stops to stroke a cat that melts like a spoonful of marmalade on a sunny wall. It presses its triangular face against her hand, purring deliriously. Yes. Good has been done. Nadia tickles the cat's ears. Dan and Celia are together. No evidence of any rift. No scrap of Simon to be seen. And the baby effectively Dan's. *To both of you. For ever.* Nadia is comforted by those words, which have never been spoken to her. Which are actually nonsense, for what is 'ever'? And who can promise it? But it is the promising that is crucial. Simon would never say that to her. *For the foreseeable future* is more like it. Now, perhaps he would, perhaps he has changed enough to say that. But does she want him, changed? She strokes the cat from the top of its head, down the hot fur of its back to the tip of its tail and then walks on.

246

On the way home, she stops at the supermarket to buy Simon some strawberry yoghurt, bananas and custard tarts, all the sweet babyish things he craves as he lies on the sofa all day, watching schools broadcasts on the television. Standing in a queue at the checkout, she is amazed at herself, at how she had the nerve to do what she did. She feels dirty, as if there are smuts on her face; her hands are grimy and hot. But as far as it is possible to see, there is no danger of Celia wanting Simon. That is good. A sort of relief. She fidgets behind a woman who fumbles with her chequebook, drops her pen, tries to chat to the dazed-looking assistant. Somewhere behind her a baby wails, a thin and desperate sound. She looks round and meets the eyes of the child, a solid baby with fat red cheeks, a white plume of hair and a demonic expression. But does *she* want Simon? Or doesn't she?

*   *   *

In order to please and surprise Nadia, Simon prepares lunch. Eggs Florentine and new potatoes. In the illustration in the cookery book, the eggs nestle in their spinach nest, glistening and buttery. There is a bottle of Chardonnay in the fridge. He wants it to be all ready when she gets home. If they had a garden he would lay a cloth on the lawn, a red and white checked cloth. If they had such a cloth.

But still, it will surprise Nadia, this initiative, it might open her up to him again.

He can't take it for much longer. Her eyes have turned to stone. If he puts his finger under her chin to tilt her face up to his, if he looks into her eyes, he sees polished granite. He cannot look deep into her eyes, beyond the shiny flecks, for there *are* no depths, there is only light reflected back, the tiny slivers of his own twin reflections. And the stone eyes gaze past him these days, always past him at the door. Her way out.

He turns on the cold tap and tips the potatoes into the sink. They are tiny new potatoes, prised early from a heavy soil, caked with red clay. He scrubs the potatoes with a brush but the clay is hard. He picks at the scabs of it with his fingers until it softens and comes away. The potatoes slip in his fingers and the water clouds with the dissolved mud. His hands are cold in the water. The floating mud leaves a reddish tide-mark round his wrists.

No use trying to peel these potatoes. He scrapes away at the tender skin, which sticks like wet tissue-paper to his fingers. He scrubs the potatoes hard until they are pale, glistening and bare; pokes out the tiny specks of eyes; and drops them in a pan. He tips the water out of the bowl and watches it flow sluggishly away, the plughole clogged by the wad of muddy skin.

He goes to the window, waiting, wondering

whether to begin cooking yet. It is still early for lunch. If he begins cooking now, he might have to keep things warm; the potatoes, the eggs. But if he leaves it, Nadia might return before it is ready and he wants it to be ready. He wants to surprise Nadia with a well-timed, a perfect meal. To prove that he is better. Prove that he is capable, at least, of this gesture.

But what if she doesn't return? What if he is left with the embarrassment of a wasted lunch? Eggs congealed on stiff lumps of spinach, potatoes sad and cold. She might be lunching with a friend. She might be doing anything. There is no reason why she *should* return.

The sunshine is golden, even the green of the leaves in the park is a golden green, as if everything has been blessed. The trees stir, not as if there is a breeze, but as if they are luxuriating in the weather, stretching their leaves like fingers, wriggling with pleasure.

'Go out,' Nadia said. 'You can't stay in on such a lovely day.' He is nervous, but she is right. Nadia is always bloody right. Experimentally, he takes his car keys from the hook where they have dangled for weeks. There is a letter he has to post. He could have asked Nadia to post it, but she would have asked questions. It is a letter he wrote weeks ago, when he came to a point of resolve, though not a deep enough resolve to go out and post it. Now he has made the decision. The car keys feel friendly, familiar in his hand. Yes, he has. He'll do that, post the letter and then tell Nadia its content. He cannot guess her reaction. And if it is over between them, which is the message he gets from her stony eyes, if it *is* over, then it is none of her business.

The sun sparkles on the rich green of the rhododendrons in the valley and between them is the shimmering clash of brilliant grass and bluebells. The air above the road far ahead shivers in the heat and the cars wobble out of it on the road before him. The windows of the car are open and Simon's hair is blown back by the rush of hot polleny air. It is strange to be out in this real technicolour world, everything is so wantonly bright and fat and lush. The road spins towards him like a rope someone is letting down to free him. Or like a video game: he is the driver and he has to steer, no matter how fast the road furls up at him he has to steer, and veer, in order to win another life. Where is he going? Wherever it is, he is going too fast. His foot presses down as if it is not real, all this metal and rubber and hot tar road, not real but a simulation. But suddenly another car is there in front of him. He is overtaking another car on a bend and suddenly it is there, this real car, this metal box which holds a real driver. He swerves, avoids collision, almost plunges off the road, wrestles with the steering wheel, pumps his foot on the brake and the car grates to an ugly squealing stop. His heart trampolines in his chest. He

250

stops by the edge of the road on the gravel and leans forward on the steering wheel, his face in his hands.

What he saw was a glimpse of terror on the face in the car he almost hit, man's face, woman's face, he doesn't know. He recognised only the terror.

His heart, which almost let him down, patters and thumps. Eventually it slows so that he can no longer feel it, only imagine it like the regular tail-wag of a faithful dog. His heart will be all right, they told him, no need to worry, carry on as normal, but what the fucking hell is normal, that's what Simon would like to know.

He has stopped near a pub—The Hawk. He gets out of the car and looks up. The sky is a nonchalant blue. That means nothing, it would be just as blue, flaunting its wispy clouds like so much frilly underwear, if he was dead and buried, if he was mangled in a ton of steel. His face is wet, he wipes away whatever it is, the sweat or the tears, and feels the roughness of his cheeks. He could have shaved. Nadia told him to shave. And now here he is, what is he doing *here* with the sky so open and the heat shimmer on the road and the hot smell of tar mingled with the lacy scent of some white flower that grows along the roadside? What is he doing here? What is he doing out at all?

And there is sound everywhere now that the engine has stopped, bird song, insect buzz, whispering leaves and, as he shifts his weight, the sound of his own feet on gravel. A motor bike snarls past, its noise a shock that sets his heart bounding again. He needs to go in. He needs a roof over his head.

The landlady is big and blonde and brittle. Her voice grates as she greets him, but he is comforted by her familiar type. The beer is good, he has not drunk bitter for weeks. Nadia brought some cans of lager home but he could not swallow it, it was like drinking liquid tin. This beer tastes entirely brown and runs down his throat so easily he has to hold himself back from swallowing it all at once. There is a baby's rattle on the bar, and a photograph of a plain, sallow baby in a fancy bonnet pinned on the wall among the darts fixtures.

Nadia has never spoken about Celia's baby, not again. It is there, a small squalling bundle between them, it is always there, in the air, and there it will stay. Nadia dreams about babies, he has heard her muttering. But what can he do? What can he possibly ever say? If there was a way of going back ... He licks a rim of froth from his lips. But the past is set now like a swarm of flies in amber and there is no way of freeing it. He has blown it with Nadia and there is not a bloody thing he can do about it. Eggs Florentine!

He swallows the last of his bitter and goes back outside into the sunshine. A group of bikers have congregated outside; their black leather glistens, their polished bikes gleam. He passes them, intimidated by their togetherness, their uniform, their collective gaze, and walks back to his car.

* * *

The door is locked. Nadia lets herself in and at once knows the flat is empty. She inhales and stretches, smiling in the luxury of a solitude where it is possible just to let go. She goes into a trance when she is alone in the house, a rhythm of working and wandering around, gazing in the mirror and watching not her face but her ideas, making coffee and leaving it undrunk. With another sensibility in the house, tracking her every move, expecting to be offered coffee, wondering what on earth she's doing in the bathroom, she cannot get into this trance and therefore she cannot properly work.

She breathes easily, glad for Simon that he has gone out in the sunshine. It is over a month since he last went out and today is perfect, the weather safe and golden and blue, the air fragrant and caressing.

There is a postcard from her mother on the mat. She is on a coach trip of the Scottish Highlands. The card shows a salmon leaping up a waterfall, and confirms her intention of visiting Nadia on the way back—tomorrow. Nadia at once notices the grime on the skirting boards, and sticky jamjars begin to jostle in the cupboards of her mind. June will have to sleep on the sofa-bed in the sitting room, which means cleaning in there, under things and behind things—and she winces, thinking of the state of the bathroom. She switches on the radio and puts on her rubber gloves, throws open the windows and sets to work.

*   *   *

Simon does not turn back as he meant to, because of a sudden stream of traffic; he does not want to cut across it and so he joins its flow. This time he drives irreproachably, keeping the bumper of the car ahead at an even distance. He drives out of the valley, rising up on the silvery ribbon of road between the hills. Last time he drove this way it was dark. Not real dark but the dark of surface night. He remembers the grinning moon emerging from between the edges of the ragged clouds. Now he drives towards the cave again. The car ahead of him turns off and suddenly behind him are bikers, a ragged leather stream, gaining on him until for a moment he is surrounded and momentarily blinded by sharp blades of sunshine on chrome. He holds his breath and his hands tighten on the wheel, but they speed off, leave him behind, only an insignificant motorist, they roar away revving and swerving theatrically. And Simon is left feeling lonely now, driving high over the moorland.

Half-grown black-faced lambs follow their mothers, who bustle away from the road at the approach of his car. He stops just off the road in the place he stopped before. He parks and gets out. The first sound he hears is a curlew's cry, and then the insect buzz which is the colour of the moorland air.

He walks down towards the cave entrance. The sky is the same insouciant blue and now a skylark lassoes him with its loop of song. He looks up into the dazzling sky. All this light is an illusion, he knows, because he has seen the darkness. He has seen the darkness that is there behind the light, that is the absence of light, that is the threat. It is the darkness to come. And he knows Roland's last hour. He experienced it himself. A little longer and he would have become stone himself, would have remained in the utter darkness, dissolved his skin and blood and sinew into darkness, left his stone scattered among the stone.

He recalls the seductive rush of the underground river. How easy it would have been to slip into it, join it, because then there would be no decision, no more struggle. There was that root down there, that slender white probe threading its way through miles of crevices in the rock in search of the river. Such force, such soft, insistent force.

He sits on the heather in front of the cave entrance, looking into its coldness. He sits there while the sun warms his skin and his hair.

The sun moves in the sky, but Simon does not move. Ants crawl on him, a butterfly settles on his shoulder but he does not see it. He is thinking about Nadia and about the letter he posted, which slipped so easily into the letterbox slot. It was a letter of resignation. He has finished with geography, finished with teaching. That much was easy. But now ... he cannot take Nadia's distance. She is pulling herself away, thread by thread, and soon she will be loose.

Last night he sat in front of the television while Nadia worked. What he watched has gone now, the flicker in his memory as shallow as the coloured flicker on the screen. And as he watched, dazed, he was partly aware of Nadia working behind a closed door, her purpose a mute rebuke. And later, in bed, the smell of henna had made him nauseous and he had held his breath as he entered her from behind, turned his face away from the false bright bush. And she had lain still, hardly even breathing as far as he could tell, only moving his fingers away when he tried to touch her. She had said nothing and sleep had muffled his sadness like a heavy feather pillow.

And what is he to do, now? There is no going back. He heaves himself up, stiff with hours of sitting, slapping at the flies that have settled on his sweater. How long has he been sitting? He's lost track, no watch, weeks since he wore his watch. There is a simple way to be out of it. He walks towards the cave entrance. There is that way. He cheated the earth before. After all, the earth won, fair and square. It beat him. That squashing stone ... he breathes in, fills his lungs with a gasp at the memory. It is only because others risked their own lives that he is here at all. He could, perhaps he should, play fair. Now, like this, on a golden day when the air is warm and complex with the smells and songs of spring, he could leave and join Roland. This is his choice now. The two ways, the dark door—slit—silly gaping mouth—that leads to the dark, or the bright road that rises up over the moor like a silver string. Leading where?

Roland is stuck for ever, arrested in the coldness of utter dark. Poor sod. No, that is not for Simon. That would be the easy thing now—the quickest relief. Simon stands up and flexes his legs and arms, feels the warm flux of blood. He goes to the cave mouth and breathes in the dead mushroom smell. No. It is not for him—that cold intimacy. The sun is warm on his hair, he strokes it, the back of his own head, feels the slight coarseness, the warmth against his hand, hair, skin and skull. He is a live and separate thing.

'Goodbye,' he whispers, and then says more loudly, calls into the gloom, 'Goodbye.' There is the faint beat of an echo after his voice like a distant reply. Simon turns away, closing his eyes briefly, wondering whether it is Roland that he is bidding farewell, or something else.

*   *   *

Nadia lifts the lid of the saucepan. There are potatoes, scrubbed and yellowish under a starchy scum of water. She blinks, puzzled, replaces the lid. The kitchen floor is damp, the insides of the windows clean, the food lined up neatly on clean shelves. The cleanliness makes her light-hearted, as if something dusty within herself has been wiped. But Simon has been gone for hours. There is no note. She remembers with a shudder the last time he left a note. She notices that the car has gone, tries to recall what he said this morning. He didn't mention going out. She suggested it, and as he nodded a little skin of insincerity filmed his eyes. He didn't plan to go out then, she's sure. What did he say? He asked her not to go, that was it. The lightness leaks from her heart. He asked her not to go and she did, just to escape his need. She switches on the kettle for a cup of tea, hoping that Simon will be back soon, wondering whether the potatoes are supposed to be some sort of sign, chasing out the small thread of worry. She wanted him out, didn't she?

There is a crash against the kitchen window and she jumps. A bird has landed on the sill, a big, clumsy bird that scrabbles awkwardly at the sill—and there is shouting from outside.

258

Nadia looks out of the window and can hardly believe what she sees. It is like a sort of miracle, Derek, upright and outside, lumbering, calling in his pure high voice, 'Darling, Darling,' and looking upwards at the bird on Nadia's windowsill. Seen from above, he is a great pyramid of a man: peaked head, cascading beard, wide belly, splayed feet in great spreading slippers. Iris hovers anxiously behind him, her hand to her open mouth, her sparkly shawl falling from her shoulders, her wig glistening like black snow.

The crow's clumsy claws cannot get a grip on the narrow sill and he flaps his wings against the glass so that feathers rain down. Nadia catches his eye, bright through the glass. He looks desperate, pathetic, his bald head a startling shrimpish pink. Nadia slowly opens the other half of the window and Darling hops in, regaining his dignity immediately, squawking, scattering a feather or two in the sink. He flaps to the floor and hops jerkily around the kitchen, leaving a long greenish dropping on the clean tiles.

Nadia leans out of the window. 'All right,' she calls to the two upturned faces. 'Got him.'

*   *   *

Darling sits on Iris's shoulder. He is fretful and embarrassed by his silly display. His head leans weakly against her cheek, his eyes are half closed.

'Naughty boy,' Iris scolds fondly. 'Dirty little bugger. Never seen Dad so worried, have we?'

'First time I've seen Derek outside.'

Iris smiles proudly. 'Not much stirs him.'

'Well,' Nadia says. She is aware of the time, of Simon's absence, of the cold potatoes snuggling in the pan. The clean kitchen is beginning to smell of crow.

'Spring cleaning?' Iris asks, nodding towards the bucket and mop and the bottles of detergent.

'My mum's coming.'

'Made it up, then?'

Nadia shrugs. 'Anyway, she's calling in. First time I'll have seen her for ...'

'That's good, duck. And Simon?' Iris screws up her face.

'Out.'

Darling makes a growling sound and rattles his feathers. Iris clucks absently at him. 'You should go,' she says with sudden intensity.

'Go?'

'To Simon.'

'But ...'

'If you want him. Go, duck. He's waiting.' Nadia opens and then closes her mouth. Iris's eyes are so intense, the light and the dark, they search Nadia for a response and she closes her eyes against them for a moment, sees Simon, his hair bright in the sun. 'It's all up to you

260

now,' Iris adds.

'Yes.' Nadia opens her eyes. 'I think I see.' She does not, quite, see. But there is a fizz in the air around her, a sense of anticipation, risk, the exhilaration that precedes a leap.

'Then you'll go?'

'Yes.' Nadia does not ask where. There is only one place.

*   *   *

But when Iris has gone and she has cleaned the signs of crow away, she waits, hoping that Simon will return, giving him time. She tries to read the paper and, when that fails, to watch children's television. She drinks a glass of wine. Unable to sit still, she goes into her tidy studio. She lifts the damp cloth off her first sculpture. She cannot decide whether it is complete and so she does not let it dry. A species of mould has grown on the strange foot/root thing, delicate blue-green tentacles like branching veins. She smooths her finger down its surface. It has an inner coldness that seeps out like breath. Nadia is waiting to cast her other sculptures, first in plaster and then, if she can afford it, in bronze. And then they will last for ever, for bronze will not corrode or shatter. She relaxes for a moment with the satisfaction of that thought. But there can be no denying that she is worried about Simon.

Nadia fidgets through the misery of the six

261

o'clock news and then she calls a taxi. She waits outside, the evening is still and glorious, muted gold now, the air pungent with wallflowers. As the taxi arrives, she turns and sees Iris watching her through the window. She has taken off her wig and her grey hair is fluffed out around her head. Nadia waves and gets into the taxi. The driver is young and beautiful and knows it. He has the air of a cheeky, beloved child. 'Hello beautiful,' he says. Bloody cheek, Nadia thinks, but smiles.

'Where to?'

'I'll direct you,' Nadia says. 'I'm going out into the country, looking for someone.'

'Great,' the driver says. 'Nearly as good as "Follow that car." It'll make my day when someone says that.'

Nadia laughs. She settles back. The windows of the taxi sparkle dustily. Once they are through the busy traffic, she watches the houses rush easily past, remembering her laborious pedalling through the rain last time she came this way. It is like another world now, a picture-book world of flowers, children on bright bicycles, and ice-cream vans, even someone trying to fly a kite. They drive through the valley and out past The Hawk. Nadia averts her eyes as they pass. The driver attempts to engage her in conversation, but the nearer they get to the place the more difficult it is for her to move her mouth. Eventually he gives up and leaves her in peace.

She squeezes her hands together in an attitude of prayer, but it is not prayer, it is will. She is willing him to be there. To be waiting. They rise high over the moorland road. Low shafts of sunlight are dusty on the grey-green heather, exaggerating stunted birches with great sprawling nests of shadow. Nadia holds her breath as they take the last curve round to the place: and there is Simon's car.

'Thank God,' she breathes.

'Beg pardon?'

'We're here. Stop here. Just by this car.'

'You sure?'

The driver switches off the engine and Nadia opens the door and steps out into the thin, clear air. It is utterly quiet and still, not a breath of wind to stir the heather, not like last time, when everything was a confusion of shivery shifting brightness. Her eyes dart around, avoiding the entrance to the cave, but she cannot see Simon.

'Should I wait?' The taxi driver regards her curiously.

'No, no.'

'You sure you want to be left? Alone?' He gets out of the cab and stands looking around him. 'Bloody nothing out here.'

'It's all right,' Nadia says, her voice gone loose with relief. 'There's my friend.'

Simon is standing in front of the cave. Her face splits into an idiotic grin which she cannot control as she counts out her fare.

'Right then,' the taxi driver says, also

263

relieved, shivering and climbing back into his seat. 'Be seeing you.' He slams the door and starts his engine. Nadia runs towards Simon.

'Hey!' she calls, and he lifts his arm in greeting as he comes forward to meet her.

'Must have cost a fortune,' he says. 'Fancy coming in a taxi!'

'How else?'

Simon shrugs. They're awkward together. Nadia notices the little wisps of blond hair at the neck of his shirt in the tender hollow between his collarbones. His face, so indoor-pale lately, is pink from an afternoon of sunshine.

'Come here,' he says. He takes her hand. There is a strange look in his eyes and she is frightened. Absurd to be frightened of Simon, but still.

'How long have you been here, Simon? Why here? I was worried ... Iris's bloody crow got free while I was cleaning the flat—my mother's coming tomorrow ...'

'Shut up.' Simon holds her hand tightly. 'Come with me.'

'Where?'

'Into the cave.'

'No!' He pulls her but she stands her ground. 'Simon! Are you mad?'

He lets go of her hand abruptly and she staggers. He turns his back, and she can see his shoulders moving, sense his struggle. She looks at the evil slit in the earth, the single empty eye.

'I only wanted ...' he begins. She puts her arms round him from behind, pressing her face into his back. Through his shirt she can feel his warmth, smell his skin. Through the thin white material she can faintly see his scars.

'Wanted what?'

'Please come with me.' Nadia closes her eyes. The colour of terror really is yellow. It is there behind her eyelids, an ugly shitty yellow. She can feel the cold of the evening now that the sun is setting, undramatically, a greenish goldness in the west. There is a breeze and goosepimples rise on her arms.

'All right.'

Simon pauses for a moment and then turns. She doesn't meet his eyes. He puts his arm round her shoulders. She walks with him, down the lumpy slope. Last time she was here he was underneath. That is what she thinks, remembering how it felt to walk here when he was down there. The irrational fear that her feet were compounding his compression. Now he is out, safe, and she has him. Has she? She puts her arm round his waist and squeezes, feeling the slip of the ribs under his skin.

They reach the entrance. There is a dripping, a stickiness, muddy slime on the inner walls; the hole is the height of a door but wider; above it tussocky grass and heather sprigs are silhouetted against the sky.

'No,' Nadia says, stopping. 'I really don't want to.'

'Don't be afraid,' Simon says. And she lets him pull her out of the light and into the shadowy gloom. She breathes in the dank wetness, the smell of old urine. There is rubbish on the floor, crisp packets, cigarette ends. She breathes very shallowly and lets him lead her in, afraid of what she might be stepping on. Simon gets a torch out of his pocket. It is a small feeble thing, but it serves to light the viscous-looking walls.

'Please, not far,' Nadia whispers. There is a small scramble down and though Simon steadies her she has to put her hand out to stop herself falling and she touches the cold stone. It is unfriendly. More than that, it feels hostile. The beam of the torch flickers ahead, bouncing and sliding in time with Simon's footsteps. He lets go of her and walks in front. She follows. She cannot speak. She looks back at the smear of light behind her. Stops. 'Simon, I ...' She is embarrassed by her voice, ineffectual, a rodent squeak.

'All right,' he says. He speaks softly. His face is lost to her in the darkness.

'I can't see you.'

He turns, but still she cannot make him out, only the deeper darkness of his mouth as it opens, he has the torch pointed downwards, only the edge of his chin is clear. 'This is as far as we can walk,' he says. 'After this there is a chimney—a pot ...'

'No!'

'It's all right, we'd need a rope. I only wanted to tell you ... I was going to ... All afternoon I've been deciding whether to go in, go back.'

'No.'

'Wait. To go back. Roland's in there, you know.'

'I know.'

'No, I mean I saw him.'

Nadia gives an audible shocked shudder. 'What ...'

'I saw something that I believe was his skull.'

Nadia turns back towards the little visible light. 'I want to get out.'

'Wait. I want to ask ... It's over, isn't it? Us.'

'I don't know, I ...'

'Because if it is, I'll go.' He sounds so lonely when he says this. And something in Nadia rebels against his loneliness. She reaches for him. Puts her arms round him, rubs her face into his warm neck where she can feel the throb of his pulse. He presses her bottom tight against him. And in the darkness she feels a terrible shock of desire. It is the strongest desire she has ever felt. It hurts. It is like electricity. And when he touches her she moans. 'No, not here.' He cups her sex in his hand and squeezes and it is as if milk is oozing from her breasts, from every pore. 'Simon, no,' she says, dizzy with the sensation.

'Go on then.' He pushes her out ahead of him, but when the light is a solid thing in front of her, a safe thing that she can attain in seconds, she turns back.

'I do want you,' she says. 'But I don't know how... how we get over... how can we...?'

Simon doesn't answer. What could he say? Outside the cave he pulls her by the hand, up the hill above the cave to the very place she stood waiting for him, where she stood with Celia on a skittish day that seems years ago. The sun has gone. The sky is pale blue still, but darkness is leaking from the ground. Simon pulls her down.

Anyone could see them there, anyone driving past and straining their eyes for the sight of lovers on a hill in the heather. And anyone who heard Nadia's voice would ponder for a moment on the oddness of the call: bird? Wild creature? And then forget.

We hope you have enjoyed this Large Print book. Other Chivers Press or Thorndike Press Large Print books are available at your library or directly from the publishers. For more information about current and forthcoming titles, please call or write, without obligation, to:

Chivers Press Limited
Windsor Bridge Road
Bath BA2 3AX
England
Tel. (0225) 335336

OR

Thorndike Press
P.O. Box 159
Thorndike, ME 04986
USA
Tel. (800) 223-6121
(207) 948-2962
(in Maine and Canada, call collect)

All our Large Print titles are designed for easy reading, and all our books are made to last.